THE VALUE OF EQUALITY

CRISTIE M. LOCSIN

authorHOUSE®

AuthorHouse™
1663 Liberty Drive
Bloomington, IN 47403
www.authorhouse.com
Phone: 1 (800) 839-8640

Published by AuthorHouse   01/31/2017

ISBN: 978-1-5246-6951-5 (sc)
ISBN: 978-1-5246-6952-2 (hc)
ISBN: 978-1-5246-6950-8 (e)

Library of Congress Control Number: 2017901397

To the best storytellers, Daddy Joe and Lolo Peding. Your vibrance and enthusiasm in telling a tale have allowed my imagination to soar and inspired me to be my own storyteller …

CHAPTER 1

There were different shades of blue in the sky above Hacienda Corazon after the sugarcane season ended. The air felt cleaner. The greenery, though gone, made the land soft and gentle under the horse's hooves, the perfect path for a gallop. Daria Hernandez and her horse Silvestre were in for a good ride. As she slightly released the reins, her heels firmly kicking the brown gelding's belly, the twenty-one-year-old hacienda princess felt peace and let go of the distraction of preparing for the sixtieth birthday of her beloved father, Señor Enrique Hernandez, that filled her mind.

Her peaceful thoughts were interrupted when she heard the approaching sound of a blue Toyota Land Cruiser and the high-pitched voice of *Yaya* Helen calling her. "Daria!" cried the chubby middle-aged lady who had been taking care of Daria since she was baby.

Daria pulled the reins, let out a sigh, and turned to the vehicle. She saw Yaya Helen rushing toward her.

"We have a big problem. The pigs that we need for the *lechon* were stolen," worriedly reported Helen.

"All of them?"

"No, probably ten, but for sure Toto, Nonoy, Nene, and Neneng were stolen. What are we to do?" asked her worried nanny.

"Let's head to the piggery to find out what happened."

On the way to the piggery Daria noted that Hacienda Corazon was one of the prime farms in the province of Azusa, spanning one thousand hectares. It had been in the Hernandez family for more than five generations. The progress of the farm reflected the rise of power of the family. Sugarcane was the most abundant crop, the star crop that shouldered the province's economy and ten percent of the country's economy. The sugar industry, which enjoyed free trade with the United States, was one of the most powerful industries in the Philippines.

Hacienda Corazon's beauty did not rest on sugarcane alone. In its orchard, fruit trees were lined up uniformly. The family enjoyed the *rambutan, lanzones, tambis,* and mangoes. On the north side of the farm was a picturesque view of historic Mt. Mansilay and a riverbed that ran along the farm, contributing easy irrigation. The hacienda's *azucarera, the* sugar refinery, which milled the majority of the province's sugarcane plantations, stood firmly on the eastern side of the hacienda.

When they reached the piggery, the workers were in an uproar. The pig pens and wire traps were all dismantled. What concerned Daria the most were the fearful faces of the workers.

"Miss, the pigs were stolen, but not by ordinary thieves—it was the rebels," Nelson, the man in charge of the piggery and chicken farm, fearfully explained. "According to the people on guard last night, ten armed men came and took some pigs and chickens. We have about twenty pigs left, and only ten are mature enough to be butchered."

"Was anyone hurt?" asked Daria.

"Yes, miss. Some of our men were wounded when they tried to hold off the rebels. Because they were armed, our men couldn't do much," answered Nelson.

Before Nelson finished describing the workers' ordeal, a voice no one wanted to hear at that moment roared. "You imbeciles! How could you let this happen? You should have guarded the place with your lives!" cried the hacienda's señora.

"Mama, please calm down. As you can see, people got hurt. I am sure Papa will understand," said Daria. "My friends the Aguilars have a piggery. I think they might sell us some pigs at a reasonable price in time for the party."

"Oh, please, Daria. You intend to buy from those people at the market? Who knows what they feed their pigs! Nelson, go to Señora Linda and ask if we can purchase twenty pigs," ordered Señora Estefania Hernandez.

"But Señora, we all know that Señora Linda buys pigs from the Aguilars—" Nelson stopped midsentence.

Señora Estefania Hernandez pretended she did not hear the comment. "Daria, see what happens when I put you in charge? This is a mess. I hate coming to this stinky place," Señora Estefania sternly said to her daughter. "I need to go back to the city. I have a prayer meeting and *merienda* with my *amigas*."

The capital of the province of Azusa was the city of Castellana. The city plaza was across from the Church of St. Thomas de Aquinas. Next to the church stood the government center that housed the courthouse and the mayor's office.

Señor Enrique Hernandez was deemed an honorable and distinguished gentleman. His tall, husky frame and clean-shaven face were well known to all the citizens of Castellana. The señor was also known for his generosity and uprightness. Señor Enrique was also one of the strongest driving forces for providing jobs in Castellana. He owned one of the province's productive haciendas, as well as his azucarera, which employed close to a quarter of Castellana's population.

It was a rare occasion at the city hall. The people in the mayor's office were on their best behavior, as though the president of the country had arrived. Not once had Señor Hernandez set foot in city hall to see the mayor. The public servants usually came to him instead.

"Señor Hernandez, to what do we owe the honor of your visit?" Mayor Karlos Vasquez smiled and gave the señor a firm handshake. "Please come in to my office." He then looked at his secretary, nodded, and closed the door.

The tone inside the mayor's office changed from formal to familiar. Mayor Karlos Vasquez was no stranger to Señor Enrique Hernandez.

Karlos's father was Hacienda Corazon's *encargado*, the haciendero's right-hand man, who had been killed by the rebels while trying to protect his señor, orphaning then-fourteen-year-old Karlos and his younger brother. Señor Enrique took in Karlos and his brother and gave them educations and a chance for success. Karlos proved himself to be an extraordinarily hardworking student. He graduated with honors and became a lawyer. After two years practicing law, Señor Hernandez made Karlos an offer that changed his life: to enter politics.

Mayor Vasquez was in his second term as mayor. The forty-year-old mayor was well loved by the haciendaros and his constituents alike. He was an honest mayor and often showed compassion to the workers and the poor. He frequently served as a bridge to establishing good working relationships between the land owners and their workers.

"*Tito* Enrique, how are you? You should have called me. I would have dropped everything to come to you," said the mayor to his benefactor.

"Well, my boy, as you know, my birthday is coming up, and Daria and Señora Estefania fill the air with much tension. I need some breathing space. Not to mention to gain some control," weary Señor Hernandez said.

"The party of the year, Tito!" commented Karlos. "Turning the big six-oh. Daria should hurry up and get married!"

"I am glad that my daughter is in no hurry to get married. I am enjoying my little princess. Besides, I see no man fit for her at for the moment."

"Well, if that's the case, Tito, I wish you a long and healthy life," added Mayor Vasquez.

Señor Enrique smiled. He then took Karlos's seat behind the mayor's desk.

"So how may I be of service?" asked Karlos as he sat across from the señor.

"Are there any developments in capturing the Communist rebels that attacked the Jison and Daza haciendas?"

"To tell you the truth, we still have no clues," answered the mayor. "Most of their people have joined the rebels, and that is something that even the police office can't control. The anger of their workers might have led to this too."

"The rebels are getting more aggressive. I have to admit there are hacistenderos that treat workers like slaves," said Señor Enrique. "However, if burning farms along with their owners is their idea of equality, this makes them worse. They are murderers."

"I have heard that the Jisons and Dazas had been refusing to pay the rebels' stipend, which angered the group and led to this," Mayor Vasquez told Señor Hernandez.

"That is why we need the government to take action. What the rebels are doing is no longer in accordance with what they are aiming for. They have become extortionists and murderers."

"Which is why the people of Castellana and your workers love you," Karlos Vasquez said with admiration. "You have given jobs and opportunities to many, and you have treated your workers, especially the field workers, with dignity and respect. I am glad my family worked for you, and I will never forget what you have given me."

"Well, my family members would not be where they are today if not for people like Karlos, your father," proudly said the señor. "I just need you to promise me that as long as you are in this position, or any other, you will always protect Hacienda Corazon."

The Hernandezes house was in a state of disorder. Every year on the day prior to Señor Hernandez's birthday they prepared a feast for the workers of Hacienda Corazon and the azucarera. Packages for the workers' family were prepared. Each package included a bag of rice, canned goods, sweets, laundry soap, noodles, and a rosary. For the feast, the cooks prepared *pansit, adobo,* chop suey, and, of course, *lechon,* all topped off with *suman,* a sweet sticky rice dessert, *leche flan,* and other native sweets.

Daria and Yaya Helen were busy delegating and helping with the packing before they were interrupted by the entrance of Señora Estefania's obnoxious twenty-four-year old niece Jocelyn Gonzaga.

"Well, well, look at St. Daria on the go," quipped Jocelyn as she stood looking at Daria, her wavy hair straightened to a fault.

"Bad hair day, Jocelyn?" asked Daria as she stood up. She wiped her brows and swept her soft wavy hair into a ponytail.

"So how are the preparations going? I am sure you are doing a wonderful job with the people in the hacienda. I do not expect much from you for the main event though. After all, what does a country mouse like you know about class?" Jocelyn challenged Daria.

"I am sure more than you do," Daria said with a smile.

Just then Señora Estefania entered with a big smile on her face.

"Why, if it isn't my favorite niece, Jocelyn! My love, you should have arrived for the party tomorrow. Leave the azucarera celebration to Daria," said her aunt.

"I have to be here for you, and of course Tito," answered Jocelyn.

It was an unspoken fact, a topic no one dared to speak about openly. Daria was not Señora Estefania's biological daughter, a truth made known to Daria when Jocelyn blatantly told her that her real mother had passed away after giving birth to her. Her father couldn't bear to lie to his daughter and explained the mistake of his past. This moved Daria to love and appreciate her father even more.

Señora Estefania De Paz's family was once one of the most affluent families in the province. Her father was the former governor of Azusa. After her father and mother were killed in a car accident, her brother went on to gamble away the family's fortune. Señor Enrique Hernandez's family purchased the De Paz Hacienda, which lead to the marriage of Enrique and Estefania. Estefania's brother was murdered by his creditors, leaving the Hernandez to pay for his debts. Estefania had two sisters. Her younger sister, Jocelyn's mother, married a doctor and sadly passed away after childbirth. Her older sister, a nun under the Order of St. Dymphna, passed away from tuberculosis. Estefania took care of

Jocelyn when she was a baby and wanted to adopt her after she married Enrique, but her husband refused. Enrique then had a love child and took in his child, Daria, to be their legally adopted daughter.

"Come inside, please, Jocelyn. Have something to eat. The food we prepared for the workers may not be to your liking," Señora Estefania said, putting her arms on her niece's waist.

As niece and aunt went into the main house, it looked as though they were mother and daughter. They had the same round eyes, mestiza complexion, and voluptuous built. That was probably the source of the hidden hatred that Jocelyn had for Daria, that Daria was chosen to be the Hernandez's daughter, not her.

"Daria, come on. Let's go back to work. It's as if you are not used to them," said Yaya Helen.

Daria smiled at her dear nanny and had started the final count of the packages when the doorbell rang.

"Good morning! How is everyone?"

The greeting came from Father Jose, the parish priest of the Church of St. Thomas de Aquinas.

"Daria, you're looking pretty as always. You are the spitting image of your dad, minus the temper, should I say?" teased the priest.

"Father, I'll take that as a compliment," replied Daria.

Brother Armando Vasquez had come along with Father Jose.

"Hello, Brother Armando," Daria greeted him.

"Daria, how are you?" said her friend, who also happened to be Mayor Karlos Vasquez's brother.

Señora Estefania and Jocelyn stepped out to greet the priest and invited him to come in with them. Brother Armando excused himself by saying he wanted to help Daria with the packages.

"Daria! My dear, I miss you. Even in this condition you still look marvelous," said Armando.

"Shhh! Father Jose might hear you," warned Daria her friend.

"You know Father. Once you give him sweets he is in his own world. He forgets he has diabetes," Brother Armando said. "So I see Jocelyn is here too. Why am I not surprised she is not helping? She does have the face of an angel but a total—"

Daria interrupted her friend and put her finger on his lips. "Mando, let me finish for you. You are going to be a man of God soon. *Maldita.*"

"I can't believe my brother has been in love with her. He just goes for the looks, not for what is inside. He is such a—

Daria stopped her friend again. "Shhh. Blinded by love?"

"God bless you, dear."

"We better stop before we get caught. You want to come with me to Hacienda Corazon to help prepare first?" asked Daria her friend.

"Surely, dear. I'd rather go with you than commit a sin."

The view of Mt. Mansilay was beautiful. Its perfect shape and peaks, covered with white clouds, were a sight to behold. According to legend, the mountain rose from a war between two tribes that lasted for ten years. When no treaty between the tribes developed, the gods could no longer overlook the evil that engulfed the people. A great earthquake came and swallowed the tribes. A mountain formed over the dead, serving as their memorial.

Perhaps the legend held some truth. Deep inside the mountain a new tribe had risen, a tribe of men, women, and children who spoke of oppression and viewed equality differently from the world. Their ideals and ideology were, in a word, too perfect. Mt. Mansilay was the home of the rebels.

The rebels were all over the country, supported by the Communist Party. They earned their money from the stipend they imposed on the land owners. They were united under the communist platform, and their passion, fueled by anger, was directed at the rich and the government that offered no changes to their impoverished state.

"My brothers and sisters, tonight we will feast courtesy of Hacienda Corazon!" Ka Abel, one of the rebel leaders, cheered.

"This is providence! We will have enough supplies for a month," Ka Eden, Ka Abel's partner, said.

"Tatay, did you steal the pigs?" Egoy asked his father.

"No, son. This is our share. You see, son, the land that the Hernandezes have does not solely belong to them. It also belongs to us. While they became rich, our forefathers worked their bones on that land. It is only fitting to get our share. So tonight, on the eve of the señor's birthday, we too shall feast. But first let us prepare some fireworks to honor Señor Hernandez.

CHAPTER 2

"I cannot believe I get coaxed into riding a horse every time I see you," whined Brother Armando.

"I still can't believe you are entering the priesthood," returned Daria.

Armando directly looked at his friend with a deeply sullen face. "I feel this is the only way to atone for my desires. I felt like I sinned, and I need to repent. I told you before about my so-called sickness, right? I feel I need to pray over and over just to be forgiven."

"You are being too hard on yourself, Armando. It is not too late to leave. If you feel your reasons are not the right ones, then don't."

Before Armando could answer, the horses were startled by a loud honking from a Land Cruiser. A man yelled to Daria.

"Daria! Princess Daria!"

Daria pulled the reins and trotted Silvestre toward the vehicle.

"Vicente? You are here! I thought you were arriving tomorrow." She dismounted and greeted her tall *moreno* cousin with a big hug.

Daria's cousin was the closest to a sibling she could ever have. He was the son of Señor Enrique's sister, Christina Valderrama, who lived in Manila. Vicente had been sent to Castellana to be disciplined by his uncle due to series of schoolboy mishaps and mischievousness. Vicente had spent his entire high school years with the Hernandezes and grew to love Daria as his little sister.

"My Daria, how I missed you!"

"Me too, Vicente! So what presents did you bring me?" demanded Daria.

"Well, Mama sent you some clothes, which I think are just your taste." He was teasing his cousin. They both knew that Vicente's mother definitely had a unique fashion sense. "I also have my own present for you." The passenger door opened and out came a dashing young man, neatly dressed, mestizo, about five foot ten, in his late twenties. He cleared his throat to get the cousins' attention.

"Oh, my apologies." Vicente pushed Daria to face his friend." Daria, this is my friend Marco, Marco Gutierrez. Marco, my princess Daria Hernandez."

"Pleasure to meet you. I heard a lot about you from Vicente," Marco said, extending a hand to Daria.

"Good things I hope," Daria said, smiling and accepting Marco's hand.

Her smile, her eyes, caught Marco's interest, and instant fondness and affection leaped in the young man's chest.

"Excuse me." Brother Armando was trying to get his horse to walk toward them. "Don't forget someone else is here too."

"Mando—I mean Brother Armando. Here, let me help you down," Vicente said.

"Vicente, my child." Brother Armando offered his hand to Vicente so Daria's cousin could show his respect.

Everyone burst into laughter.

"This certainly does not suit you, Mando. I will never go to confession or attend mass if you are the priest," said Vicente.

"By the way, Marco, this is our friend Armando. Please address him as Brother Armando."

The delight of seeing her cousin made Daria forget the time. She was reminded by Silvestre's persistent nudge.

"Oh no. Your surprise caught my attention, but we need to head to the azucarera to prepare for the party. We better hurry," Daria said as she mounted her horse again.

"If you mean hurry on the horse, sorry Daria. I am riding with Vicente. I cannot gallop down the hills on a horse," Armando complained.

"Don't look at me! I'm driving," added Vicente.

"I can ride," Marco offered.

"You ride?" Daria asked with a quizzical look on her face.

"I play polo. I don't think it will be much different," Marco answered, taking the reins from Brother Armando.

"All right. Let's put your polo skills to the test then," Daria challenged

"Challenged accepted," Marco confidently answered.

"Are you ready, Marco?" asked Daria.

"Yes, ma'am!" smiled Marco.

At the same moment, almost synchronized, they kicked and yelled and galloped toward the azucarera.

The courtyard of the azucarera turned festive. Colorful small flags were hung from tree to tree, and a birthday banner with Señor Hernandez's picture occupied the entire wall on one side of the yard. Buffet tables had been set out to hold the food. They were expecting at least eighty families. The packages were stored in the sugarcane trucks to be handed out after the party.

Daria, Vicente, Brother Armando, and Marco were greeted by Lourdes, the office secretary.

"Miss Daria, everything is ready. Its two thirty, and people are starting to arrive," Lourdes informed Daria.

"Can you escort Vicente and our friends, please? I just need to freshen up," Daria requested.

On cue, Yaya Helen ran alongside Daria to her office to change.

"So, Marco, what do you think of Daria?" Vicente looked at his friend with a smile. "She is something else, isn't she? You won't find anyone like her in the city."

Marco smiled. "She can surely ride a horse. And from looking around here, she sure knows how to throw a party."

"Pretty girl too, isn't she?" Brother Armando added.

"That is a given," Vicente answered.

Before Marco could make a remark, his thoughts were disrupted by seeing Daria walking toward them.

Daria joined them and asked, "So what did I miss?"

"Nothing much, just talking about you. I think Vicente is setting you up with Marco," answered Brother Armando.

Before anyone could continue, the mood tensed when the high-pitched, stern voice of Señora Estefania rang in the courtyard.

"My, it is so hot! You over there—make sure there are no flies around," ordered Señora Hernandez. "You know how the señor hates flies. Bring more people to fan flies away from the food."

"Hello, Tita Estefania. How are you?" Vicente greeted her. "Hello, Jocelyn and Father Jose."

"Vicente, what a surprise! I thought you were arriving tomorrow," Señora Estefania said. "And who do you have here?"

"Tita, Jocelyn, Father, may I introduce my friend Marco Gutierrez to you. His family owns the firm I work for, Gutierrez Developers."

"Pleasure to meet you, Señora Hernandez," Marco respectfully said. "Father Jose, Jocelyn, nice to meet you."

Jocelyn had a flirty smile on her face.

"The pleasure is all mine. So what does your family build, Marco?" asked Jocelyn

Daria and Armando snickered, prompting Señora Estefania to give them both stern looks.

"We are into real estate development," answered Marco politely.

The conversation was interrupted as the man of the hour stepped inside the courtyard.

"The birthday celebrant is here!" Señor Hernandez said, announcing his arrival.

"Papa!" cried Daria as she ran to her father, giving him a big hug.

"My mischievous girl!" he answered, hugging her back. "What trouble did you make today?"

"Trouble to make you happy, Papa," answered the delighted Daria.

No one could deny Daria was Señor Hernandez's daughter. They had the same smiling eyes, round dimpled faces, and rosy complexions.

"I love you, Daria!" said the señor to his daughter. "Wow, look at all this! Let the celebration begin!"

Daria's smile radiated as she saw her father laughing and enjoying the program the workers had prepared for him. It seemed to her that Señor Hernandez was more relaxed as he enjoyed partying with the workers than at the formal parties at home. The male workers sang a medley of Frank Sinatra songs, and the female group showed off their skills with theme songs from various movies. There were also dance numbers, including the cha-cha and tango. Even the workers' children sang and dance for their señor.

Daria went to the stage

"Papa, all of us have made this event special for you because we love you. Thank you. Thank you for being generous toward others, for being fair, and for being kind. I know I am lucky to have you as my dad, and the people here are lucky that they are working for you. With that, this song is for you." Daria sang her father's favorite song, "All the Things You Are."

Señor Hernandez stood and walked over to embrace and kiss his daughter.

"Thank you, my dear daughter. And everyone else, it has been a pleasure working with all of you," Señor Hernandez said in gratitude. "Hacienda Corazon would not be what it is today or maintained its prestige over the generations if not for the workers who stood beside our family. Our success is your success. May God bless us, every one."

The night continued with feasting and laughter. The workers and their families were appreciative, and the atmosphere was comfortably happy. Even Señora Estefania and Jocelyn seemed to relax. As the night was about to come to an end, Lourdes asked the people to convene at the truck lot area.

At the truck garage, Daria, Yaya Helen, Vicente, Brother Armando, and even Marco began handing out the packages to the families. The festivities took on a different tone when a thunderous sound was heard outside the azucarera.

"Señor, Señor, get down! Take the señor and his family to safety!" cried Felix, Señor Hernandez's bodyguard.

Daria was fazed but recovered fast and ran toward her father's side. The señor stood steadfast and headed toward the entrance of the azucarera, followed by his guards.

"Daria! Where are you going? Stay here," called Señora Estefania.

Daria did not hear her mother and continued to follow her father. What they saw outside the azucarera was a sight that had often been reported on the nightly newscasts when haciendas were attacked and overtaken by rebels. Tonight was the start of the outcry for war by rebels against Hacienda Corazon. They presented their gift to Señor Hernandez: the heads of the stolen pigs on stakes and a banner written in the pigs' blood that read HAPPY BIRTHDAY SEÑOR ENRIQUE HERNANDEZ.

"Clean this up *now*!" Señor Hernandez ordered. "Felix, get to the bottom of this."

Felix, the head of Señor Enrique's private army, nodded and called his men to clean up and to convene inside to strategize about finding the rebels.

"Daria, go inside," ordered her father.

"What about you, Papa?"

"You go home with your mama, and Vicente too. I'll see you there later."

Señor Hernandez furiously went inside his office at the azucarera, followed by Felix and his men.

"Señor, we have been checking the boundaries, but we saw no rebel activities. They are becoming more aggressive, sir. Before their arms were just homemade guns, but now it seems that somebody has been giving them better weapons," reported Felix.

"Just this week, two haciendas lost their wars against rebels. Felix, we have been reliable about paying our stipend to make those rebels leave us alone. What happened?" angrily asked Señor Hernandez.

"Señor, we made sure that our borders were covered. The stipend has been delivered. This caught us by surprise too," answered Felix.

"I will have a talk with the other hacienderos and the mayor tomorrow. We need to do something about this."

The rebels at the group's hideout in Mt. Mansilay were having their own celebration. The threat they'd sent to Hacienda Corazon was considered the first act in starting their war over Hacienda Corazon.

"Cheers to us, my brothers! May this serve as a warning to the hacienderos that their governance over the land will soon be over. Land, my brothers and sisters, is for all. No one man should reign over it. Equality for *all*!" Ka Abel proclaimed.

"Equality for all!" the brotherhood of rebels chanted.

"Our efforts at gaining the haciendas of the Dazas and the Jisons, as well as our stand against Hacienda Corazon, would have not been successful if not for our patron, who for now I can not name. To our patron!"

"To our patron!"

"Hacienda Corazon has always been on time paying their dues. Don't you think this might cause them to stop their stipend?" said Ka Emok.

"More reason for us to keep attacking them. Remember, my brothers, Hacienda Corazon is the most powerful hacienda in Azusa. If we make them shake in fear, the other haciendas will become afraid, and surely more stipends will come," answered Ka Abel.

CHAPTER 3

D aria barely got any sleep after the night's events. She got up and headed toward the dirty kitchen to see if she could help with breakfast. On her way out, she noticed the guards were doubled and the kitchen bustling and busy. Daria turned her head toward her father's studio outside the main house and noticed the lights were on. She heard the voices of men in heated discussion streaming out from the room.

"Your papa and the hacienderos were here since four in the morning," Yaya Helen said. "The politicos are here too."

Daria sighed, hoping that last night's events would not lead to the fear that everyone was too afraid to talk about.

In Señor Hernandez's studio, the air was as thick as in the peak of milling season, when fumes would belt from the exhaust of the refinery's smoke stacks. Arguments over what to do with the rebels and the higher government's failure to reply were the central frustrations.

"Puñeta! Why don't we all put our private armies together and invade the rebels?" remarked Señor Montevista. "After what they did to the Dazas and Jisons, I cannot believe the president is turning his back on us. Did he forget who placed him in his position?"

"President Mendoza has his hands full. His health is deteriorating, and it seems Vice President Aragon has been running the show. Have you read about the rallies and the opposition against him, left and right, in Manila?" added Governor Escalante.

"Who funds these peons anyway? We are already being forced to pay stipends to stop their attacks, but look at what happened. We need to show them that we are not afraid," Señor Jamora angrily huffed.

"It does not matter who funds the rebels. I agree we should put our private armies together. However, if we shed blood, would that stop other rebels from attacking? It would only give the other rebels power to prove their cause," said Señor Hernandez.

"We rightfully own our land! It is our birthright, and we have the right to do as we please. The people who came with the land and worked for us have the choice to stay or leave. It is not up to these so-called rebels to decide," said Señor Jamora.

"My friends, I understand how you feel. I too am a haciendero. I have spoken to the president about our concerns," Congressman Saison remarked. "The president has been steadily losing support of the people. He will not run again in the upcoming election, and he does not care anymore."

"Clearly he forgot that votes from the haciendas, especially from our province, made him president," said Señor Jamora. "We inform our workers who to vote for. With what is happening to the haciendas and the entire country, if all hacienderos would unite we could choose the next president.

"Well, it seems you have pointed out a solution to our problem, Señor Jamora," said Señor Hernandez. "I think it is time for us to choose the new president of the country."

It was not until after lunch that Daria got a chance to see her papa. After the preparations for the party and the events of the prior night, Daria tried to make sure that the atmosphere had calmed down before she greeted her father. She walked toward her father's studio, her present in hand, and knocked softly.

"Papa, are you awake?"

"Come in, my love," said her father, who was waking from a nap.

"Happy birthday, Papa!" Daria ran and kissed her father. Her papa happily accepted her greetings and gave her a warm embrace.

Daria handed him a present wrapped in plaid with a green bow and a card.

Dear Papa,

God blessed me with so much, but my greatest blessing is you. You are my inspiration and my moral compass. You will always be my first love. Happy sixtieth birthday.

Your Daria

"Daria, if God permits, your only love," smiled Señor Hernandez. "What made you say this? Oh, wait a minute. In all the chaos I forgot to notice. Is this because of the young man, Vicente's friend—what's his name again? Marco, was it?" teased her father.

"No, Papa!" Daria blushed. "You are my only Prince Charming. Open my gift," urged Daria.

Daria's present caught Señor Hernandez by surprise. It was a picture of him and his daughter, but not just any picture. It was a picture taken when Daria was just a young infant.

"Daria, where did you get this picture?" a teary Señor Hernandez asked her daughter.

"I got it from Mother Superiora when I delivered our donation to the asylum they are building next to the monastery," answered Daria. "I don't recall seeing a picture of you and me when I was a tiny baby. I think I was probably a newborn."

Her father cut short Daria's thoughts. "I will treasure this forever," said Señor Hernandez. "Now, go ahead and change. We don't want to be late to our event, right?"

"Okay, Papa. I'll see you later. I love you."

As Daria closed the studio door, Señor Hernandez picked up the picture frame. Tears formed in his eyes. He remembered Daria's mother as though it was yesterday—a day he wished had never happened.

Daria never knew her mother. She never knew her name or identity or had seen a picture of her. All Daria knew was that she'd died after she was born. Señor Hernandez, with all his power and fortune, had made sure that Daria's mother's identity would never be known to her daughter and would be forgotten by the people of Castellana.

Daria's mother was an orphan raised by the nuns in their orphanage. When she was eighteen she entered to become a novitiate in the Order of St. Dymphna. One of her tasks was to teach catechism at the Hacienda Corazon. She was supervised under Mother Felicia de Paz, Señora Estefania's sister. Señor Hernandez was captivated by the simplicity of the young catechist. Her kindness and sincerity were refreshing to Enrique after the snobbery and the materialistic side of Estefania. They fell in love, and Daria was conceived. When the Order found out that Daria's mother was with child, she was placed in solitude. Mother Felicia, a woman of virtue, told Enrique the truth about the novitiate's condition. On the day of Daria's birth, Enrique stormed the monastery. Holding his baby girl and letting go of the woman he loved were bittersweet.

The Hernandez house in Castellana was a two-story Spanish-style house like any other mansion in the city, but what stood out was the massive garden that surrounded the front of the house. It was almost a copy of a palatial garden in Europe. Tropical flowers were in bloom. Orchids of different colors, sizes, and shapes shone, the lights accentuating their beauty. The bushes were perfectly trimmed to uniform length. The green grass was mowed in perfect lines. White lanterns at the perfect height adorned the palm trees.

The servers, dressed in white shirts and bow ties, were being prepped and given final instructions by Yaya Helen. The tables were set to perfection on fine embroidered tablecloths; the hand-polished silverware matched the fine china. The menu was set: *lechon*, prime rib, paella, and corn soup.

The band tuned their instruments and started with a medley of Beatles music.

Jocelyn, dressed in a royal blue beaded dress that hugged her too tightly and her father, Dr. Feliciano Gonzales, were the first to arrive. Her hair was in a bun to keep the frizz from showing. She wore high-heeled shoes and emerald chandelier earrings given by Tita Estefania.

Vicente and Marco headed to the garden in their suits, their hair gelled neatly, looking like a perfect catch for any of the elite Castellana daughters.

The guests started arriving: the hacienderos and their wives, politicos and their partners. It was a night when everyone came to show off their cars, jewelry, purses, and shoes. Mayor Karlos Vasquez arrived and gave his respects to Señora Estefania. Ignoring Jocelyn, he headed toward Vicente and Marco.

But the night belonged to Señor Hernandez and his daughter. Señor Hernandez entered the garden in his Barong, looking distinguished, dashing, and refined, with his most precious gem on his arm. Daria was wearing an off-the-shoulder emerald green A-line dress. Simple diamond earrings complementing her long, wavy hair.

Vicente playfully nudged Marco, to the dismay of Jocelyn.

Señor Hernandez greeted his guests. "Friends, thank you. It is my great pleasure to celebrate the sixtieth year of my life with all of you. Tonight, may the air be filled with laughter and may all of us be blessed. *Salud*!"

"*Salud*!" cheered the guests.

The guests, all in a celebratory mood, ate, drank, and danced.

Marco took the chance and approached Daria. "I think you should go to Manila and be a party planner. I must say, you did an excellent job," praised Marco.

"Well, thank you. I'm glad you are having fun," said Daria.

"How about you dance with me?" invited Marco.

"You know it's my dad's birthday, and Vicente is watching us right now." She waved at her cousin.

"I'll take my chances," Marco said confidently.

Marco took Daria's hand and led her to the dance floor. The band started playing "Fly me to the Moon." The couple seemed to catch the attention of the guests, especially Señor Hernandez. After the song played, the crowd cheered. The band then turned mellow and started playing "The Way You Look Tonight."

Marco turned to Daria to change to waltz position but was interrupted by Señor Enrique. "Now it's my turn to dance, young man." Marco courteously bowed and handed Daria to her father. Other dancers left the stage as well to allow father and daughter to have their moment.

Mayor Vasquez approached Jocelyn. "Jocelyn, may I dance with you?"

"Karlos, please. Not a chance." Jocelyn left for the garden, leaving the mayor dumbfounded and embarrassed.

Señora Estefania heard the conversation and pulled Jocelyn aside in the garden.

"Jocelyn, for goodness sake, be nice to the man," advised Jocelyn's aunt.

"Tita, I don't care if he is now the mayor or will be president. To me he is that strange boy in the hacienda who gives me the creeps when he looks at me. He is beneath me."

"Well, just act nice. We don't want people talking about your attitude before we find you a prospect for marriage," pointed out Señora Hernandez.

"You know what would be perfect, Tita? I think Karlos and Daria would be perfect for each other. Me, I am interested in Vicente's friend Marco," Jocelyn said.

Their conversation was interrupted as Governor Escalante clinked his glass.

"I would like to make a toast. To my dear friend Enrique, happy birthday. The province is grateful to you and your family for providing jobs and opportunities to the people of Azusa. I'd say that if you have a love for politics you would probably be the perfect governor, or perhaps president of this country." The guests cheered for Señor Hernandez.

"You are the true epitome of what a haciendero should be," continued the governor. "Your love for the land and for your people, your generosity and kindness, are what we all aspire to."

Governor Escalante paused before the tone of his speech turned serious. "That is why, my friend, what happened on the eve of your birthday was indeed a travesty." The crowd became silent. "We, your brothers, and our haciendas are here to support you and are ready to lend you a hand, as is the entire province of Azusa, in remembrance of our fallen brothers. We are here beside you. Salud!"

"Salud!" The guest raised their glasses, drank, and cheered.

"Thank you, Governor Escalante. I am truly touched and honored by your words." Señor Enrique paused and looked up. "Yes, the eve of my birthday was indeed something I do not wish to bring up tonight. However, as I look at all of you present here today, I miss the Dazas and the Jisons. What happened to them and their land deserves justice. We tried to bring justice and peace to our beloved Azusa, especially our Castellana, but President Mendoza seems to be focused on other things, and he forgot his promise to protect us.

"President Mendoza seems to have forgotten that our country's economy is driven by our haciendas. The food that is put on the table in every Filipino household is from the farms cultivated by the haciendero," said the señor, showing his dismay at the current administration. "Therefore, along with Governor Escalante, the Association of Hacienderos in Azusa and the entire Visayan region and parts of the Mindanao region have come together in agreement with the Nationalist Party to choose a candidate for presidency who we believe will protect our lands and interests," announced Señor Hernandez.

"My friends, tonight we would like to announce our candidate. Ladies and gentlemen, may I present to you the next president of the Republic of the Philippines, our very own native Azusan and Castellanan, Karlos Vasquez."

CHAPTER 4

S eñor Hernandez's birthday party appeared on the society pages of the local papers, but it was overshadowed by the headline Nationalist Party and Hacienderos of Visayas Announce their Presidential Candidate. The phones were ringing left and right in the azucarera's office. Telegrams arrived, and errand personnel were dropping letters every couple of minutes, asking for a statement or an appointment to speak with Señor Hernandez.

Señor Hernandez's office in the azucarera displayed the accolades he'd received as a businessman. Recognition from different government and charitable organization adorned his walls, as well as photographs of past Philippine presidents and international leaders. Behind his chair hung a picture of his parents, Doña Rosario and Don Federico Hernandez. On his table, his name was engraved on an eighteen-carat gold plate. There was a picture of him and Daria.

Señor Hernandez was on the phone talking to Mayor Vasquez, but he hung up when he heard a knock on his door.

"Enter, Vicente," Senor Hernandez said. He was expecting his nephew.

"Hello, Tito. Insanity has arrived at Hacienda Corazon," Vicente said. "Remember my friend Marco?"

"For the future of the haciendas and the future of our country, I will take insanity," Señor Hernandez warmly answered. "I do apologize I was not able to give you enough of my time and attention as I promised, but what can I do for you? I heard you had a proposal for me, but before that, I forgot to ask you how are your mother and father, Vicente? Has your mother finally grown up and accepted the fact that she is an adult?"

Vicente laughed. "Mama is still Mama in love with Papa. Loves to shop, loves the theater and now the movies, and still can't cook. As for Papa—Well, as you know, he has been appointed ambassador to the United States and travels a lot, and Mama seems to be enjoying going around the world with him."

"My little sister," smiled Don Enrique. "So let's get down to business. Marco, I heard your family is into construction and real estate?"

"Yes, Tito Enrique. The Gutierrez Group of Companies are builders and developers. We buy and develop lands and subdivide them into lots for housing. We are also starting to plan condominiums around Metro Manila," Marco proudly shared.

"This seems to be the trend in Manila. People are moving to the city, and I can see why this is quite profitable. How did your family start, Marco?" inquired Señor Hernandez.

"Quite humbly, Tito. My father inherited land from my grandfather in Manila. My father is an architect, and he started with one apartment complex in Manila," Marco shared. "Fortunately, it was a success. He bought more land. When he purchased a huge property he decided to divide the land and sell the land per square foot, ideal for small homes. From there we started our own construction company too," added Marco.

"This is where my proposal comes in, Tito," Vicente cautiously added, trying to read his uncle's face. "Thanks to you, me, Mama, and my family have lived very comfortable lives because you run Hacienda Corazon and the azucarera really well."

"No doubt about that," Señor Hernandez said.

"I was hoping that with your blessing, I can have Mama's share in the land divided into a subdivision," said Vicente.

Señor Hernandez was quiet.

Vicente carefully continued. "I am asking for the land on the west side that is closest to the city, at least fifty to one hundred hectares, to develop."

"And I expect my sister said yes to this proposal," said Señor Hernandez. He stood and turned his back to Vicente and Marco, looking at the picture of his parents.

"Yes, Tito," Vicente answered nervously.

"Marco, I don't know if Vicente ever told you the story behind Hacienda Corazon. Being the owner of this land is not an easy task," Señor Hernandez said. "To keep the land as a whole has required blood, tears, and sweat," said his uncle. "It pains me, my dear nephew, that you are asking me to sell parts of it—for what? For profit? Fifty hectares may not seem a lot, but if this progresses would you ask me for the quarter of your mother's share too?"

"Tito, I do not mean any disrespect. Hacienda Corazon is part of my roots too. I am just looking toward the future," said Vicente.

"So you think that sugarcane and farming will no longer be in the future?" challenged Vicente's uncle.

"Tito, the world is changing. People are changing. We are progressing and moving forward," answered the señor's nephew. "Yes, we do need farming, but the number of professionals is increasing, and they want to have homes for their families."

"I understand your desire, Vicente. I am not saying no, but give me time. I am a fair man, as you know. Let me study your proposal and see, but for now let's end here," finished Señor Enrique.

It was close to four in the afternoon, and Daria was in her office, trying to focus on reconciling the expenses for the end-of-the-month report. Between the phones ringing and the people hustling back and forth, she was not up to the task and could not accomplish her work for today.

Her thoughts had kept wandering all day to why her father and the other haci0enderos chose Mayor Vasquez to run for president. Daria had no interest in politics. She grew up seeing her father create politicians, which led her to view politics as a game where the winner earns power, and not to serve the people.

"Lourdes, I'm done for today. Can you radio Nelson to saddle up Silvestre and tell Yaya Helen I'll be back in an hour or so?" Daria requested.

As she was heading out she saw Vicente and Marco by the azucarera office entrance, looking serious.

"How did the meeting with Papa go?" Daria asked curiously. "What exactly did you ask him, anyway?"

"Well, business. Business that could make Hacienda Corazon a frontrunner," smiled Vicente, not giving many details to avoid worrying his cousin.

"Did Papa agree to your proposal?" asked Daria

"He said he will consider it," answered Vicente.

"Well, best of luck, gentlemen. I am off to the stables. Care to join me?" Daria asked, expecting a no from her cousin.

"I'll join you," Marco offered.

This caught both Daria and Vicente by surprise.

"I think after all the events this week a breath of fresh air would be good for the mind and body," remarked Marco.

Vicente, unsure if he would leave Daria and Marco alone, thought and gave in. "All right, you two go. I am heading back to the house to relax. See you both for dinner."

Unbeknownst to the trio, Señor Hernandez was looking at them at his office window. His thoughts turned toward Marco and Daria. *Perhaps. Perhaps.*

At the stables, Daria was surprised to see Marco was capable of putting the saddle on the horse. He picked the mare Paris, and he handled the grooming quite well for a city boy.

"Who would have thought? I thought when you play polo, the horses are already tacked up and ready to go, but look at you!" remarked Daria.

"Yes, they are, but I want to learn how to get things done, not just done for me," answered Marco.

Daria mounted Silvestre, and Marco got on Paris. They walked out of the stables and then trotted toward the hills. The workers had started replanting the sugarcane, and the buds burst from the soil. The *tambis* trees bore red fruits. Daria reached for two and tossed one to Marco.

"What is this?" asked Marco.

"You never had *tambis* before? Try it."

"Hmm, not bad. Tastes like apples. I thought at first they were bell peppers, but I know bell peppers don't grow on trees," remarked Marco.

Daria smiled at Marco's willingness.

"How does it feel to own such a huge piece of land? I mean, this is massive for just one owner," commented Marco.

"Nobody's asked me that question before. I was born in Castellana, and I grew up with Hacienda Corazon as my playground."

"It's quite a playground," said Marco. "The workers—have they been working for your family for generations as well?" inquired Marco.

"They have. We are grateful for their work. Without them, there would be no crops, no sugar, no products," Daria said with a smile.

"My family business is in land too. However, we give people we call the working class or the middle class the opportunity to own homes. Would you be willing to give up part of your land to give it your people to build their own homes?" asked Marco.

Daria was caught off guard by Marco's question. She'd never had a conversation with anyone about her opinions. She'd always been treated as a fragile girl whose views were irrelevant and naïve.

"It still boils down to business, right? Whether giving them an opportunity to own land or work for the land, it is still a matter of making profit," answered Daria. "But, to answer your question about selling a piece of Hacienda Corazon for homes … Was that what you and Vicente asked my papa?" asked Daria.

"Proposed, yes. You think he will say no." Marco tried to get a feel for what Señor Hernandez would say from his daughter's point of view.

"Don't judge Papa. His answer might surprise you," Daria answered.

The two continued on to the trail and lost track of time. Marco pointed to the majestic mountain.

"So this is how Mt. Mansilay looks up close? It's beautiful." He looked at the mountain and then at Daria.

Daria noticed how far they'd traveled and felt uneasy.

"I think we should head back now. It's almost sunset. I think Yaya Helen is probably worrying about now."

"Can we stay for the sunset?" asked Marco.

"Perhaps some other time?" said Daria, looking around.

"Are you okay? You look a little nervous," Marco asked with a concerned look on his face.

Before Daria could answer, three gunshots rang out. Paris panicked and threw Marco. The mare ran toward the open field, and another shot was fired. The horse dropped to the ground. Daria was shocked as she watched the dying mare struggle for life.

Marco picked himself up and reached for the radio in Silvestre's saddle pocket and called for help.

"This is Marco and Daria."

"Yes, sir. This is Felix."

"Felix, Daria and I are close to Mt. Mansilay. Gunshots were fired. My horse was shot. We need help."

"Roger, sir. We are on our way."

"Daria, snap out of it," Marco said, shaking her gently.

Daria's thoughts wandered back to the events that happened in her father's birthday.

Marco mounted Silvestre, pushing Daria forward and had the gelding walk back to the trail of the hacienda. Daria regained her senses and was about to speak, but Marco covered her mouth.

Voices of men murmuring headed toward the struggling mare.

"This is one of Hacienda Corazon's horses. Horse meat is quite a delicacy," one of the man said, laughing.

Marco pulled the reins and asked Silvestre to quietly head back toward the woody trails. Silvestre, however, started trotting and captured the attention of the rebels.

"Hey, who's there? Stop!" yelled one of the men.

Marco kicked Silvestre's belly hard to make the gelding gallop. The men tried to run after them. One of the men shot in the air, but Silvestre continued to gallop. When the men saw Felix and his men coming to rescue Marco and Daria, they retreated.

"Miss Daria! Sir Marco! Are you both all right?"

"Yes, Felix," Marco answered as he helped Daria down. "Daria, you are safe."

Daria looked at Marco, placed her head on his chest, and started crying. Marco wrapped his arms around her. "You are safe. We are safe. Let's take you home."

Yaya Helen paced back and forth, waiting anxiously for Daria's return. As she saw the blue Land Cruiser enter the gate, she made the sign of the cross and hurried down to meet them.

"Daria, my Daria. Are you hurt? Let me look at you." Yaya Helen started crying, filled with worry. "Let's go inside."

Señor Hernandez walked toward his daughter and embraced her. "It's all right, Daria. No one will harm you. As for the horse, we can always buy a new horse."

"Papa, I am okay but Marco fell off Paris and ..." Daria said, trying to fight back tears.

"I am all right, Señor. I am more concerned about Daria. The event might have shocked her," Marco said, trying to avoid worrying Daria.

Vicente came up to his friend. "Dr. Jimena is here. Let's have him check you."

"Helen, where's your señora?"

"Oh, Señor, the Señora and Jocelyn went on a retreat. They won't be back till Friday," answered Helen.

"I am okay, Papa. I will be all right. I am all right," Daria assured her father.

"Daria, look at me." Señor Hernandez turned his daughter toward him. "No one in this world will harm you as long as I am alive, do you understand?"

Daria nodded. "Yes, Papa, I know that. I am tired though. May I go to my room? Yaya Helen, can you prepare my bath, please?"

Daria gave her father a kiss and quietly walked to her room.

Señor Enrique looked at his daughter as she left. For the first time in his life, the haciendero felt fear. He walked toward the bar and poured himself a shot of brandy. The people who'd threatened his daughter's life needed to pay.

He picked up the phone. "Karlos, I need you to come to my house. Now."

Mayor Vasquez left his desk without hesitation and headed to the Hernandez residence. As soon as he arrived he made his way to Señor Enrique's studio. Señor Jamora, Señor Montevista, and Congressman Saison were present as well.

"Tito, I heard what happened. Is Daria all right?" asked the mayor.

"Yes, she is still shaken, but she will be all right," replied Señor Hernandez.

"I sent the police to patrol the area and work with Felix," reported Karlos.

"I trust that your men and Felix can handle this," said Senor Hernandez. "My concern now is your filing for candidacy."

Mayor Vasquez was caught off guard. He thought the señor would be more concerned after what happened to his daughter and that his candidacy would be secondary.

"In the next few weeks the Commission on Elections is opening its office for presidential candidates to file," Senor Hernandez informed Karlos. "Señor Jamora has arranged with his contacts in the press to get you coverage, and Señor Montevista and the governor ensured pledges from other families to fund your candidacy.

"I will be in Manila with you when you file," added Congressman Saison.

Mayor Vasquez was quiet for a moment.

"Señors, I appreciate your appointment and your trust, but I am not sure I am ready. I have only been in politics for a couple of years. How do I gain the public's trust?" an unsure Karlos Vasquez said.

"Which is why you are the perfect candidate, Karlos," interrupted Señor Jamora. "You are young and, pardon the expression, come from humble beginnings. The youth who cry for new blood in politics will adore you. The laborers and the union will feel you are with them. Even the rich can empathize with your ordeal as a young boy whose father was killed by the rebels."

"Karlos, when you were a boy I knew from the start that your life would not be confined here in Castellana," Señor Enrique shared to boost Karlos confidence.

"I promised your father that I would make you the man that he hoped you would become. I will not fail that promise," said Señor Hernandez.

"Very well, I will do as you ask. I will file my candidacy, and I will be the next president of the republic."

"This is it! I can feel our victory rising." The enthusiastic Congressman Saison rose and poured four shots of brandy. "Here's to the next president. President Karlos Vasquez."

The rebel's hideout was on full alert. After the incident at Hacienda Corazon the rebels could not risk attracting attention. Fortunately, they have their patron sent an informant about the police and the Hacienda's private army that they were able to move their group further into the mountains.

"Hacienda Corazon has doubled security, and the police will investigate soon. We need to regroup and wait for our next move," Ka Abel advised his group. "Also, since the national elections are coming up, we have to remain vigilant and see which candidate will be willing to listen to us."

"The haciendero's puppet, Mayor Vasquez, is running for the presidency. The hacienderos and the Nationalist Party are in this, and we must do something about that," cried Ka Emok.

Ka Abel was silent, as though he knew a secret, a secret from the past that he hoped someday would be of good use to him and their cause.

Daria was unable to get to sleep and decided to attend first morning mass. She joined Father Jose and Brother Armando for breakfast.

"Daria, my child. I am glad that you are all right. Pray God is always with you and looking after you," said Father Jose. "Now if you will excuse me, I need to attend a parish meeting. Brother Armando, stay with your friend."

"Thank you, Father," said Daria.

When Father Jose was out of sight, Brother Armando stood up and, in tears, hugged his friend.

"My Daria! I thought I would lose you. Thank God Marco was there to save you," said Mando, teasing his friend and hoping to cheer her up.

"Of all the things to say, Armando! Please, there's no need for dramatics." Daria smiled at her friend.

"I just couldn't help thinking about the rebels. Why are they doing this? What are they trying to prove? Are we really being selfish about owning so much land?" Daria asking her friend for some insight.

"Daria, after what happened it is only natural to seek answers, but my dear, you are the victim here. Rest your mind, and don't think too much about it. Let's talk about Marco," Brother Armando said, trying his best to get a smile out of Daria.

"Did I hear somebody say *Marco*?" Vicente interrupted.

"Vicente, were you eavesdropping? Do you know that it is a grave sin to listen to someone's confession?" warned Brother Armando.

"Mando, you are no priest, and no, I was not eavesdropping. I knocked and no one answered, so I let myself in," Vicente defended himself.

Daria blushed. "Is Marco with you?"

"The Lone Ranger, you mean?" joked her cousin. "He's on his way. He was unable to escape Father Jose, so I guarantee you he did not overhear your conversation," Vicente informed her.

When Marco's footsteps could be heard approaching, Vicente announced his friend's arrival. "Here's our hero!"

"Which hero are you talking about?" Marco tried his best to walk straight and placed his hand on his friend's shoulder.

Daria put her hand in her chest. For some reason, she suddenly felt awkward around Marco, an uneasy feeling that she had not felt before. It made her self-conscious.

"Of course you are the Lone Ranger! Thank you for saving our Daria. You shall be rewarded generously. She will probably have to name her first-born son Marco in your honor," teased Brother Armando.

Daria looked horrified.

"Stop with the Lone Ranger joke please." Marco looked at Daria and smiled. "I am glad to see you are all right, Daria."

"Thank you, Marco. I guess there'll be no riding around the hacienda for now," answered Daria. "Knowing Papa, he will probably have Silvestre come live with us and make me ride my horse around the garden."

"Well, at least no one got hurt and it happened when Marco was with you," pointed out Vicente. "This has been a memorable trip, right, my friend? I am sure this excitement will make you visit Castellana again," he said, poking his friend.

"Oh, that's right—you are leaving tomorrow." Daria was surprised at the disappointment in her voice. "Did Papa give an answer to your proposal, Vicente?"

"After yesterday's events, I will not push it. Mama will be back in a few days from America. I will ask her to help convince Tito Enrique."

"I do hope she can convince him. It would be nice to see you both again." Daria spoke her thoughts out loud.

Marco smiled, and his heart fluttered.

Señor Hernandez and Mayor Vasquez were having coffee in the Hernandez garden, discussing Daria and Marco's encounter with the rebels and how to proceed with the mayor's filing for candidacy. The conversation turned to a much lighter note. Señor Hernandez had noticed that some things were missing from Karlos's life.

"Karlos, not that I am prying, but I notice you don't have a girlfriend," Señor Hernandez said, putting his coffee on the table. "Are you dating or pursuing anyone? Do you have a lady in mind?"

Karlos coughed, surprised by the señor's question.

"If you become president I would not mind you marrying Daria," Señor Hernandez said jokingly.

"Señor, Daria is like a little sister to me. It is hard for me to think of her as a woman. Though she does have qualities that would make her fit to be a first lady," said Karlos.

"I agree with that, but I was just joking. I would never force my daughter to marry a man she does not love or who does not love her," Señor Hernandez said.

"However, Señor, I do have a lady in mind. I think you might have noticed my fondness for Señora Estefania's niece, Jocelyn," Karlos shared.

"I did notice. Would you really want a materialistic brat like her? It is quite obvious that she snubs you and dislikes you," pointed out the señor.

"Who knows, Tito? If I become president things might change," Karlos replied with a hopeful look on his face.

"You are free to dream, my boy, but Jocelyn should not be given the position and power as first lady of this land. Some people are too greedy for that," advised Señor Hernandez.

"Papa, Mayor," Daria said as she entered. "Vicente and Marco are here to greet you before their flight tomorrow for Manila."

Señor acknowledged the men and had them sit, gesturing for the maid to serve them coffee.

"I'll excuse myself," Daria said, not wanting to join in.

"No, Daria. Please, my dear, sit," suggested Señor Hernandez. "There is something I need to ask you to do for me. Daria, I would like you to go to Manila with Vicente," Señor Hernandez ordered.

"Papa, if this is because of what happened yesterday …" Daria said to protest her father's suggestion.

"I think it would be a good idea for you to have a vacation. Also, I would like you to learn about and see what Vicente and Marco are working on in Manila," said Señor Hernandez. "See if their business might bring some good to Hacienda Corazon."

"Vicente, Marco. I thought about your proposal," said Senor Hernandez, capturing the attention of Vicente and Marco. "You have to understand that business and politics are inseparable, no matter what others say. Marco, if you want to invest in Hacienda Corazon's land, I ask for your support for Mayor Vasquez's candidacy. Vicente and Marco, if you can assure me of your company's support, then we have a deal."

The three youngsters were surprised.

"I know that Mayor Vasquez is an intelligent and capable man," said Marco. "I will for sure put in a good word for him with the business sector."

"Thank you for the opportunity, Tito. We will do our best. We won't let you down," Vicente said, shaking his uncle's hand.

Daria remained quiet. She could read her father quite well, but for the first time what her papa was plotting seems a mystery to her. All she could do for now was agree.

CHAPTER 5

Manila, October 1969

The hustling, bustling city was not really Daria's environment. She felt relieved when she saw they were at the village where Vicente lived, an exclusive gated community with modern houses and finely manicured front lawns that almost looked too uniform. Vicente's house was contemporary. The signs that his parents were indeed well traveled showed in the house. The entry resembled a resort. There stood Vicente's mother, Christina Hernandez-Valderrama.

"My children, I am so glad to see you are here," Señor Hernandez's younger sister said. "Come inside. We have so much catching up to do."

Christina Valderrama, or Tita Chris, as she wanted to be fondly called, was a woman of the city, a socialite with a fun, likable personality who loved to live life. She went to a boarding school in Manila and had lived in the city from then on. Her husband, Jaime Valderrama, was the Philippine ambassador to the United States. Tita Chris loved Daria and Señor Hernandez but was estranged from Señora Estefania.

"So Daria, have you met Marco? What do you think of him?" She led her niece to her all-white living room, decorated with Lalique crystals and Fernando Amorsolo paintings.

"Mama, you surely know how to ask the most pertinent questions. You have not even said hello to your only son," Vicente approached his mother, giving her a kiss.

"My son. My perfect son. I know you are well, so no need to ask. I got a call from my brother, and he told me about how your proposal went. You got what you wanted, so I know you are doing fine. I don't know about Daria and Marco though. I heard he saved your life?" said Tita Chris with a mischievous smile

"Marco is a gentleman, Tita. Yes, he got us both away from an encounter with the rebels," Daria shared with her aunt.

"Well, let's invite him over," her aunt suggested with a mischievous grin.

"Mama, we just got back. Don't you think we should let the poor guy get some rest first? Besides, I'll see him at work on Monday. I am taking Daria too," Vicente told his mother.

"Oh, good! Daria, why don't you rest up a bit, and then we can go shopping. You need a whole new wardrobe while you are here in Manila," her aunt offered, ushering her to the guest room.

The weekend was fun yet chaotic for Daria. Her aunt's energy was at a level that is probably equivalent to her horse Silvestre's gallop. Daria had fun shopping with Tita Chris. Her aunt's taste was beyond Daria's simplistic style, but her aunt was respectful enough when her niece declined a suggestion. Daria was treated to elegant restaurants and the ballet. It was noticeable that she caught a lot of attention from the city's young men.

It was not until late Sunday afternoon that Daria was able to call Señor Enrique about her arrival in Manila, to the dismay of Señora Estefania. Daria received news that she thought quite amusing.

CASTELLANA

Señor Hernandez's Home

"*Por Dios*, Enrique, why did you send Daria to Manila without a chaperone? You should have waited for me to come back. Jocelyn should have gone with her," the irritated Señora Estefania said.

"I did not want to disturb your praying, Estefania. And besides, Daria will be with Vicente and Cristina. They will take good care of her," Señor Enrique told his wife.

"Your sister is on another planet! What ideas she might put into your daughter's head!" Estefania said, not hiding her dislike for Enrique's sister.

"Something that would make Daria laugh, I hope. And besides, there is something I want to discuss with you and Jocelyn and, of course, my brother-in-law Dr. Gonzaga," Enrique said, changing the topic to avoid a fight with Estefania.

Jocelyn sat up straight, intrigued by what her uncle had to say. Dr. Feliciano Gonzaga, Jocelyn's father and the town doctor, put down his coffee cup and looked up at Señor Hernandez.

"As everyone knows, Karlos is up for the presidential seat. We also know that he has always been interested in Jocelyn," started Señor Hernandez.

"Tito, if you are implying—" Jocelyn interrupted.

"Jocelyn, let me finish," her uncle said, looking at her sternly.

Señora Estefania placed her hand on Jocelyn's waist and shook her head, telling Jocelyn not to interrupt.

"As I was saying, since Jocelyn has no prospects or proposal for marriage, I suggest we accept Karlos's proposal to be engaged to Jocelyn," Señor Hernandez said, stating it more like a business proposal than anything else.

"Tito, how could I marry that person? The poor boy from the hacienda?" whined Jocelyn.

"Jocelyn, please. He is no longer that poor boy. He is our mayor now, not to mention he will be running for president," her father said calmly, knowing where Señor Enrique was trying to get to.

"Your father is correct, Jocelyn. Do not be stubborn or too proud to think of Karlos's past. Think about the future. He could be the next president of our country," Señora Estefania said, trying to encourage her niece, aware of the benefits Jocelyn might receive. "And you, my child, will be the first lady of this country," Señora Estefania added, beaming.

"First lady. Would that mean I could be the richest woman in the country?" inquired Jocelyn.

"One of the most powerful and perhaps one of the most catered to if he wins," Señora Estefania said, trying to reassure her niece. "You see, my child, a man needs a woman next to him to win the presidency. Not just any woman but a beautiful, intelligent, and graceful woman who would awe people. I think that is why your uncle is trying to convince you—because you have those qualities."

Señor Hernandez tried to hide a laugh because he knew all Jocelyn had was beauty. But to make Karlos happy and agreeable, he needed Jocelyn to agree.

"I think you should pray and think about it, Jocelyn. Marriage is a responsibility, let alone if you become first lady," Dr. Gonzales said, trying to ponder on things.

"Oh, hush, Papa! What do you know? I think Karlos would not be a bad husband if I get this in exchange," Jocelyn said, realizing that the life she had been dreaming of could be achieved. *Well, if he wins. If not, then I will still be the first lady of Castellana.*

"Good! It's all set then. Let me call Karlos and invite him to come over for dinner. If it all works out you will join him in Manila to file for his candidacy," beamed Señor Hernandez.

MANILA

Vicente took Daria to his office, where he was the chief engineer for Gutierrez Group of Companies. GGC was the company owned by Marco's family; Marco was the director of land development and acquisitions. Vicente and Marco met in one of Ambassador Valderrama's parties in New York; Marco was a student at Yale. Vicente had earned his degree in engineering from Santo Thomas University, and his career seemed to be a given because he had a fascination with industry and technology.

"Vicente," greeted Marco. "Daria, welcome to our office."

Daria smiled and shook Marco's hand. She was amused that the office environment exuded a different air from the azucarera. The modern amenities and the organized cubicles, as well as the employees in their suits, looked stiff and monotone compared to the busy and colorful characters that came in and out of Hacienda Corazon.

"Would you want to have coffee first?" offered Marco.

"I would love to, but I have a lot of work that needs to be taken care of," Vicente said. He winked at his friend. "Marco, since you are the boss you can get away with many things, so I leave Daria in your hands."

Before Daria could refuse, Marco led her to his office. On the way, Daria noticed the office staff looking at her. All she could do was give them a small smile. The elevator ride was uneventful. Daria was uncomfortable when more employees greeted Marco and her, staring at them because Marco still held her arm.

When they reached his office on the tenth floor, Marco asked his secretary to bring them coffee and then opened the blinds, giving Daria a view of the Metro.

"So what do you think so far?" Marco asked.

"You have a really nice view from your office. It must be nice, seeing the vastness of the city and Rizal Park from here."

"Yes, but the greenery and the mountains of Hacienda Corazon are sights to behold too," Marco said.

"So where should we start? Vicente told me about the proposal, but to be honest I have no idea what am I supposed to do or what I am here for," Daria said openly.

"How about I show you what goes on outside the office? As you can see, there is nothing here but people working, taking calls, and having meetings. Let me take you to where the action is," suggested Marco.

One of GGC's worksites was about twenty minutes from Marco's office. One of Marco's projects was to create housing for middle-class families, places to call their own offering respite and an investment for the middle-class workers. As they approach the site, Daria felt like it was harvest season at the Hacienda. Instead of people and water buffalo working on the field, heavy machinery plowed the land to make way for concrete. Tractors were filled with concrete blocks and sand instead of sugar cane. This made Daria smile.

"This is one of my pride projects," Marco beamed. "And Vicente's vision on how to branch out Hacienda Corazon to different businesses."

"So you think that farming and sugarcane are outdated?" asked Daria.

"No, Daria. Not at all. However, the world is changing. We need farming, but people are changing and becoming educated, having careers. They will not want to work in the fields anymore. However, people always need land. Wouldn't you want to share your land and make a profit too?" Marco asked, trying to challenge Daria.

Daria smiled. *Of course I would want to share the land*, she thought to herself, *but for profit?* That was something she'd never thought of. Deep inside, in her most honest and deepest thoughts, she would love to give part of the hacienda to the people for no profit at all. She shook her head, for she knew her thoughts were naïve.

"Are all the workers here working for you, Marco? They sort of remind me of the people who work the fields, but instead of crops they carry blocks," observed Daria.

"Yes, in the construction part of the company, which is what Vicente handles," replied Marco. He carefully added, "We handle them quite differently from how you handle the workers at the hacienda."

"What do you mean by that?"

"Well, I know that the people in the hacienda are given wages, but here we follow government and labor regulations that are not applied to the haciendas. I mean, we pay social security and overtime, and they get time off work. They are protected by the union too, and we try our best to abide by the union," Marco shared, trying to be careful not to offend her.

"But despite abiding by the union, I still read on the news that the laborers are revolting against companies. It seems to me, even with the law, the union will never be satisfied," Daria said. "I did talk once to Papa about benefits for the workers, Marco," shared Daria. "When the law was passed, the haciendieros were exempted. I told Papa maybe we should set an example. He told me that for now, we can give benefits in other ways. I guess if one hacienda starts giving its workers benefits, the other haciendas will be forced by their people to follow."

"This is also probably why Vicente is presenting this project as a way to protect your family," Marco added thoughtfully.

"Marco, there you are." A broad man in his late fifties approached.

Marco waved at his father. "Dad, I did not know you were out here today. Let me introduce to you Daria Hernandez, Vicente's cousin. Daria, my dad, Miguel Gutierrez."

"It's a pleasure to meet you, Mr. Gutierrez."

"Please, call me Tito Miguel," Marco's dad said, smiling warmly at Daria. "Marco, your words describing this beautiful young lady were too pathetic. Daria, thank you. Please do extend my thanks to your parents for being such gracious hosts when my son visited Castellana."

"Will do, Mr. Gutierrez... Tito Miguel," answered Daria.

"Marco, why are you taking this young lady to such a hot and dusty place as our work site?" Miguel Gutierrez scolded his son playfully. "I feel I did not raise you as a gentleman! Forgive me, Daria."

"It's okay, Tito. I am glad Marco brought me here. After all, I am here to learn about Marco and Vicente's project." Daria was trying her best to maintain her composure.

"Well, young lady, would you do me and my wife the honor of joining us for dinner tonight? I will extend the invitation to Cristina and Vicente as well," invited Mr. Gutierrez.

"If it is fine with Tita Cristina, Tito, I don't see why not," Daria courteously replied.

"All right. Then we will see you tonight. We are only a few blocks away from your aunt's house, and my wife is a great cook," beamed the older Gutierrez. "Marco, why don't you drive Daria back to her aunt's house?"

"Yes, Dad. Shall we, Daria?"

Before they left, Miguel Gutierrez pulled his son's arm and teasingly whispered, "Do not let this one get away."

CASTELLANA

Señora Estefania was checking the dinner table, making sure that the setting was perfect. Tonight, Karlos Vasquez would formally ask for Jocelyn's hand. Their engagement excited Estefania.

Jocelyn and her father arrived. Jocelyn quickly rushed and twirled in front of her aunt.

"Do I look like a first lady, Tita?" asked Jocelyn, her nose in the air.

"You surely do!" She gave her niece a hug and kissed her brother-in-law. "Your dress fits you perfectly, and the jewelry! What can I say? Your aunt definitely has taste."

Father Jose entered, Brother Armando following behind. "Well, I am in awe. Jocelyn, may God bless you, my child. Hopefully I will be officiating at your wedding."

"Father, it surely depends. It might be the bishop, or perhaps the cardinal, if Karlos becomes president."

"He has not formally proposed yet, Jocelyn," Brother Armando added.

"Why, Armando, my future brother-in-law. How lucky am I! I will have a priest for a brother. If I become first lady, I will do everything in my power to send you to the Vatican," said Jocelyn airily.

"Brother Armando will be returning to the seminary to conclude his training and hopefully, with God's blessing, he will be ordained in December," shared Father Jose.

Before Armando could reply, Señor Hernandez entered the room along with Mayor Vasquez.

"Everyone, here is the man of the hour!" Señor Hernandez announced. Señor Hernandez nudged Karlos Vasquez forward.

"Good evening, Dr. Gonzales, and of course Señor and Señora Hernandez, Father Jose, Mando." Karlos nervously greeted them and approached Jocelyn.

"I am grateful for all of you being here today. As you know, aside from Mando, I consider you family. Jocelyn, you have always captured my admiration. To me, you are the most beautiful woman in Castellana. That is why, in front of everyone who loves you, I would like to ask if you would do me the honor of becoming my wife," Karlos proposed quickly.

Jocelyn smiled. "Where is the ring, Karlos?"

"Oh, the ring!" He took out the box and opened it to show her a three-carat marquis-shaped stone in a ring that made Jocelyn gush. "Señora Estefania picked it out. I hope you like it."

"Of course I do! Yes, Karlos. I hope you will make me the first lady of the country," Jocelyn answered.

Manila

"So Estefania's niece is engaged to Karlos. I like Karlos. He is such an intelligent man, but I must say he has poor taste in women," said Christina Valderrama, rolling her eyes.

"Karlos has been in love with Jocelyn for as long as I can remember. I'm glad that they are getting married," Daria replied.

"If Karlos were not running for the presidency, I doubt this would ever happen. For sure Estefania is smiling from ear to ear right now," added Christina.

Before Christina could continue, Vicente announced their arrival at the Gutierrez residence. Marco was waiting for them at the front door, pacing back and forth, looking nervous.

Everyone exchanged greetings with Marco before he escorted them inside the house. The Gutierrez house was simple and to the point, comfortable, with few frills or valuable collections. What caught Daria's attention was the array of musical instruments: a piano and cello in the living room, a drum set with a couple of guitars on the veranda that overlooked the swimming pool. Their home was decorated in a contemporary style and was quite inviting.

"Christina, Vicente. And you must be Daria. I am Marie Gutierrez," said Marco's mother, a petite, slender, brown-eyed lady. "It is a pleasure to meet you. I heard so many good things about you."

Marco's mother was half American and half Filipino. She'd met Marco's father when he traveled to New York. Marco had two younger brothers who were currently in college in the United States.

"I hope you like American food," Marie said as she ushered the guests toward the dining room, where she served pot roast and fresh baked rolls.

"This is awesome, Tita Marie!" Vicente exclaimed. "It's amazing how you can prepare all of this on such short notice, while someone I know can't even make rice with a week's notice."

"My son, it is not polite to point out your mother's weaknesses to others," Christina Valderrama scolded her son, which sent the whole room into laughter.

The dinner was relaxed and filled with good food and fun conversation, mostly about the boys' visit to Castellana. Daria was amused to see that the Gutierrezes conducted themselves with humor and did not act aristocratic, considering their status and success in business. It was refreshing to see humility among the elites.

"So Daria, how are you liking Manila? We should take you to the polo club," Marco's mother suggested. "Marco has been telling us how much you love horses."

"Of course, Mom. I mean, if Tita Chris permits," Marco answered his mother cautiously.

"Absolutely! I do not expect Daria to stay with me the whole time and not have fun while she is here," Christina said.

Christina Valderrama noticed that Marco started to look nervous and anxious.

"I must say, Marco, you look flustered, and you are all red. It does not seem hot in here," teased Vicente's mother.

Vicente burst into laughter and was about to comment but was interrupted by Mr. Gutierrez, who announced dessert would be served in the backyard.

The teasing halted as they enjoyed the night breezes and the chocolate cake baked by Marco's mother. Christina Valderrama had one glass of wine too many and urged everyone back inside to hear her sing, asking Mr. Gutierrez to accompany her on guitar and Mrs. Gutierrez on piano. Vicente escorted his mother inside, leaving Marco and Daria alone.

"Your parents are so much fun. Thank you for having me," Daria told Marco, smiling.

"Thanks. It can get crazy here. I think my parents like you. I mean, you are probably the daughter they never had." *That came out wrong,* Marco thought. "Daria, I have been meaning to ask you ..." Marco said in a serious tone.

Daria turned to Marco. He smiled and lost his train of thought for a second.

"You know, every time I look at you I am lost for words," Marco said, trying not to act nervous. He told himself, *"No, Marco. You like this girl so much—do this right."*

"I really like you, Daria," Marco continued. He took Daria's hand and looked her in the eye. "I think you are special and that you are an incredible woman who can bring so much to this world. I really want to get to know you better."

Daria looked stunned but tried to smile to encourage Marco.

"I have never done this before with any woman, but you are not any woman, so I will do this the traditional and right way. Miss Hernandez, would you give me the opportunity to pursue you, with the hope that one day I can ask your father to marry you?"

Such a formal and honorable proposal left Daria speechless. Though she had known Marco for only a short time, she could feel the young man's sincerity. Deep inside her heart she knew that she was falling for Marco too.

Daria nodded, looked up, and smiled at Marco. "I accept, Mr. Gutierrez."

Unbeknownst to them, four faces were peering through the living room window and smiling at them.

Daria told her father about Marco's intentions, and Señor Hernandez also received a phone call from Marco and Christina, his sister. Señor Hernandez seemed pleased. Marco gave his word to pay his respects after All Souls' Day. Señora Estefania brushed Daria's news aside; local and some national papers had picked up the story of Mayor Vasquez and Jocelyn's engagement.

Three weeks into Daria's stay in Manila, in the midst of her fluttering heart and joy over Marco, she was reminded that Mayor Vasquez and Jocelyn were arriving in Manila to file for Karlos's candidacy. Her joy was interrupted when Jocelyn appeared.

"Daria!" Jocelyn greeted her, flaunting her ring. "Say hello to the future first lady."

"Hi, Jocelyn. Congratulations. I am happy for you and Karlos," Daria told Jocelyn sincerely, giving her cousin a hug.

Christina Valderrama welcomed Estefania's niece. "Jocelyn, how are you? Look at that ring of yours—it's as big as your hair."

"Hello, Tita. Thank you for having me," Jocelyn said, mindful of her manners. She knew that Daria's aunt did not favor her.

"So what is the plan for us ladies? Is Karlos in the Nationalist Party's office? I suppose he will be staying at Señor Jamora's?" Cristina asked Jocelyn without allowing her to answer. "How does the Nationalist Party want you to appear for the press tomorrow? What image do you want to project?"

Jocelyn waited a couple of seconds before answering. "They will be sending some people to dress me. I would like to thank you for organizing the dinner tonight so Karlos can meet with the Gutierrezes. They could really help us."

"Anything for my brother. Well, you have to thank Daria for that. After all, she is their future daughter-in-law."

Jocelyn smiled a fake smile.

The dinner Christina Valderrama prepared was simple yet intimate and elegant. The Gutierrezes, representatives from the Nationalists party, and members of the Manila Business Club were present. The food was catered by one of Manila's finest chefs, and a pianist accompanied by a violinist filled the dining room with classical Filipino music.

It was apparent that Mrs. Gutierrez had become fond of Daria. She pulled her away from Marco and started introducing her as her daughter-in-law. Daria was worried about Jocelyn. She felt for her cousin, who stood in a corner, not knowing anyone. People passed her by as Karlos was introduced table after table by Congressman Saison.

"Excuse me, ladies and gentlemen, I would like to thank Mrs. Christina Valderrama, wife of our ambassador, for hosting this wonderful dinner," Congressman Saison started. "On behalf of our Nationalist Party and the members of the Manila Business Club, I would like to introduce to all present our future president, Karlos Vasquez."

Karlos waved and smiled confidently. "Thank you, Congressman Saison. Ladies and gentlemen, I am Karlos Vasquez, and yes, I am the Nationalist Party nominee for president. "I know some of you might ask about who I am and my purpose for becoming president. Who is Mayor Karlos Vasquez? He has neither a pedigree nor a name. Is he running because the hacienderos are behind him? Is he worth my support?" Karlos paused for a second to look at the crowd. Some businessmen seemed uninterested in what he was saying. Karlos thought to himself that he needed to say something catchy to get their attention.

Karlos started again "All of these questions are valid. True, the hacienderos are supporting me, but I will not be their puppet. I support their cause because without them I would not be where I am today. However, because they made my nomination possible, that does not mean that I will follow their whims. No, I will do what is best for the progress of our country, and I made that clear to them." Karlos noticed he was starting to get the crowd's attention.

"I will be the bridge between the old and the new. I will bring industry and progress to the fields and opportunities for business to flourish for both the hacienderos and those who are in the business sector," Karlos said, his momentum growing.

"I was born poor. My father was killed by the rebels. I was given the opportunity of an education, and I did not waste it. I became a lawyer. I defended the poor, which led me to become a public servant to serve those in need. This was embraced by the people of my hometown," Karlos Vasquez shared.

"The world is changing. Opportunities are opening, and all of us have to embrace the changes. My countrymen want the opportunity to improve their lives, and that is why I turn to you, the businessmen of Manila." Karlos stretched out his arms to encompass the businessmen. "Without your corporations, factories, innovations, I cannot do enough on my own to help this country. I need you and your businesses to provide jobs to better the lives of those in need. This is why I ask those who are present here to stand with me and the Nationalist Party, for the future our country."

The guests were silent before the president of the Manila Business Society applauded. The rest followed suit, and the Nationalist Party members started chanting, "Vasquez for president." Jocelyn rushed to Karlos's side and raised her fist.

Daria started clapping too, but she noticed that there was something different about her old friend. Daria saw a confident and direct man. She was surprised about his line about the hacienderos. She tried not to think about it too much. She just told herself it might be just a strategy to get the Manila business sector to support him.

COMMISSION ON ELECTIONS OFFICE

The day of filing for the presidential candidacy came, and the door of the Commissions on Elections was opened. The election focused only on the presidential and vice presidential seats. Karlos Vasquez was the Nationalist Party presidential candidate, running against Vice President Manolo Aragon of the Democratic Party and his vice president, Congressman Alfredo de Guzman of Tarlac.

Karlos's running mate, former senator Aristotle Lacson from Zamboanga, a veteran in politics, waved to the reporters and walked slowly with the support of his cane. Señor Jamora was also present, along with Congressman Saison and Governor Escalante, all wearing blue, the party's color, to show support for Karlos Vasquez.

Jocelyn was in a blue Filipiñana dress, her hair up, enjoying the attention of Karlos's supporters. Daria, escorted by Marco, wearing a simple A-line dress, was wishing she did not have to be there, but as the dutiful daughter she was, she'd honored her father's request.

The filing was amicable, and different candidates from different parties greeted each other and shook hands. Even Karlos and Vice President Aragon greeted each other and posed for the cameras. When they were about to part ways, a bomb exploded a block away from the Commission on Elections' office, dispersing the panicked crowd. People frantically ran left and right. Vice President Aragon's bodyguards rushed him into his bulletproof vehicle. The police started a formation to prevent the protesters from entering the Commission on Elections grounds. Señor Jamora's bodyguards escorted the Karlos Vasquez entourage, including Jocelyn, to a safety vehicle.

Marco and Daria couldn't pass through the crowd. Daria tugged on Marco when she saw Karlos trying to head toward the protesters. Karlos took the megaphone from one of the police officers, saying, "My countrymen, I am Karlos Vasquez. Today I filed my candidacy for president. I am not leaving until I hear the reason and the cause of your protest."

"Liar! You are like the rest of them! You are nothing but a puppet!" a protester roared.

"You may think what you want, but if I become the president of our country I will be in the service of the people, not for the interest of those who would not benefit all," Karlos said, reassuring the crowd. "May I know what your group is and what is your cause? What are you trying to achieve?"

"We are from the labor union groups!" cried one of union heads. "We are here because we labor and toil, but not all of us get the benefits and pay mandated by law. The government offers no consequences to those who do not follow the law."

"My father died after working on a construction site. We received no help from the company he worked for. We have many debts from trying to keep him alive, and all the company said was that my father was the one violated the law because he worked that day. No one forced him," cried one of union members.

"My wife and I worked for a factory. There was no ventilation, and we inhaled fumes the whole day. When we complained we were told to find a new job. My wife caught pneumonia and died, leaving me with our three children," cried another voice from the crowd.

Karlos made his way in front of the police officers so that the people could see him. He raised the megaphone and said, "I am the son of a farmer. I grew up seeing my grandfather and father wake up at four in the morning to work in the fields and come home at sunset. I too worked in the fields to help my parents when I could, thinking that my efforts would ease their burdens. I do understand your pain."

The crowd quieted, and Karlos continued. "I was fortunate that the señor of the hacienda was a good man. He gave me the opportunity to study, to become a lawyer. I took it upon myself to become a public servant. My brothers, I understand that you long for equality and for change. I hear your voices. So that is why I ask you to grant us a peaceful election. Let us show them that we can win with negotiation, not hostility. If I become president, I, the son of a farmer who has lived in poverty and stood in your shoes, will make sure your voices are heard."

"How do we know that you can be trusted?" asked a protester.

"I invite your leaders to come meet with me at the office of the Nationalist Party," encouraged Karlos Vasquez. "My door is open to discuss your needs. I would not have stayed here to face you if I were not sincere." Karlos then pointed out his opponent's response, "I would have ran away like a coward because I did not want to be bothered. I would make empty promises."

Daria and Marco were both astounded by what they heard from Karlos. They saw the protesters start to back off and disperse. The crowd calmed down, and they heard people saying, "Karlos Vasquez deserves to be the next president."

The evening paper, radio, and evening news covered the candidacy filing and the candidates, but that was outweighed by what Karlos Vasquez had done with the labor and union protesters. The front page of the national papers the next day featured Karlos's photo taking on the crowd; the photos of the candidates occupied the second half of the front page. Most of the editorial pieces were written about his heroic act, though a few were skeptical. The office of the Nationalist Party was bombarded by the press and followers trying to get a glimpse of the new sensation.

"Karlos, my boy, you did it! Old man Aragon better retire now. What you did was brilliant! Free advertising, free publicity, free media coverage—brilliant, my boy, brilliant!" praised Señor Jamora.

"At first I was doubtful if you could pull it off, Karlos, but even before day one of the campaign you have made your name known around the country," added Governor Escalante. "You played the game well. Good choice of words."

"I just did what needed to be done," said Karlos. "What is our first course of action when we start campaigning?"

"Well, first we have to observe All Soul's and All Saint's days. Visiting your father's grave would be fitting and good publicity," suggested the governor. "Then we can play around with your love story with Jocelyn."

"The first campaign stop is Mindanao in November. This is where Aristotle Lacson will come into play," added Señor Jamora. "We then head back to Castellana for the Christmas season, where we can showcase your love for your town and, of course, your province."

"You make it sound so easy," commented Karlos.

"We have a lot of support in Mindanao and the Visayas, which is why you need to head to Manila and go around Luzon after the holidays and travel around the Visayas for the last part of the campaign," continued Señor Jamora.

"I have to add that I want to meet with the rebel leaders, as well as labor and union leaders. I want to show them that I hear and understand their concerns," added Karlos.

"Of course. We can arrange that. We can bring in actors if they won't cooperate," thought Señor Jamora out loud.

"Let us try to get the real leaders," Karlos challenged. He looked out the window and saw the media and his supporters. He took a deep breath and closed his eyes. For the first in his life he felt he had found his true purpose.

CHAPTER 6

D aria arrived in Castellana early the day before All Saint's Day, before Karlos and Jocelyn. She was glad, for it would give her the chance to catch up with her father. The drive from the airport to her house made Daria realize how much she missed Castellana. The sight of Hacienda Corazon's coat of arms in front of the hacienda's entry made her think about what she had seen and learned in Manila. Her thoughts then turned to Marco, and she felt a certain longing in her heart. Daria shook her head. When she looked up she saw Yaya Helen waving happily.

"Daria! I missed you, my baby. Yaya is happy that you are back. Did you have a good time?" Yaya Helen asked excitedly.

"There was definitely a lot of excitement. I will share the details later," Daria answered. "Are Mama and Papa having breakfast?"

"They are in the señor's studio," answered Yaya Helen.

Daria headed toward her father's studio. She missed her papa but was a bit anxious to see her mama. With presents in tow, Daria knocked and then opened the door to the studio.

"Good morning, Mama, Papa. I am home," she announced.

"My Daria, how I missed you!" said her papa. "Next time I will send you on vacation for less than three days. I can't wait to hear about all the events and trouble you got yourself into in Manila."

Daria went up to her papa to give him a kiss and then approached Señora Estefania cautiously. She did not looking up but accepted Daria's greetings.

"Yes, Papa, there surely were a lot of things that happened," Daria said. "Tita Christina sent gifts."

"Oh, my sister! Hopefully it's not something too exotic." Señor Hernandez accepted the blue box Daria handed him and opened it. Inside was a leather cowboy hat with a note saying:

Brother dearest,

I hope this helps give you the John Wayne look when you go around Hacienda Corazon.

Love, your baby sister.

Enrique tried the hat on and turned to Daria and his wife to jokingly ask, "Do I look like John Wayne?"

The ladies giggled.

"Enrique, don't even show yourself around in that silly hat," said Señora Estefania, trying to hold her laughter.

"And this is for you, Mama." Daria handed her mama a red box with a bow.

"A red box? Christmas is not even here yet." Señora Estefania accepted it, and her stern look softened when she saw the brand on the box. "Well, Christina does know how to shop. We will call her later to thank her." She tried on the beige Salvatore Ferragamo pumps.

"Daria, a lot of things happened in Manila, but the first thing I want to discuss is the most important." Señor Hernandez looked at his daughter affectionately. "I received a phone call from Marco, and I have to commend the boy for being traditional and honorable enough to ask me to pursue you. Do you like this young man?"

Daria's face turned hot and felt embarrassed by her father's question.

"We will be expecting him three days from now. He will be staying at Governor Escalante's home since Vicente won't be here and the circumstances are now different."

"Yes, Papa. I understand. I met with his family too, and they were kind and welcoming," added Daria.

Señora Estefania tried to act uninterested. "Did you learn anything while you were there?"

"I got a chance to go see how they run the business. The way they run things is something businesses should follow," cautiously answered Daria. "When Karlos was filing for his candidacy, Marco and I heard the protesters complaining about how companies treat workers. Marco's companies are doing their best to head toward equality."

Señora Estefania seemed unamused by Daria's answers and about to challenge her, but she was interrupted by Señor Enrique.

Señor Hernandez asked one question after another and looked his daughter in the eye. "Daria, do you like Marco? Do you think he will make you happy? Would he honor your thoughts and consider your opinions?"

Daria smiled and embraced her father. She knelt next to him and said, "Yes, Papa. I like Marco, and he does have the qualities of a good man. In God's good time everything will fall into place."

Señor Hernandez patted his daughter's head. "Your happiness is mine. All I want is someone who will be good to you and treasure you as much as I do."

Señora Estefania was silent. She had been married to Enrique for more than thirty years and never once had she felt love from him. When Daria was born all his love went to his daughter. She let out a sigh and looked the other way, taking a sip of her coffee.

In the Philippines, remembrance and paying respect to the deceased happen on November 1, All Saint's Day, deviating from the Roman Catholic calendar, where the second day of November was hailed as All Soul's Day. Both days were observed as religious and national holidays, and people returned to their hometowns to visit their loved ones who had passed away.

There were two burial grounds in Castellana, the Catholic cemetery and the government, or public, cemetery. The Hernandezes arrived early at the family's mausoleum, where the remains of Señor Enrique and Señora Estefania's parents rested. It also housed the memorial for Daria's great-grandparents and other family members who had passed. The mausoleum was filled with arrangement of white carnations and white lilies. Señor Hernandez lit a white candle for his parents and in-laws, and Señora Estefania and Daria did too. Father Jose started his blessing, and everyone prayed in silence.

Daria thought of her mother. "Wherever she may be, may she have everlasting peace," prayed Daria. On moments like these, she wished she had a picture or a memory of her mother.

On the other side of town stood the public cemetery, more chaotic than its Catholic counterpart. While the Catholic cemetery had well-kept grounds, organized lawns, and palatial mausoleums and flowers neatly adorned the tomb sites, the public burial grounds were filled with candle and flower vendors. People wandered around the unkempt grounds, not knowing where their families' tombs were. Sepulchers instead of mausoleums stood high on the walls of the cemetery.

There were more people than usual in the public cemetery. It was not because the number of dead had increased but because the son of Castellana was with the people that day. Karlos Vasquez, along with his brother Mando, visited their father's grave. Their father was buried in one of the sepulchers, and the brothers lit a candle and offered a prayer to their father. After paying their respects, Karlos Vasquez greeted his constituents, shaking hands and gesturing them to follow him to the cemetery's entrance. At the entrance was a truck loaded with *suman,* a sweet sticky rice treat wrapped in banana leaves and mangoes prepared for especially for All Soul's Day.

"My friends, today we remember our loved ones. Let us remember all they have done and do what we can to have a better future. As a son of a farm worker from Castellana, I hope that I will have your support to become the leader of our country. Please let us celebrate our traditions by eating suman. As we were told, if we eat sweet sticky rice, unlucky souls will not stick to us," Karlos invited the crowd.

"You are indeed a good man, Karlos. May God bless you," cheered a man in the crowd.

"You have not forgotten where you came from. We will support you," said one of his constituent.

Karlos waved and ushered the people toward the truck. Brother Armando started handing out the food. The people were overjoyed by his gesture.

"Thanks for helping me out, Mando. Tatay would be happy, and I am sure he is proud of both us. I wish you well and will be praying for you," Karlos said affectionately, gripping his brother's shoulder.

Brother Armando smile and touched Karlos's hand. He thought, *My calling to be a priest may very well be God's plan so I can act as my brother's conscious and moral compass when he feels alone and if his direction to help the people is going astray.*

One limping man holding a cane came up to Karlos with his son and caught the mayor by surprise.

"Your father would be very proud of you. You will be the one who will fulfill this country's destiny, and we are here behind you to help you," the man said, patting Karlos's chest.

"Thank you. I appreciate your support," Karlos answered, shaking the man's hand. As the man left Karlos noticed that the man had left a note in his chest pocket.

The rebels in Mt. Mansilay had been quiet. Almost too quiet. Ka Eden was cooking a big batch of *valenciana*, sticky rice with meat, what the elites called the poor man's paella. Ka Abel and Egoy went to town to observe All Soul's Day and then to head to Mindanao to meet with another rebel group.

"Ka Eden, the men are getting uneasy. Why are we not moving? All we do is monitor the movements of the haciendas," complained Ka Roger.

Ka Eden covered her large wok with banana leaves, leaving it to dry, and faced Ka Roger.

"We have to be patient. Especially with elections coming up. We need to plan accordingly and follow the group leaders' instructions. One mistake and everything will fall apart."

"Do you think Mayor Vasquez will win? The news about him handling the protesters was impressive. Maybe he will be willing to talk with us too."

"Of course he did well," Ka Eden murmured quietly. "Ka Roger, for now let us act according to plan. Continue to talk to the hacienda workers and convince them that our cause will better their lives and invite them to come and join us."

Ka Eden went back to her cooking. She thought about Mayor Vasquez becoming president and smiled. A poor man's son becoming the most powerful man of the country—that was something new.

The holidays passed, and Daria was relieved. All Soul's Day was always hard on her. Suppressing her emotions through the remembrance of the dead made her sad about not knowing her mother. She was also saddened by the departure of her friend Brother Armando and prayed that her friend could overcome the fear that was in his heart.

Daria tried to distract herself with Marco's visit. To her surprise, his parents were arriving in Castellana, insisting they wanted to formally meet Daria's parents. Daria sat in the back patio looking at the garden. She noticed that the flowers were blooming; the weather had begun to cool down. She started to walk toward the flowers but looked back when she heard Señora Estefania calling her.

"Daria, can you come here? I need to talk with you," requested Señora Estefania.

"Yes, Mama," answered Daria. She approached her mother and sat on a garden chair.

"It is quite a surprise to have Marco's parents come over to meet us," said the Señora. "I suppose this is something serious. I thought he was just courting still, not proposing or anything yet."

Daria was surprised at her mama's inquiry, especially with her actual effort to try to have a conversation with her.

"There is no proposal for engagement yet, Mama. Marco's parents were really accommodating and very nice to me during my stay in Manila. I think Mr. Gutierrez is interested in talking business with Papa too," Daria said to her mother carefully, trying to avoid any conflict.

"You know, Daria, you and Vicente are the only heirs to Hacienda Corazon. It may be in the province, but it earns very well. Its income can compete with big corporations in Manila. I just want to make sure that it is not what they are after," Señora Estefania warned.

"Mama, I don't think money is the issue with my relationship with Marco. I don't see him having any interest in the hacienda. In any case, I think he and Vicente would want to invest in making it better," answered Daria.

"I am glad that Jocelyn is engaged to Karlos, because if he does win the presidency I know the hacienda will be protected. You might not believe me, Daria, but I do want what is best for you," Señora Estefania said, taking a sip of her coffee.

Daria could not believe what she just heard. Before she could reply Yaya Helen entered and announced the arrival of the Gutierrezes.

Señora Estefania and Daria went to the house and greeted their guests in the living room.

The señora introduced herself. "Welcome, Mr. and Mrs. Gutierrez. I am Estefania, Daria's mother. Marco, nice seeing you again."

The Gutierrezes exchanged pleasantries with Señora Hernandez. Marco made his way to Daria, handing her a bouquet of yellow and pink tulips. As he was about to embrace her, Señor Enrique stepped in. Marco took a step back.

"Welcome to Castellana, familia Gutierrrez," greeted Señor Enrique.

"It is our pleasure to meet you, Señor Enrique Hernandez," said Miguel Gutierrez. "We heard great things about you and your town from Marco. We were so enamored of your daughter that we could not resist joining our son."

"Marco is such a charming young man, and quite a businessman too. I am glad you came so we can discuss his proposal for Hacienda Corazon and perhaps also some politics," Señor Hernandez said to Mr. Gutierrez.

"Business, yes, Señor, but politics—let's just say I leave that to the people and to the experts," said Mr. Gutierrez.

"Well, before the gentlemen discuss business, let's head to the dining room. Karlos, Jocelyn, and Governor Escalante will be joining us," said Señora Estefania as she ushered her guests to the dining room. As they entered Karlos, Jocelyn and Governor Escalante arrived as well.

As the guests seated themselves around the luncheon table, Jocelyn whispered to her aunt, "Tita, how come you did not use the Chinese plates and the silver spoons and forks? We need show these people how rich you are."

Estefania pulled Jocelyn back to make sure the guests didn't hear them, "My dear, the china and the fine silver are only used for formal occasions. Besides, to show class and elegance one does not need to show off."

Señora Estefania sat on her husband's right, and Daria was seated on her father's left. Governor Escalante occupied the seat opposite the *cabisera*. Marco sat next to Daria, and his parents sat next to Señora Magarita. Karlos took his seat next to Marco and had Jocelyn sit next to him. Estefania Hernandez rang the bell, signaling the maid to start serving the tomato soup. As the maid made her rounds, Mrs. Gutierrez could not help but comment, "Oh my, this is like in the Jane Austen novels that I read."

Señora Estefania smiled, trying to show she was not amused by the comment. "Here in Castellana we still have a certain culture and lifestyle that we follow."

"Estefania, I think it's just a way of Marie saying that you have a fancy way of presenting a luncheon," commented Governor Escalante, trying to break the tension.

"So, Karlos and Jocelyn, when is the wedding?" asked the governor, knowing that this would divert Estefania's attention.

Karlos laughed. "It is really up to Jocelyn. We have not set a date yet. It will probably be after the elections."

"I would want it after the elections. If Karlos wins the presidency it would be an elegant affair, our gift to the people," Jocelyn said dreamily.

"How would it be a gift to the people, Jocelyn?" asked Marie Gutierrez. "It should be a simple affair if Karlos becomes president. As the servant of the people, he should show humility, not extravagance."

Estefania defended her. "Well, it's not like Jocelyn comes from a poor family. If the people question the cost and the luxury of her wedding, we can say that her family paid for the wedding."

"Daria, what about you? How do you envision your wedding?" Marie tried to avoid further aggravating Estefania and Jocelyn.

"Mom!"

"Marie!" Marcos and Miguel Gutierrez gasped in unison.

"Son, it's just a conversation. I want to hear Daria's thoughts."

"Daria, I too would like to know," Enrique said, smiling. "I want to know how much money I need to put away for you."

"Papa!" a wide-eyed Daria said.

"Daria probably has no idea. I always thought she would become a nun before Marco came along," Jocelyn said, which caused Señor Hernandez to look at her sternly.

Seeing her father's temper rising, Daria answered. "I just want a simple wedding. I want to get married here in Castellana. If Mando is a priest by then, he can officiate at my wedding. We'd have the reception here at home and have another celebration at the hacienda with the people."

"And we can have another grand celebration in Manila," added Mr. Gutierrez, which made everyone laugh and broke the tension a bit. "Marco, the ball is in your court now, my son."

Luckily for Marco, the maids started serving the main dish.

The ladies made their way to the library. Señora Estefania showed Marie Gutierrez the family heirlooms and artwork decorating the walls of the Hernandez home. The gentlemen were left in the dining room for coffee and started with chatter about the upcoming elections.

"Karlos, you are heading in the right direction. The entire country has been talking about you and your efforts. The rich and the poor seem to agree that you are the man for the position. You're giving Aragon a run for his money," started Governor Escalante.

"We have not started the campaign yet, Governor. I am sure they have a lot of propaganda ready, and I am the underdog. Vice President Aragon has been in politics for years. His name is known by the people all over the country," said Karlos.

"Like everybody said, they want change, right? Out with old and in with the new—figuratively and literally speaking," answered the governor.

"Well, if that is the case, you might get kicked out of your position soon, my friend," joked Señor Hernandez. "How did the business league view Karlos, Miguel?"

"To be honest, I have no taste for politics. What the union asked Karlos our company put into practice after the labor law passed," said Miguel Gutierrez. "Our company's philosophy is that if our employees and workers are taken care of, they will be motivated to work better."

"I admire you for what you stand for, Miguel." Turning to Mr. Gutierrez he added, "At the end of the day we need to earn profits to keep businesses going and to continue to provide jobs."

"There will never be satisfaction for everyone," Marco said, trying to make a point. "If there is complete equality for all then there will be no democracy. What we need in our country is to bridge the gap between the rich and the poor by creating professions to strengthen the middle class."

"Marco, Western thinking has influenced you too much," said Governor Escalante.

"I agree with Marco." Everyone turned to Karlos. "The middle class is the key to strengthening the economy. The more educated people become, the more they strive to better themselves. I am an example of that."

"There you go, Karlos—you can use that for you campaign. I think that would work well with the student voters and professionals, especially in the urban areas," suggested Miguel Gutierrez.

"That would not work for majority of Visayas and Mindanao though," countered Señor Hernandez. "Parts of Luzon and the majority of Visayas and Mindanao are still farmland. Karlos needs to connect with the land owners because they dictate who to vote for. The entire Hacienda Corazon alone can already produce at least five hundred votes compared to individual student voters and the professionals. United haciendas can make a president."

"I agree, Tito, but as I was talking to the protesters, a thought came into my mind," Karlos shared. "The businesses in Manila are targeted by labor and union groups, and the hacienderos' nightmare are the rebels attacking and claiming their land. To be honest, I do not see any difference between what both parties are asking. If I could get the trust of the unions and the rebels, I could probably negotiate with the business community and the hacienderos. I bet that is something Aragon cannot do."

"How on earth can you do that? The protesters were a blessing in disguise, but what about the rebels? Especially the militant Muslim group in Mindanao? Good thing we have Aristotle help us out. His farmland has troubles with both rebels and Muslims militants," stated Governor Escalante.

"As the traditional politicians say, let the people hear what they want to hear," said Karlos, standing up. "Now, gentlemen, if I may be excused, I have a meeting at the city hall."

"All right then. Next stop for you is Mindanao, and I need to be heading home too. Miguel, Marco, shall I meet you at home?" asked the governor.

"I'll join you, Governor," Miguel said, standing up and heading toward Señor Hernandez. "Enrique, pleasure meeting you. I hope to get to talk you and enjoy your company."

"Same here, Miguel. Let me show you the way to the library." Señor Enrique pushed back his chair but was interrupted by Marco.

"Tito, may I have a moment?" asked Marco.

"It's okay, Tito, I'll take them," Karlos offered.

Daria's father and her suitor returned to their seats. Señor Hernandez rang the bell and asked the maid to make them a fresh batch of coffee.

"Tito, thank you again for having us. I do apologize that my parents arrived on such a short notice—" Marco was interrupted by Señor Hernandez.

"Get to the point, Marco," Señor Hernandez said sternly.

"Right. My intention for visiting, sir, is not to talk about business or politics but to formally ask if I might date Daria," Marco directly said to Daria's father. He then shook his head, for he knew the words did come out wrong.

Señor Hernandez looked at Marco and leaned toward him. "Marco, I know you spent your college life in America. The word *date* does not apply here in Castellana," a stern-sounding Enrique Hernandez said. "Daria told me you want to pursue her, but just to date her? Young man, you'd better stop if 'dating' is your intention. I want my daughter taken seriously, or I can easily have Felix track you down."

Marco was trying to figure out if Señor Hernandez was being witty or testing him, but Daria's father seemed to read his mind.

"Marco, when it comes to Daria I take things seriously."

Marco took a deep breath. He tried to calm himself down and caught a glimpse of a picture of a young Daria smiling. "Tito, I know Daria is the love of your life. She is the most special woman I have ever met," Marco said. "I admire her for her humility and wit, and I have to say I have fallen in love with your daughter. I do not see myself being with anyone but her. I know it has only been a short time since we met, but from the first time I met her, a part of me could not let her go. Señor Hernandez, I am asking for your blessing. I would like to ask for your daughter's hand in marriage."

"When are you planning to propose to her?" asked Señor Enrique.

"With your permission, I would like to propose to her on Christmas Eve here at her home, before Noche Buena," Marco replied earnestly.

Señor Hernandez was quiet; there was no expression on his face as he tried to overcome his emotions. The day a man came to ask to take his daughter away had become a reality. Then he thought about Daria, about how she smiled when she spoke about this man and the glow that radiated around her when this man was standing next to her.

Señor Hernandez took a sip of his coffee and looked at Marco. "Someday, my son, if you have a daughter, make sure if someone asks for her hand in marriage you remember the exact words you said to me. For now, let's keep it a secret between us."

Marco processed, word for word, what Enrique Hernandez said.

"It's yes, Marco. You have my blessing."

Marco Gutierrez, lost for words, stood up. Instead of accepting his soon-to-be father-in-law's handshake, he embraced Enrique Hernandez. Both men tried to fight back tears.

CHAPTER 7

D aria returned to her usual routine after Marco and his family went back to Manila. She made her rounds at Hacienda Corazon with Silvestre, but the gelding was annoyed by the sound of the Land Cruiser trailing behind them carrying Felix and Yaya Helen. Daria was not fond of the idea, but this was the only way her father would allow her to ride her horse around the fields. Daria noticed that cold breeze coming in; the sugarcane was getting taller. She signaled Felix to make a right so she can check the fruit trees.

Daria headed toward the orchard and saw children throwing their slippers on the lanzones trees, trying to hit the fruit. The children saw Daria approaching and started scrambling. She saw a little boy trip on his slippers and smack his face on the ground. Daria got off Silvestre and approached the frightened boy.

"Are you okay?" Daria asked softly.

Felix started yelling at the children to leave, but Daria stopped him.

"Yaya, can you help this boy, please?" Daria directed Yaya Helen toward the boy. "Children, come back. We are not upset with you."

When the children headed back toward Daria, she noticed that she have not seen their faces before. Felix approached her and said, "Miss, leave this to me. I will tell them to go away. They are not from Hacienda Corazon. They are probably illegal settlers."

"Felix, let me handle this. They are just children."

"Are you here because you want some lanzones?" Daria approached the kids cautiously. She reached for a branch filled with the small, round, yellow-skinned fruit and handed some out the children.

"Yes, miss. We do not mean to steal. We are hungry, and when we saw the fruits we could not help but take some," the little boy replied.

"Where are you kids from?" asked Daria.

"We came from the Jisons' hacienda, miss. Please, miss, do not send us away," pleaded one boy wearing tattered clothes.

Daria looked at the emaciated, dirty faces of the children. Some wore no shoes nor slippers, and their clothes were inadequate.

"Tomorrow at around eleven in the morning, I want you to tell your families to come to the azucarera in Hacienda Corazon. No need to be afraid. Tell them Daria Hernandez wants to talk with them. Father Jose will be there too. For now, I am giving you permission to take some fruit with you, but remember—it is not right to steal. Do you understand?"

"Yes, Miss Daria," the children answered in unison.

The little boy tugged Daria's shirt and said, "Thank you."

Daria turned to Felix. "Does Papa know about this? How long have the people been staying in the hacienda? How many families?"

"Miss, your papa is aware of the situation. About thirty families have settled close to the northern side of the hacienda. They claim to have been with the Jisons before, but we are not sure if all of them are indeed from there," said Felix. "The surrounding haciendas seems to have a lot of illegal settlers on their lands too."

"Well, rebels or not, they are still people, and they are hungry. I need people to help feed them tomorrow and give them supplies," ordered Daria. "Yaya, I believe we still have leftover packages from Papa's birthday?"

"Yes. When we get back home I will check how many we have. I believe we have more than enough. I will go to the market after so I can make a big batch of chicken rice soup," offered Yaya Helen, knowing that Daria was on a mission.

Daria looked back at the kids, who were busily picking fruit and devising ways to carry as much as they could. She waved at them and mounted Silvestre. Daria could not help but feel empty. She started to think differently about the massive amount of land that her family owned and the children who did not even have a small piece of land to build a home on.

Daria passed by the parish office on her way home to ask Father Jose to help her on her mission with the children and their families. The priest happily agreed. When she arrived home, she headed straight toward her father's studio. She did not hear her mother calling her.

"Daria, Daria!" called Señora Estefania.

"Oh, sorry, Mama. I was in a rush to see Papa," said Daria. "Jocelyn, hello."

"Hold on, Karlos is with your papa. Jocelyn is leaving for Zamboanga tomorrow."

"Yes, Mama, but I need to talk Papa first," Daria said, hurrying toward her father's studio. "Hi, Karlos, Papa. I was out with Silvestre today, and I saw some poor children. They told me they were from Hacienda Jison, and they are settling on the north side of our hacienda. Would you believe there are at least twenty families there? They are hungry and sickly. I visited Father Jose today. I told the children to bring their families to the azucarera tomorrow. I had Yaya Helen prepare food for them, and I will give them the remaining packages from your birthday," Daria reported, out of breath, amusing her papa.

"My darling, you never cease to amaze me. Do what you must," said Señor Hernandez.

"Yes, Papa, but I feel feeding them is just not enough," Daria mused. She sat in the chair in front of her father's table. "I feel I need to do something more."

"Do you want to run for president, Daria?" Karlos asked, trying to cheer Daria up.

"Not funny, Karlos," Daria replied. "I just can't help but think about what Vicente and Marco have been planning. Creating new jobs besides farming for the people. Providing benefits in case they get injured or are too old to work. Opportunities for children to go to school. Karlos, you should do something. After all Hacienda Corazon is your home too."

"Daria, I must say I am impressed by your actions but more so by your thoughts. You have grown up," Karlos said.

"Maybe you just miss Marco so much, my darling. That's why you keep hearing his words in your head. Go ahead with your project for tomorrow, and I will handle the settlers, okay?" Señor Hernandez said to comfort his daughter. "Now go change for dinner."

Daria shook her head in defeat and left her father's studio. Karlos thought about Daria for a moment. She was no longer the little girl running around the hacienda but a woman who wanted to improve the lives of others. Karlos was impressed.

The next morning Daria headed to the azucarera with Father Jose. She asked Jocelyn to join them, but Jocelyn declined, saying she had an appointment. Daria thought this might have been a good opportunity for Jocelyn as she wanted to become first lady.

Felix and his men were helping Yaya Helen unload supplies. Daria noticed that some of the men were heavily armed.

"Felix, tell your men to remove their arms, please," demanded Daria.

"Miss, if there is an attack we need to be ready. Señor Enrique ordered us to make sure you are safe," answered Felix.

"If the rebels attack we will offer them food," Daria said calmly. "Please, at least no weapons bigger than the kids."

Felix complied and instructed his men to remove their rifles and only to keep hand guns.

Before long the children Daria had met at the orchard were running toward her, happily yelling, "Miss Daria! We are here, and our families are here."

The little boy who'd fallen walked up to Daria to say hi.

"Is your ankle better? I forgot to ask your name." Daria knelt to check the boy's foot.

The boy nodded and smiled. "My name is Lito, and my mother and baby sister are here with me."

Lito's mother came up to Daria and thanked her for inviting them.

Father Jose clapped his hands to catch the crowd's attention and asked them to form a line. He then led a prayer. After the prayer, the crowd formed a line, and Yaya Helen and a couple of Felix's men handed out the rice soup.

Father Jose and Daria walked among the crowd, trying to see if they could gather any information from the people without frightening them. Daria saw how hungry they were; no one wasted a single grain of rice. The children were very happy to have their own shares and sat quietly and contently.

"Father, this breaks my heart," Daria whispered to Father Jose.

"Daria, God will bless you for your generosity. Hacienda Corazon is not the only farm that is experiencing this problem. These people are blessed because you did not turn your back on them," answered Father Jose.

"Vicente and Marco presented a proposal to Papa to subdivide the southern part of the hacienda. Come to think about it, if they can start, the sooner the better. Their project could offer people jobs," Daria said to Father Jose.

"In God's perfect time, my child." Father Jose patted Daria's back and headed toward the children to play with them.

Daria and Yaya Helen started to hand out the packages, a total of fifty. Some women approached Daria but were blocked by Felix. Daria shook her head at Felix and smiled at them. The women meant no harm. They just wanted to thank Daria and ask her if she had any work for them or their husbands. Daria instructed them to leave their names with Yaya Helen.

The children gathered around Daria and gave her hugs and thanked her for their meal. They told her that they hoped they could see her again and that she would bring treats for them. Daria laughed and told them if they attended Sunday school at the parish she would.

A group of rebels from afar were observing Daria and Father Jose. They were surprised that Daria had come out to help the illegal settlers and wondered why Señor Hernandez agreed to allow her to help them.

"Having those people join our cause would make our job a bit harder," Ka Roger said. "Maybe we should go and scare Señor Hernandez's daughter away."

"No, let her be," Ka Eden said sternly. "I got word from the patron not to touch her. Let her help the people."

Daria arrived home exhausted, happy, but unfulfilled. Her mama and papa had left to attend one of their friend's anniversary party, and she was glad to have the whole house to herself. After taking a bath, she changed into her pajamas and went to the library.

One thing Daria appreciated about her mama was Señora Estefania's love for books. The library was decorated with burgundy draperies and white shelves. The books were categorized by genres and alphabetized meticulously by Señora Hernandez herself. The polished and shining antique silver cherub bookends were her mama's precious treasures, for they once supported Señora Estefania's father's books. Daria decided to choose a fun book to read, Mark Twain's *A Connecticut Yankee in King Arthur's Court*. She made her way to the white sofa and placed a cushion behind her back. As she settled down the phone rang. When Daria picked up the phone, she was pleased to hear the voice on the other line.

"Marco!"

"You sound enthusiastic to hear from me. Do you miss me that much?" Marco teased. "I bet your parents are not home, right?"

"Yes, they are attending an anniversary party. I am just glad to have somebody to talk too after a long day," said Daria, trying to avoid saying how much she missed him. Daria told Marco about the illegal settlers and the children and how helpless she felt for not doing enough to help them.

"You and Vicente need to hurry up and get your project started so we can give people jobs," Daria said.

"Well, I think maybe next year. Don't you think we should get married first? What's your ring size? I know how you want our wedding to go, and it seems easy. We can probably get married in two weeks," Marco teased.

"I'm hanging up now, Marco," Daria countered.

"Wait, Daria, I am only half joking," Marco said in self-defense. "So Christmas … What are your plans for Christmas and the New Year?"

"Tita Christina and her family will be spending the holidays with us, and I believe Tito Jaime will be home too. What about you?"

"Me? My parents are flying to New York next week to spend Christmas with my brothers, so I guess I will be alone here."

"You are welcome to join us if you want. Oh, Armando's ordination will be on Christmas Day. He would be delighted to have you," Daria said, hoping Marco would say yes.

"I wish I could, but with my dad and Vicente out of the office, I really can't leave work," Marco said calmly. "Sorry, Daria. I miss you, and I will make it up to you."

"I miss you too, Marco," said Daria, trying to cover the disappointment in her voice.

MINDANAO

Karlos Vasquez arrived at Zamboanga's airport with Jocelyn and her father, Dr. Feliciano Gonzaga, early afternoon. Karlos was expecting a quiet arrival, but he was astonished to see that a crowd of people filled the airport exit. The press made their way toward Karlos. The *Zamboanga's Inquirer* reporter came up to him. "Mayor Vasquez, what plans do you have for Zamboanga and Mindanao?"

"I would like to see the beauty of Zamboanga and make connections with the people of Mindanao and our Muslim brothers and sister."

"There are rumors that the Muslims leaders want to meet with you. So do the rebels after they observed your concern for the common people. Would you meet them even if it puts your life on the line?" The reporter held his recorder near Karlos's face.

"Of course, but I do not want to worry my loved ones, especially my lovely fiancé, Jocelyn." Karlos waved to Jocelyn and held her with his arm. Jocelyn smiled when she saw the cameras start flashing. "I am running for president with a mission and the promise to help my countrymen. If my Muslim brothers want to meet with me, I am willing to hear their thoughts and concerns."

Aristotle Lacson came up to Karlos and gestured to the press. The crowd started yelling Karlos's name and started chanting, *"Vasquez for president!"* The people seemed bewitched by Jocelyn too. Some women came up to her and adorned her with a local jasmine garland. Jocelyn, enjoying the attention, reached out for Karlos and clung to his arms.

Zamboanga reflects Spanish colonial rule and its Muslim heritage. The geography has been ever-changing throughout history, but the beauty of the land had been abandoned by the government's political decision to divide the land and remove its title as the capital of Mindanao. The people in that part of Mindanao were torn and divided. The Muslim movement protected its territory against the migration of Christians to the area.

The scenery on the way to Nationalist Party's vice presidential candidate's home reminded Karlos of Azusa, though he thought that Zamboanga was more beautiful; one side reflected the deep blue ocean and the other side the picturesque mountains. Spanish architecture was also prominent, but the feel of the town was more humble and simpler than Castellana.

"Is it safe here, Tito Aristotle?" asked Jocelyn when she saw women covered with headscarves. "I heard that the Moros openly kill Catholics here."

"Jocelyn, mind your words," scolded Dr. Gonzaga.

"There are attacks here and there, but we manage to survive," Mr. Lacson said to Jocelyn. "Not all of them are bad people. Same with Catholics—not all Catholics are good people."

"Jocelyn, my dear, that is why I am so glad you accompanied me here," Karlos said, trying to inspire Jocelyn and get her involved. "I am sure the women of Mindanao want to see their future first lady as a sign of hope and a model of peace."

The guests from Castellana was surprised to see the home of Aristotle Lacson, a former senator and a farmer. His house did not seem to suit his stature.

"Are you surprised my house is not a mansion like the hacienderos in Azusa?" Aristotle asked frankly but kindly. "Life is different here. After my wife passed away, I decided to let go of our house and to live a much simpler life. Not to mention that because of the ongoing problems my province is facing, luxury has no place here," added Mr. Lacson.

Jocelyn walked toward the bungalow house, her father following her. A chicken coop occupied the lot adjacent to it, and coconut trees surrounded the area.

"This reminds me of our old house before," commented her father. "There was a time when I thought I should start selling eggs in the market since my patients would bring them as payments all the time."

"That's why you never became rich!" Jocelyn rudely said to her father.

The doctor tried not to hear his daughter's comment, and Karlos trying to pacify the situation. "Dr. Gonzales, I remembered how you used to treat the people in the hacienda, wanting nothing in return. You are a generous man, and I believe deep inside Jocelyn has a heart as giving as yours."

"Welcome to my humble home," said Aristotle cheerfully as they entered his house. "Jocelyn, you and your father will be staying here with me in the main house, and Karlos will be staying in the guest house in the back."

From Karlos's perspective, Mr. Lacson home was cozy and comfortable. There were no valuable or breakables, only the basic necessities. The simple house contained a living room, dining room, and three bedrooms.

"This is Conching. If you need anything just let her know. She will do her best to help," said Mr. Lacson.

Jocelyn was not amused about the accommodations, but she told herself that she needed to do what she needed to do to help Karlos win the presidency. "I notice you don't have any bodyguards," Jocelyn said, a concerned look on her face. "Knowing the rebellion is around here, I just don't feel safe."

"I have a couple of men and nearby workers, not to mention Jerome and Apollo." He pointed to the two German shepherds lazily sleeping in the backyard.

Karlos and Dr. Gonzaga laughed.

"Pa, we are ready," Aristotle's son Alexander said as he entered. The former senator's son came up to Karlos and introduced himself. "You must be our future president, Karlos Vasquez. It is an honor to meet you."

"Pleasure is mine. I would like to thank your family for your hospitality. May I introduce my fiancé, Jocelyn, and her father, Dr. Gonzales," Karlos said, shaking Alex's hand.

"Please, my wife and I have prepared a simple welcome dinner for all of you," said Alex, gesturing to the Castellanans to follow him.

Karlos found the setting refreshing and comforting. It was like a scene from his childhood. There was a long wooden table lined with banana leaves that were covered with rice, milk fish, *tilapia*, crabs, shrimps, and charcoal-cooked chicken. There was no fine china and no silverware. Karlos couldn't help but throw his fist on the air.

"Yes! This is what I call a feast!" Karlos said, heading toward the table, leaving behind a dumbfounded Jocelyn.

"I am glad you like it, Karlos," his running mate said. "The rice here is grown on our land, the seafood was brought by the fishermen who

are here, and the chicken—well, I guess you saw their home earlier."
The people started laughing, and Karlos waved and bowed at them.

"Also, Karlos, I would like to introduce my wife, Yasmin." Alex
escorted his wife toward Karlos. "This is our son, Ali, and our daughter,
Maya."

Karlos courteously bowed his head toward Yasmin and gave each
of Alex's kids a pat on the head. Karlos beckoned to Jocelyn to join
them, but Jocelyn seemed surprised to see a woman covered by a black
headscarf. Dr. Gonzales nudged his daughter and held her hand, almost
dragging her to meet Alex's family.

"I'm Dr. Gonzales, and this is my daughter, Jocelyn," politely said
the doctor.

"Jocelyn, you are a beauty. It is so nice to meet you," Yasmin said
warmly.

Jocelyn forced a smile and nodded.

"Dr. Gonzales, it has been awhile since we had a doctor in our area.
I hope you can spare some of your time for the people while you are
here," Yasmin said with a hopeful look in her eyes.

"Yasmin, they are here to campaign—"

Dr. Gonzales interrupted Alex. "Sure, I would be happy to be of
service. Karlos and you father-in-law can surely handle the campaign
without me. I think I could be of good use here."

"All right, let's sit and eat!" invited Aristotle.

Jocelyn was quiet during the entire meal, thinking of a million
excuse to go inside. Karlos, on the other hand, was enjoying himself.
He looked comfortable eating with his hands and talking to the people
about his experiences at the hacienda when he was a young boy. Yasmin
noticed Jocelyn was looking anxious and brought her a warm wash
cloth.

"Here, Jocelyn, to clean your hands," said Yasmin, offering her a
washcloth. "This must be something new for you. You need not worry.
My father-in-law is well respected by the people here, and we are here
if you need anything."

Alex noticed that Jocelyn was uneasy when Yasmin approached her. He turned to Karlos. "So Karlos, how long have you and Jocelyn been engaged, and when is the wedding?"

"Here, here!" the crowd cheered. Mr. Lacson opened the vinegar wine and started pouring drinks.

"We got engaged a couple of months ago. Hopefully we'll marry after I win the presidency," Karlos said, turning red.

Jocelyn was thrown off by how bold Karlos was. She wished her aunt were around to save her.

"Yasmin and I, as you can see, came from different worlds," shared Alex. "But love, as they say, can overcome anything."

"Is Yasmin Catholic?" asked Jocelyn curiously.

"We did not get married by Catholic or Muslim rites," stated Alex. "It was *papang* who married us." He raised his drink to his father.

"You see, Karlos, Yasmin is the daughter of a Muslim farmer here in Zamboanga," continued Alex's father. "My son fell in love with his daughter and vice versa. Though Alex is not Muslim, they saw he is a good man, a man who would make their daughter happy. They disowned their daughter not out of hatred but from love to set her free to make her choice."

"I am happy with my choice," Yasmin said, looking at Alex. "I am grateful, too, that Alex's parents accepted me. Every day I visit my parents and have my children meet them, regardless of what my people say about me."

"You see, Karlos and Jocelyn, status, religion, or government should not be a hindrance to your happiness," added the former senator.

"Let's drink to that!" cheered Karlos.

The dinner ended. The people said they would stand by Karlos to make him president. Alex and Yasmin headed home with two sleepy kids in tow. Jocelyn and her father excused themselves and headed for the house.

"You know, Karlos, I was surprised when Congressman Saison asked me if I could be your vice president," said Aristotle. "I really have no desire to go back into politics, and I was adamant about you."

"I can understand that." Karlos turned his head and looked up. "You probably thought like everyone thought, that I would just be sitting as president and the hacienderos would actually be pulling the strings."

"Yes. I have been in politics for a long time. From the highest head office to the minor seats, everything seemed to be set up by those who have money and power," replied Aristotle. "There are a lot who started with true and honest desire to serve the people, rich or poor, but most are tempted. With the power to govern over people, let's be honest— who would not want it?" added his running mate.

"Is that why you decided to retire?" asked Karlos.

"Aside from the stage makers behind the political arena and the corruption, I feel I can't serve the country wholeheartedly anymore." Aristotle poured himself another drink. "The reasons that convinced me to run behind you are Alex and Yasmin. I feel our government has been turning a blind eye on the real problems we have here in Mindanao. They sent their armies to kill without talks or diplomacy."

"If I am elected president, do you think I can stand for the people and not be a puppet?" asked Karlos.

"You will be the most powerful man in the country. If you are given the seat, remember that you are the president and do not allow anyone to tell you otherwise," answered the former senator.

CHAPTER 8

T he province of Azusa and the neighboring provinces were on high alert as heavy rains and wind started to enter the Visayas. The howling winds crushed the windows of the Hernandez home. Castellana was in darkness after lightning struck a major electricity pole. The citizens of the city barricaded their homes with sandbags to prevent the flood waters from entering, and families are huddled in prayer, asking to be spared by the incoming typhoon.

Señora Estefania and Daria, together with their household staff, were in the library praying the rosary, trying not to panic after they heard the tempest arrive, breaking branches off the trees.

"Hail Mary, full of Grace..." Señora Estefania continued.

Daria was trying to focus but could not help but think about the people of Hacienda Corazon, as well as the settlers at the foot of Mt. Mansilay. She tried to get back to praying, only to hear Yaya Helen's nervous scream after a loud crash outside.

"I think the tree has been uprooted and hit the greenhouse," Yaya Helen said, making the sign of the cross.

Daria reached out to her nanny, trying to calm her.

Daria heard her father's voice in the living room but looked down when her mama gave her a stern look. "Holy Mary, mother of God..." Daria continued.

When the rosary was over, Señora Estefania told the maids to replace the candles. She also instructed them to put ice on the meats and not to leave the house.

Daria sat in the living room with her father, who was listening to the radio.

"Felix, do we still have extra batteries? And the generator—when can we use it?" Señora Estefania voice reached the living room from the kitchen.

"Your mama's voice can compete with strong winds, but instead of breaking windows, our eardrums," Señor Hernandez said, shaking his head.

Daria let out a laugh. "Papa, do you have a plan for the people in the hacienda? For sure they are the ones who will be most affected," Daria asked her papa.

"This is not our first big typhoon, Daria. Every year we have small ones, and in the past we had bigger ones, and we always managed to survive," Señor Hernandez told his daughter.

The radio started to regain its signal, and the broadcaster announced that the typhoon had passed the province.

"Oh, thank God!" Daria heard the maids saying. Daria was thankful too but fearful about what the typhoon had left behind.

MINDANAO

Zamboanga was hit with heavy rains, but the typhoon spared the province. The phone lines in Castellana were damaged by the typhoon, leaving Karlos with no choice but to send telegrams to Señor and Governor Escalante.

Karlos and Aristotle were about to have an interview with Zamboanga's local radio station.

"Karlos, I know it is a difficult time right now, but you need to focus on your goal," Aristotle reminded him.

Karlos nodded and stood up as they saw Rudy Magbanua, the radio host, enter the room.

"Senator Lacson and Mayor Karlos Vasquez, what an honor," started Rudy. "So this is how it works. The show is thirty minutes. I ask the questions, you give me your answers—simple."

Rudy handed them each a pair of headphones and tapped his mic. The show producer gave the host the thumbs up, and the red light turned to green, signaling the start of the show.

"Good evening, Zamboanga. I hope you enjoyed your dinner. Thank you for joining me and my guests, Zamboanga's pride, our former senator, now running for vice president, Senator Aristotle Lacson," said the host. "And of course, with great honor, running under the Nationalist banner, presidential candidate Mayor Karlos Vasquez."

"Thank you. The pleasure is ours. Thank you for inviting us to be on your show," said Aristotle.

"So Senator, after being away from politics for a while, what made you come back?"

"Well, my love for Zamboanga, of course. I got to know this young man, and I believe his visions and ideals will help not only Zamboanga and Mindanao but also the entire country."

"Your team is, I should say, new. Mayor Vasquez is a young man, and you, my dear friend, are—how should I say this ..." the announcer said, trying to have the former senator finish the sentence.

"Old?" answered Aristotle.

"Your words, not mine," answered Rudy.

"Like you said, Rudy, I am old. Most politicians in this country are, well, my age. I think it's about time to give our country a new voice, a new leadership, and a new vision. I believe no other man is more fit for this position than Karlos Vasquez," said Aristotle. "My old age comes with wisdom though, and I am here beside him to show him the ropes, so to speak."

"Well said, Senator Lacson. Mayor Vasquez, thank you again for granting me the opportunity to interview you and share your voice with the people of Zamboanga," Rudy said, signaling Karlos to come closer to the mic.

"Thank you for having me on your show. Zamboanga and its people have been very welcoming, and this is the city I chose to start my campaign," shared Karlos.

"Why is that, Mayor? Well, we are one of the larger provinces, and my show reaches Davao City and parts of General Santos," boasted Rudy.

"When I arrived yesterday, Mr. Lacson prepared a dinner for me, and at that dinner there were no politicians, no businessmen, no hacienderos, only regular working folks. It reminded me so much of my childhood and the simple dreams I used to have. It was quite an eye opener."

"You mentioned that your father was a farm worker and that you are a scholar. What makes you think you can be the next president of this country?" asked Rudy.

"Why not?" Karlos answered back. "When I was in elementary school I learned in history that we are a democratic country. Being so, everyone who has the qualifications can run for any office in the land, so why not give it a try, right?"

"Certainly not the answer I was expecting," commented Rudy.

Karlos let out a quiet laugh. "Rudy, for years we have had presidents who hold degrees from prestigious universities. We have leaders who came from political families and rich families promising the people a better life, but how come with every election we still hear the same things? People are starving. The poor are getting poorer and the rich are getting richer—where are the opportunities for education?"

"So you say you can make a difference?"

"I can and I will," said Karlos. "My office will be open to all in need. I acknowledge the generosity of my sponsors, but this does not mean they are in control. I have to answer to my countrymen, the majority, not to one group only."

"When you filed your candidacy in Manila, you grabbed the media's attention by talking to the union and labor protesters. I am sure you are aware of the situation between the Muslims and the Christians here in

Mindanao. Will you be willing to talk with the Muslim leaders or even the Muslim movement? Would you put your life on the line?"

"For the sake of our country and for the Filipino people, I will," Karlos said with no hesitation.

When the interview was over, Rudy thanked his guests and led them to the station's waiting area, where Alex, Yasmin, Jocelyn, and Dr. Gonzaga sat. Alex gave his father a hug, and Yasmin followed. Jocelyn did not move until she was nudged by her father. She stood and held her hands out to Karlos.

"That went well. I should say, Karlos, you got my vote. At least with us small media folk, you got most of our support," assured Rudy. "It is the national media that you need to convince now. Aragon has shares in publishing, and he will use that to his advantage."

"That's why we are counting on you, my friend," Aristotle said, giving the announcer a nudge.

"If you win in the Visayas and Mindanao, it would put you head to head with Aragon," analyzed Rudy. "You need to win the farmers in Luzon, and we know that the hacienderos in the Visayas are not friendly with their Luzon counterparts."

"Well, for now let us keep our focus on Mindanao. Christmas is coming, so campaign will slow down during the holidays," pointed out Aristotle.

Rudy and Aristotle continued their conversation as they headed toward the exit. Alex went with them, escorting Jocelyn and her father to the car, leaving Karlos the opportunity to ask a favor from Yasmin.

"Yasmin, this might be too much to ask, but would there be any way I could meet with your father?" asked Karlos.

Yasmin was surprised by the request but did not deny it. "Tomorrow Dr. Gonzales agreed to come with me to see some sick children," Yasmin said to Karlos. "My family's home is not too far away. I will send word tonight."

Karlos and Dr. Gonzales joined Yasmin in the nearby town where her family lived. Aristotle and his son were arranging their trip to Davao. Jocelyn said she was too tired to go with them.

They first stopped by the health clinic, where Dr. Gonzales was more than happy to be of service. Yasmin then gave Karlos directions to her father's house.

Karlos stopped by a fruit stand to buy oranges. As he came closer he noticed women in their *abayas* trying to avoid him. A man with a cane, along with his son, then approached him and asked him if he was there to see Kaab Kalim. Karlos nodded, and the man pointed to the third house, with a brown gate. The man patted Karlos' chest and left. Karlos headed toward the house and knocked on the door.

A young boy opened the door. Karlos asked him if he could speak to the owner of the house and said that he knew Yasmin. The boy ran inside without saying a word. Then a tall man with a full beard came to the door.

"*As-Salam-u-Alaikum*," greeted Karlos, as Yasmin had taught him.

"*Wa Alaikum Assalam wa Rahmatullah*," returned Yasmin's father. "You must be Karlos Vasquez. I was expecting you."

CASTELLANA

The province of Azusa was in a state of calamity. The typhoon swept the entire province, leaving behind a swath of destruction to homes and the haciendas. Castellana was not spared. The streets around the city were covered with muddy water. The fountain in the middle of the plaza was broken into pieces and the city hall windows shattered. Even the Church of St. Thomas Aquinas was not spared; the statues of the apostles that surround the church's gate had lost a part or two.

The Hernandez house was one of the lucky few. The damage was minimal. Aside from uprooted trees and the flood that entered the dirty kitchen and the señor's studio, overall the house had survived the brunt of the storm.

Señora Estefania was busy ordering the helpers to clean Señor Hernandez's studio first. Some of the men were working in the garden, removing the uprooted tree and cleaning the damaged flower pots.

"Mama, we should let the helpers go home so they can check on their families," Daria suggested to her mother.

"Daria, we too need help. Have them finish their work first. Besides, there is no electricity yet. And what about dinner?" Señora Estefania answered, looking annoyed.

"Daria is right, Estefania," Señor Enrique told his wife. "Daria, tell Helen she can go with Felix and take the maids with him. They can come back tomorrow. When the men are done with the trees, tell them they can go when Felix returns."

Daria nodded and went to relay her papa's orders before her mama could reply.

"Enrique—" Estefania began.

"Estefania, I know how to turn on the generator, we have enough candles, and Daria knows a dish or two," Enrique told his wife. Feeling dizzy, he walked toward the sofa.

"Are you all right, Enrique? You look pale," asked Estefania as she sat next to her husband.

"I'm just tired. I'll go check on ..." Enrique tried to get up but felt weak.

"Why don't you get some rest, Enrique? You must be tired," Estefania suggested, helping her husband to stand up.

"I think a nap will help. Tell Daria to wake me up in an hour," Enrique said, leaving Estefania in the living room.

Estefania looked at her husband as he headed toward their room. She was concerned about him but did not dare suggest a doctor or medicine because she knew that would anger him. Through the years, Estefania had accepted Enrique's distant coldness toward her. She knew that she would never be first in Señor Hernandez's heart. She never stopped praying, though, for the day to come when Enrique would to look at her and appreciate her, hoping someday to hear the words "I love you" from her husband.

CHAPTER 9

F our days had passed since the typhoon hit the province of Azusa. The Hernandez household was back to its original routine, but that could not be said about other families in the city. There was still no electricity in certain parts of the city, and the telephone lines had not been fully repaired. Daria received a telegram from Marco a couple of days after the typhoon, but she was not able to reply until the next day because the station office could hardly keep up with deliveries. She sent a message back, assuring Marco that everything with her family was fine and asked for their prayers.

The damage to the city and the haciendas had begun to unfold. Father Jose and the other parish priests were waiting for government aid, but none had come, to their dismay. Governor Escalante and Congressman Saison, as well as other congressmen from the province, were working to organize aid to be sent to the province, but knowing they were supporting the Nationalist Party, the Office of the Interior and local government were making it hard for them.

The haciendas suffered, their crops destroyed by the typhoon. The workers whose homes were destroyed at Hacienda Corazon are being housed temporarily in the azucarera. Daria and Yaya Helen are running around trying to help people, but they lack medical help, and the food supply was running low.

Señor Enrique was in his office on the phone with Congressman Saison. "*Puñeta*, that stupid Aragon! This is not about politics! This is about people needing help!" shouted Señor Hernandez.

"Enrique, I am trying my best. Have you heard from Karlos?" asked Saison.

"I received a telegram. I finally got hold of him this morning. The airport is still closed. They will arrive at the port tomorrow," reported Señor Hernandez.

"We better pray that we can spin something out of this before Aragon takes advantage of the situation. How about Jamora—where is he? Can he have somebody write an editorial about this?" the congressman asked.

"I have not spoken to him. Every haciendero has the same problem right now. We can't get supplies of food and medicine. Listen, call my sister and tell her to call me," ordered Señor Hernandez. "I sent her a telegram this morning. I am hoping her husband can help us out."

Señor Hernandez placed hand on the back of neck as he felt it tighten. He felt a sharp shooting pain radiate to his head. He sat up straight when he heard Daria's voice.

"Papa, any news?" Daria asked, looking tired.

"No, my dear. I know we are running low on food, and we need medicine. It is sad to think that politics in this country comes first, before its people," said Señor Hernandez.

"Are you all right, Papa? You look a little pale, and you are sweating." As Daria walked toward her father she grabbed a tissue to wipe his brow. Placing her hand on her father's forehead, Daria said, "You don't have a fever."

"I'm all right, my darling. You look tired too. Why won't you head home and rest?"

Daria shook her head. "We are fortunate that our home is safe and we are well. I can't leave yet."

The phone rang. Señor Enrique was glad to hear his sister's voice on the other end. He assured her that everyone was safe but said the people needed help. His sister said she had contacted the Philippine National Red Cross and they had sent relief that would arrive by sea in two days. She also said if the airport would open they could send help right away.

Señor Enrique looked up at Daria and smiled, handing her the phone.

"Tita Chris, we are all okay. I hope you can find a way to send help."

"Daria, it's Marco. Thank God you are all right," said the voice on the other end.

Daria started tearing up but held back to avoid worrying Marco and her father. "Marco, I am grateful we are all right, but the people are suffering," Daria shared.

"We are doing our best, Daria. Help will come. Just pray and be patient," ended Marco. The connection was cut off.

The following day no help came. Daria went to check on Father Jose, only to see the people in town were in far worse shape than those in Hacienda Corazon.

"Father Jose, we brought clean water. I had it taken to the kitchen," Daria said, embracing the parish priest.

"Daria, let us not lose faith in what we see," Father Jose said, trying to comfort her. "God will provide, and he will heal all of us."

The radio in the church office announced that Vice President Aragon was going to send aid to the people and that they were working with the local government office to move the aid along the fastest route available.

"Why do they have to do this to the people? If they are angry with the haciendas, then so be it, but letting the people suffer …" Daria observed.

The radio commentator continued, saying that the absence of Karlos Vasquez in the midst of the calamity was an act of treachery.

"They try to put Karlos down. I know Karlos would be here in an instant if he could," Daria said, trying to hold back her anger in front of Father Jose.

"God provides our needs, Daria," Father Jose said.

Father's Jose words were prophetic. They heard sounds of trucks entering the city square. Father Jose and Daria went out and saw trucks heading toward the church. Daria wondered who was coming and was relieved to see Karlos and Dr. Gonzales.

"God has answered our prayers and delivered providence," Father Jose greeted Karlos.

Karlos paid the priest his respects and came up to give Daria a hug.

"Karlos, what is all this? How on earth did you get all of this aid to Castellana?" Darla asked, feeling a sense of relief.

"During my campaign I made friends, and they have come to help me," Karlos answered simply.

"Tito, I'm glad to see you too." Daria greeted Jocelyn's father. "Where's Jocelyn?"

"She's with your mama. She said she will join the ladies in prayer," Dr. Gonzales informed Daria. "If you excuse me, I have work to do."

The trucks parked in front of the church, and one team set up a first aid station. A tent was also set up offering sugar water, and Father Jose directed the volunteers to the kitchen.

Daria saw Karlos make his way through the crowd, holding the children and comforting the people. There was no media present, no higher-ups to impress. All Daria saw was a man who sincerely wanted to help his constituents. Daria went up to one of the tents and asked if she could be of any help. Karlos found Daria there and asked how her papa and the people from Hacienda Corazon were.

"The crops planted for the next milling season are all gone. Not just at Hacienda Corazon, Karlos, but all the haciendas. I am glad you were able to make it here to Castellana, but the entire province is in a state of emergency," Daria shared sadly. "What's worse is the present administration is trying to slow down the process for help to arrive."

Daria and Karlos were caught by surprise when a photographer started to take a picture of them. Then Señor Jamora walked toward them.

"Karlos, my boy! I knew it. I knew you would come out as the hero of this game," Señor Jamora said.

"This is hardly a game, Señor. People's lives are at stake here," Daria said to Señor Jamora.

"Yes, dear. Now Karlos, I need you to make a statement to the press and tell them how you made this effort," Señor Jamora, putting his arm toward Karlos and leading him to the reporters.

Karlos's efforts relieved the city of Castellana. Just before they ran out of supplies, the Philippine National Red Cross arrived with medical help and food. Karlos went to different cities in the province to provide aid. Daria went back to the hacienda and asked Felix to take the injured workers to town.

Daria went to her father's office and was surprised to see her father snoring on his chair. Daria closed the door and headed out of the azucarera to get some air. Yaya Helen followed her and reminded her that she was not allowed to go out without a bodyguard.

"Yaya, with the state we are all in, you still think about those things," Daria said to her nanny.

"Of course. You are my responsibility," Yaya Helen answered.

As Daria hugged her nanny, a thought came into her mind, but it had to wait till her papa woke up. She turned to Yaya Helen. "Yaya, can we go check on Silvestre, please?"

"My baby, Nelson said Silvestre is okay. The horses are safe. No, no you cannot go alone," warned Yaya Helen.

"Would it be all right if I take Daria, Yaya Helen?" a familiar voice asked.

Daria turned around and couldn't be happier to see Marco standing in front of her.

Daria ran toward Marco and jumped into his arms. Marco smiled, relieved to see Daria was all right. He squeezed her tightly, not wanting to let her go, but Yaya Helen was quick to end their greeting.

"Daria, you stand here, and Marco, you stay there," Yaya Helen warned

"What are you doing here?" Daria asked, still in disbelief over seeing him.

"When you told me you needed help, how could I sit and do nothing?" Marco answered. "I came here with aid from the Business

Association. A lot of us do not approve of the government's withholding the supplies for political reasons, so here I am."

"Marco, I am touched," Daria said and started to cry.

"What's with the tears?" Marco asked. "Tears of joy I hope. Also, your tita Christina has reached your uncle, and the United Nations will send aid too, and we will all help rebuild the province."

"Marco, my boy, this is a wonderful surprise," interrupted Señor Hernandez.

Marco went up to Daria's father and shook his hand. "Yes, Tito, more help is coming. Things will be back to the way they were."

Daria went to her father's side and hugged him.

Señor Hernandez thought to himself that it used to be only him who could make his daughter smile. In a way he seemed relieved that now she had Marco too.

More relief started coming in, and the province was slowly getting back on its feet. Along with opening the airport and the ports, reporters from all over the country also came to report on the progress of the province. Some newspaper acknowledged the heroic acts of Karlos Vasquez, and there were those who said that it was his job to do so. A handful of reporters described in their editorials the lack of government support for the province. The press started turning, though, as Ambassador Jaime Valderrama arrived in Castellana along with the aid from the United Nations. With him came reporters, and Karlos Vasquez got international recognition.

"Jaime, it has been awhile, but your presence, as always, is grand," Señor Hernandez said to his brother-in-law.

"Enrique, Castellana and Hacienda Corazon are my wife's home too. I cannot turn my back on her when she seeks my help," the ambassador answered.

"Nevertheless, thank you," said Señor Hernandez. "You met Karlos before, right?"

"Yes. When he was in law school, he would visit us in Manila. Intelligent man. Brilliant, I must say," Jaime Valderrama said, scratching his brow. "It is quite a journey from his humble roots to running for president. No one can really deny destiny. Was this your plan all along, Enrique? For him to become president?" asked Jaime directly.

"The boy has the traits of a leader, and the way things are going he is heading in the right direction," said Señor Hernandez.

"Let's say he does win. Do you think he will remain loyal and true to his word that he will protect the haciynderos? There will be other groups interested in him too, you know. He also seems to show interest toward the unions," said the ambassador suspiciously.

"I can only speak for myself. I raised that boy. I gave him an education and constructed a path for him. I cannot assure the other hacienderos, but Hacienda Corazon and Castellana are his home, and I trust that he will protect my interests," Señor Hernandez said with confidence.

"There are so many stories written about people like him. The majority turned into dictators in the end," Jaime pointed out. "When a man realizes how much power he has in his hands, it can make him insane and feel indispensable."

"So how's the US?" Señor Hernandez asked, diverting the topic.

"As long as we maintain friendship and cooperation with them, free trade with sugar will continue. There are some concerns over rebel activities, but this travesty is all over the world. We just need to show them that we can handle the rebels, retain our democracy, and deliver the goods," said Jaime simply.

"I am starting to think about Vicente's proposal. This year, due to the typhoon, we have lost a season's worth of crops. This will be a big loss for the sugarcane industry," pointed out Señor Hernandez. "If we don't recover quickly and, God forbid, another calamity strikes, the smaller haciendas will suffer."

"The azucarera will follow too," added Jaime Valderrama.

"That is why the more I think about Vicente and Marco's proposal, the more I think we should begin sooner than later," said Señor

Hernandez. "Aside from selling lots for housing, maybe we can get into construction too."

"Seems to me you just don't want Daria to move to Manila," teased his brother-in-law.

"Well, that too." Suddenly Señor Hernandez grabbed his head and started sweating.

"Enrique, are you all right?" Jaime said, checking on his brother-in-law.

"I have been having headaches, and my body is weakening lately. I think I'm just tired," Señor Hernandez answered.

"Have you seen a doctor?"

"There is no need for that. Besides, if I see a doctor, you know Daria and your wife will panic. That would be worse," Señor Hernandez said. He rang his bell to have a maid attend to him.

"Enrique, I insist. I am leaving soon. Tomorrow, we will go see our friend Dr. Jimena," his brother-in-law stated.

Enrique nodded in defeat. "All right, as long as it remains between me and you."

CHAPTER 10

I t had been more than two weeks since the typhoon had passed, and things were starting to return to normal. Electricity and phone lines were restored. People returned to their jobs, and the children were back in school. Karlos resumed his campaign in the Visayas, this time without Jocelyn. Newspapers and magazines were back in circulation. Headlines were dominated by the aftermath of the typhoon as the press continued to cover the relief efforts. The other presidential candidates couldn't deny that Karlos Vasquez was gaining momentum in the election.

Daria and Marco joined Señora Estefania at the breakfast table. Daria immediately noticed that her papa was not there.

"Mama, do you know where Papa went?" asked Daria. "He did not mention that he was heading out early today."

"He took your tito Jaime to meet with some friends for breakfast. He will be back soon," said Señora Estefania. "Marco, how long will you be staying? As you know, you and Daria are not even engaged yet. If not for this calamity, it would be improper to have you stay with us."

Marco smiled at Señora Estefania. "I'm leaving on the first flight tomorrow, Tita, with Tito Jaime."

"All right then. Daria, remember to take Helen with you wherever you go," instructed her mama.

"Yes, Mama. Are you heading out?"

"I am going to see Jocelyn. I am sure the poor child is traumatized over her stay in Mindanao. She needs me to comfort her," Señora Estefania said before she left Marco and Daria alone.

"Should I call Yaya Helen now?" asked Marco.

Daria laughed and shook her head. She saw a pile of newspapers and magazines, picked one, and handed one to Marco.

"Looks like everyone is talking about Karlos," said Daria.

"And you too," Marco added, seeing a picture of Daria and Karlos in the paper.

Daria looked up, and Marco started reading. "The team of Karlos Vasquez and Hacienda Corazon's Daria Hernandez have made the relief operations run smoothly. People reported that before Mayor Vasquez arrived, Daria was the beacon of hope for the people. She tirelessly gave aid to people, not only from their hacienda but also to others as well."

"So you and Karlos are a duo now," Marcos said with a hint of jealousy in his voice.

"Are you jealous?"

"Do I have any reason to be?" asked Marco, looking straight at Daria.

Daria stood up and kissed him on the nose, which caught Marco by surprise. He grabbed her hand and kissed her back. Daria went back to her chair, blushing. Marco picked up the paper and said, "I am confident that I have no reason to be".

The couple got the chance to spend most of the day alone, with Yaya Helen in tow. They passed by the bakery that made sweets native to Castellana. Daria made Marco try a variety of sweets, and the young man finally gave up, saying he might develop diabetes. Daria laughed. "You are in the sugar capital of the country. Of course everything here is sweet!" They passed by the city hall and the plaza, and Daria was happy to see that the fountain had been fixed. When they made it back to the Hernandez's house, Daria was pleased to see her dad and Tito Jaime having coffee in the garden.

"Papa! Where have you been the whole day?" Daria asked her father.

"Your papa and I went to see an old friend, Daria," answered her uncle. "Won't you both join us for coffee?"

Marco and Daria sat down, and Yaya Helen went inside to brew them a fresh pot.

"Tito, Tita Chris must be so happy to have you here she might not allow you to leave," Daria teased her uncle.

"You said it right. I was supposed to arrive the first week of December, but here I am!" Jaime Valderrama said.

Señor Hernandez turned to Marco. "Marco, about your project with Vicente. I read the feasibility study and the investment you need to get it started. I do have the funds for it, and permits will not be an issue. Given all this, when can you start?" asked Daria's father.

Marco was surprised by Señor Hernandez's question. He never would have thought that he would be so eager to start so soon.

"Well, I still have an ongoing project, which will end probably in February of next year," Marco said. Seeing Señor Hernandez's expression, he knew that was not what he wanted to hear.

"Why the rush, Papa?" Daria asked.

"I realized after the typhoon that real estate is the direction to go. I realized the value of it after calculating the losses of this season's harvest. Not to mention that Hacienda Corazon has an overflow and higher grounds, which makes it good place to build houses," Señor Hernandez said eagerly.

Marco was also wondering why Daria's father was in a hurry to start the project. Something inside was telling him that there something more than just the events of the past week must have led him to make this decision.

Daria was confused too. Maybe the losses had scared her papa, but this was too big a decision to make overnight. Her father could be impulsive at times, but this was really different.

"Are you all right, Papa? Are you worried that that the hacienda might not recover?" Daria asked.

Before her father could answer her uncle interrupted. "Daria, your aunt wanted me to bring her some sweets. Can you come with me to the bakery and help me pick out what she wants? She also wants some dried fish. It's not that late. Who knows? Maybe we can still find some in the market."

Daria turned to Marco, but before she could say anything her uncle whisked her away. "Don't worry, dear, Marco will be all right. I guarantee you he will be alive when we return."

When Daria and Jaime Valderrama were out of sight, Marco turned to Daria's father.

"Tito, is everything okay? Just the process alone to get this started will take at least six months. We also need to obtain materials and machinery, and we have to bid this out to contractors," Marco explained.

"I don't have time, Marco," Señor Hernandez said.

Marco looked at Señor Hernandez, hoping he'd misunderstood him.

"Marco, you told me you love my daughter and that you will be proposing to her on Christmas Eve," reminded Señor Hernandez. "I might not have enough time to settle other things for her."

Señor Hernandez saw the concerned look on Marco's face. "Marco, Daria is my only joy, and I am afraid that I may leave her soon."

Marco was stunned and couldn't muster words to speak.

"I went to see Dr. Jimena today, though I don't believe that quack. All of us must head toward our end. We just don't know when. He told me six months," Señor Hernandez said with slight sarcasm and anger in his voice.

"Tito, you have to let Daria know," Marco said softly.

"No, I do not want Daria to know, and you will not tell her anything," Señor Hernandez ordered. "I do not want your plans to be delayed. I want Daria to be happy. I want to see her get married. I want to be the one to walk her down the aisle. I want to make sure that she will be all right. I need a guarantee that she will be taken care of," Señor Hernandez said, his voice breaking.

"Señor, rest assured that Daria will be safe with me and I will love her as long as I live." Marco knelt next to Daria's father. "I will not tell Daria anything, but please don't overwork yourself. Spend your time with Daria, enjoy her smile, and allow her to be a comfort to you."

Señora Estefania overheard Señor Enrique's confession. She cried silently and quietly went inside the house. She admitted to herself that she was defeated by Daria. Somehow her hatred and jealousy toward her daughter grew even more.

Karlos garnered more supporters as he headed toward Negros, Cebu, and Ilo-Ilo. The people, the business sector, and the hacienderos and independent farmers were delighted by the fact that a person from the Visayas might be the next president. His actions after the typhoon proved his compassion toward others and his dedication toward public service. He was gaining momentum, and his sincerity made him approachable.

Ka Abel made his return to Mt. Mansilay. The rebels in the mountains had also suffered from the calamity and were slowly rebuilding. Ka Abel was able to bring funds to his comrades to help them rebuild their forces.

"My brothers, the typhoon showed us how evil and corrupt our government is," said Ka Abel. "When I was in Mindanao, opportunities opened to our group, and our movement has made ties that can help strengthen our cause."

"Ka Abel, this is a good time to attack the haciendas. The workers' morale is low. After the crisis, a lot of hacienderos are having money problems because the sugarcane crops were lost," said one of the rebels.

"Let us take this opportunity to recruit, especially the workers from the smaller haciendas. But this is not the time to make a full-on attack," advised Ka Abel. "Also, let us keep our eye on the upcoming election."

"Is there a candidate the higher-ups are asking us to support?" asked Ka Eden.

"Yes. We need to make sure Karlos Vasquez wins this election and becomes our next president."

As the Christmas season arrived, the Hernandezes prepared their home with festive decorations. The entry to the house was lined with red and white poinsettias, and Christmas lanterns painted red, green, gold, and silver made from *capiz* shells hung from every corner of their home.

Daria was in the living room, and not in a festive mood. She was still thinking about the families displaced after the typhoon. She reached toward the brown oak chest, opened the antique container, and started to carefully take out the nativity set that her family had collected over the years.

"*It's the most wonderful time of the year...*" sang Señor Hernandez as he entered the room.

"*There'll be much mistletoeing and hearts will be glowing when loved ones are near...*" Daria joined her father.

"*It's the most wonderful time of the year...*" father and daughter sang together.

"Here we go again with the Christmas decorations," Señor Hernandez said, half amused. "I remember when you were a child you questioned Santa Claus and never believed that the presents were from him."

"Well, Papa, for the simple reason that we don't have a chimney! My favorite memory is when Tita Christina gave you a new turntable and so many records, and we would stay the entire day in your office, singing until we lost our voices," Daria said to her father fondly.

"Which led to Dr. Jimena removing your tonsils," ended Señor Hernandez. "What gift do you want this year, Daria?"

Hmm... There is really nothing I need, thought Daria. "I would love to travel to Hawaii again with you, just the two of us. Our trip to Hawaii is probably my most happy memory."

"That is doable, or maybe I should send you and Marco there," teased Señor Hernandez.

Daria was happy that her father had openly accepted Marco. Daria hoped that one day Marco would propose to her. She could not think of any other man she would want to spend her life with except Marco Gutierrez.

"You seem to be in a hurry to throw me out of the house," Daria said, looking at her father and pouting.

"I guess I miss having a little Daria around," said her father.

"Papa, if Marco does propose, would it be all right if I say yes?"

"Daria, no father would say yes to that question, but Marco is indeed honest, capable, and good. I know he will take care of you and love you," said her papa.

"It's just that Manila is so far away. If only we could stay here in Castellana." Daria revealed her true concern about getting married.

"I spoke with Marco and Vicente, and they will be starting their project for Hacienda Corazon next year. This would give you a chance to see Marco more often and remain here in Castellana," Señor Hernandez told her, trying not to add more details.

Daria was happy and excited about the news. She thought that would give her a chance to be with Marco without leaving her father.

"Daria, be honest. Is there something you would really want for Christmas? Ask for anything," Señor Hernandez encouraged her.

"Well, there are a few things, but not for me," Daria said, unsure if she could continue.

"Go on, tell me."

"The house in the city that Karlos lived in when he was the mayor—if by chance he becomes president, would it be possible for Yaya Helen to have the house and the land?" Daria asked. "She has been with me all my life. She even sacrificed marriage to take of me. I just want to make sure that when she can't work anymore she has her own home."

"Daria, I can definitely do that for you," Señor Hernandez assured her.

Daria embraced her father. "Oh, Papa, that would make Yaya Helen and her family so happy."

"Are you planning a Christmas party for the people?" asked Señor Hernandez.

"Yes, but I want it to be a simple. I know how the haciendas have suffered. The smaller haciendas might not have the means to celebrate with their workers. I was thinking of inviting them," suggested Daria.

"Did Father Jose put you up to this?" Señor Hernandez asked knowingly.

"Well, partly. Plus Mando will be ordained on Christmas Eve."

"Then we should have a celebration for Mando too!" said Señor Hernandez.

"Yes. Mando offered half of the donations from his benefactors to be spent for the people of the smaller haciendas so they can have a Christmas celebration too," said Daria.

"Sounds like a good plan! Go ahead and plan the dates," Señor Hernandez told her. "Have you heard from Marco?"

"Sadly, he will be working, Papa," said Daria with a disappointed look on her face.

"Maybe I'll drag Marco here as my Christmas gift for you," offered Señor Hernandez.

"No need, Papa. I am sure we will get our chance to spend Christmas together in the future." Daria smiled. "Now that I've thought about it, I think there is a Christmas wish I would like to ask from you, Papa." Daria looked at her father, trying to be brave.

"Go ahead, my dear."

"Papa, Mama once said that Vicente and I are the future of Hacienda Corazon. It is a big piece of land, and it got me thinking." Daria saw that her papa was listening to her intently. "Papa, Vicente asked for his shares to be turned into the subdivision project with Marco. I have thought about this. I love Hacienda Corazon and the people."

"So what are you asking, Daria?"

"Papa, I mean no disrespect. You are still alive, but I am hoping that I could give my share to the workers who have worked for us for a long time and their families so they can have their own land and farm their own land. I am thinking of Nelson, Felix, Luciana, and also other families," Daria asked her father, almost begging.

"Daria, I do not know what I have done in my life to deserve a daughter like you. I will talk to my lawyers and surveyors to see how we can do this for them," Señor Hernandez said without hesitation.

"Papa, this means so much to me! I love you."

Señor Hernandez realized that moment that if indeed you are getting close to heaven's door, nothing matters more than to make the person you love the most happy. Everything else was secondary.

Karlos Vasquez arrived in Castellana nine days before Christmas. His first appearance to his constituents was during the first day of the *Misa de Gallo,* the nine-day devotion leading to Christmas Eve and the birth of Jesus Christ.

Karlos greeted Father Jose and took time to greet his constituents. Jocelyn and Señora Estefania joined Karlos, but the crowd seemed to be displeased with Jocelyn.

"Jocelyn, you need to do more to have the people like you," advised Señora Estefania.

"I really have no desire to go out and strain myself helping others, Tita. It's a waste of my time. I really wish we'd head back to Manila and have the elections soon," Jocelyn said to her aunt, letting out a yawn.

A little boy holding a cup of hot sweetened tofu ran past Jocelyn and accidently spilled the drink on her skirt.

"Why, you little brat!" Jocelyn picked up the boy and shook him. "Are you blind?"

The boy's mother went up to Jocelyn and apologized. "I am sorry, Madam. My son's slippers tore when he was running. I am so sorry for the accident." The woman bowed to Jocelyn.

"Your son is stupid!" Jocelyn yelled at the woman and pushed her. Jocelyn then picked up the drink from the ground and threw it at the boy's mother.

That caught the crowd attention. Karlos hurried to Jocelyn's side.

"You are a bad woman!" the boy yelled at Jocelyn. "We apologized for the accident. Why do you have to do this to my mother?"

Before Jocelyn could answer she felt Karlos grip her arm. Señora Estefania whispered to Jocelyn to calm her down.

Karlos walked up to the mother and son. "I do apologize for my fiancée's reaction. She is exhausted from accompanying me and helping me serve all of you."

"We did not see her around helping after the typhoon. We always see Miss Daria. She is the one who has been helping us when you are not here," the boy said.

Jocelyn became more upset when she heard Daria's name. Señora Estefania put her arms around her niece's waist and told her, "Do not say anything. Apologize and offer them money."

Jocelyn approached the boy, trying her best to act like Daria. "I am so sorry, little boy, I am just tired. Here, take this and go buy something for yourself." Jocelyn handed the boy's mother some money.

"We do not need your money," the boy replied. "Thank you. And do excuse us. We are leaving now." The boy turned to Karlos Vasquez. "I believe in you, Mayor Vasquez, but I wish Miss Daria would become your wife, not that mean lady."

Karlos smiled and apologized to them again. He went up to Jocelyn and looked at her directly. "Jocelyn, the boy was right. If you want to become first lady, you need to show more compassion and be more like Daria." He left the stunned Jocelyn and Señora Estefania behind.

CHAPTER 11

Christina Valderrama and her family arrived the day before Christmas Eve, just in time for Hacienda Corazon's Christmas party. The workers entertained the Hernandezes with Christmas carols, and the kids danced for them. Señor Hernandez stood up and commanded everyone's attention.

"My people, this year has been very rough for all of us. We have been through many typhoons, droughts, and disasters, but Hacienda Corazon is still standing because of all our hard work. So this year, though our finances may not be as strong as in prior years, everyone will still receive their thirteenth-month pay," Señor Hernandez announced.

The crowd cheered and thanked the señor for his generosity.

Christina Valderrama stood next to her brother.

"My, how I missed the hacienda. I wonder if any of you still remember me?" asked Christina.

"Of course we do. You should visit us more often, Señorita Christina!" one of the workers called.

"You might not see a lot of me, but you will be seeing more of my son, Vicente, for next year changes will happen to Hacienda Corazon that will be beneficial to you and to us," said Christina. "I hope you will support my son and Daria during their new venture."

The crowd clapped but seemed confused by what their señorita had said.

"Now, it's my turn for gift giving. In addition to my brother's thirteenth-month pay, my husband and I have started a scholarship foundation that would allow the children of Hacienda Corazon an opportunity to go to college," Señorita Christina shared.

The crowd cheered again. Daria was happy to see that even though the celebration might not be grand, they were still able to share with the people the blessings they had.

Daria approached Vicente but was distracted to see her father walk out of the room. She followed her papa when Señor Hernandez entered his office. Daria was debating whether to disturb her father or not, but decided to let herself go to him. Daria was grateful for her decision when she saw her father clutching his head in pain.

"Papa, are you okay? What is hurting you?" Daria asked, trying not to panic.

Before Señor Hernandez could say a word, he fainted. Daria caught him and slowly laid him on the floor. She was frightened at the sight of her unconscious father and started screaming for help.

Señor Hernandez woke up in his bedroom with an IV drip in his arm. He panicked and pulled the IV out while Dr. Jimena tried to calm him down. Señor Hernandez's temper flared. He started yelling at everyone in the room.

"*Puñeta*, Jimena, you quack. Take this off me!" yelled Señor Hernandez at the doctor.

Señora Estefania tried to pacify her husband, but Señor Hernandez would not have it.

"Estefania, you know how I hate doctors and hospitals. Get them out of here," ordered her husband.

"Calm down, Enrique. We are all concerned about you. They are here to help you," answered his wife calmly.

"I don't need help! Get out, Estefania!" Her outraged husband turned red.

"Enrique, please be reasonable. We just want to make sure you are all right. If there is something—" Estefania stopped midsentence when Señor Enrique threw a glass of water at her.

"I said get out, Estefania!" Enrique ordered his wife. Señora Estefania composed herself, released a deep breath, and stepped out of the room.

Daria was about to follow her, but her papa stopped her. "Daria, please stay with me," Señor Hernandez asked his daughter, visibly calming down.

Daria walked to her father's bedside and took his hand, trying to restrain her tears.

Señor Enrique asked the doctor and the nurse to leave him with his daughter.

"Daria, I am sorry for scaring you," Enrique told his daughter while holding her hand.

"Papa, are you all right? Please, if there is something that is bothering you let us help you," Daria begged.

"Daria, you don't need to be scared. Nothing is wrong," Señor Enrique assured her. "I think I am feeling my age. Past events have been chaotic, and a little rest would be good."

Daria was not convinced by her father's reply. She could tell he was hiding something from her. Daria did not pry for information to avoid her father's temper rising again.

"Papa, if you are really all right, then please talk to Dr. Jimena and follow his orders," Daria said. "That would really put my heart at ease."

Daria went to the living room and told Dr. Jimena that her father wanted to see him. Daria looked at her mother and felt sorry for her. Growing up, she had noticed how cold her father was toward her mama, and there were times when Daria felt guilty. Growing up, Señor Enrique's daughter had tried her best to get close to her mama, but she never succeeded. They had a distant relationship.

"Mama, are you all right?" asked Daria carefully.

"Why shouldn't I be?" answered Señora Estefania with no expression on her face.

Señora Estefania had accepted the fact that her marriage had been arranged and there was no love for her in Enrique's heart. "I have lived my life with your papa like this. I am used to his temper and his personality."

Daria sat next to her mother and held her hand, but her mama refused it.

"Daria, would you please ask Helen to make me coffee," requested Señora Estefania.

Daria nodded and complied. All her life she'd tried to have a relationship with her mother. *Sadly*, thought Daria, *that will probably never happen.*

Señor Enrique was feeling better the next day, and his mood improved. Dr. Jimena ordered him not to overexert himself and to enjoy Christmas. The doctor told Daria and Señora Estefania that the señor was exhausted and that everything was fine. All he needed was rest.

"My brother is as strong as a water buffalo," Christina Valderrama teased her brother. "You should learn to relax. Do you want to try yoga or acupuncture?" Christina assumed a tree pose, and Señor Enrique tried to hold back a laugh.

"My dear sister, you and your hobbies!" Enrique said. "How about you stay here in Castellana and help in the hacienda?"

"Oh, please, Enrique! I don't have the capacity or the interest to do so," said Cristina.

"Maybe you should make part of Hacienda Corazon into a shopping center. Then Christina might consider it," suggested Ambassador Lacson.

"We can add a movie theater too!" added Christina.

"You seem to want to throw away the purpose of the hacienda and our family pride, Christina," said Señora Estefania, looking annoyed.

"We are projecting the future," countered Christina, acting like a robot.

The family laughed at her comment. Señor Enrique then turned to Vicente. "Vicente, since I have approved your proposal, I will be seeing more of you here in Castellana."

"Yes, Tito. We hope to start in February," said Vicente.

"Would you be interested in running the azucarera too? Maybe Marco will be interested," mused Señor Enrique.

"Daria would be the best person for the azucarera. She knows how to run that place inside out," Vicente complimented, giving Daria a wink.

"I have no doubt about my daughter's capacity to run the hacienda," beamed Señor Vicente. "But it would be nice if she had someone she can rely on."

"Papa, we don't need to worry. You are here. Like you said, you are as healthy as an ox," Daria said to her father, also trying to convince herself.

"What are the plans for tonight?" Señor Hernandez asked to change the subject.

"We will all be attending Christmas Eve mass and, of course, Brother Armando's ordination," Señora Estefania explained. "Then we will head home for Noche Buena."

"Good! Sounds like a Hernandez family affair. Karlos said he won't be joining us, and of course Mando will be with Father Jose." Señor Enrique smiled, knowing something life-changing was in store for Daria.

Christmas was the most beloved holiday in the Philippines. The festivities happened everywhere, even in the aftermath of the typhoon. The people of Castellana did not lose hope and made the occasion festive, keeping the Christmas spirit alive.

The plaza was decorated with handmade wooden Christmas stars covered in colorful paper hung on each post. The fountain that had been destroyed by the typhoon was adorned with colored lights that made the water move like it was dancing. Christmas music could be heard all over the plaza, the children singing along.

Around ten thirty that night, the people headed toward St. Thomas Aquinas Cathedral. The Hernandezes sat up front in pews engraved with the names of Señor Enrique's parents. Karlos Vasquez joined them and received a cheer from the crowd. The church was decorated with red poinsettias, and the nativity scene filled one side of the church. Organ music played, and the choir hummed Christmas church music.

The procession began. Father Jose and soon-to-be Father Armando walked toward the altar. Daria smiled at her friend, and Mando gave a little wave. Daria thought to herself that maybe Mando had made peace with himself because he looked happy and peaceful. Father Jose gave an inspirational homily, reminding families about the true meaning of Christmas. After communion came Brother Armando's moment when he accepted his vows as a priest. He was then ordained Father Armando Vasquez, his first obligation to serve the people of Castellana, along with Father Jose.

Noche Buena, a long-standing tradition practiced by Christian families all over the country, was a feast celebrated at midnight to honor the birth of Christ. It was no different at the Hernandez household. Señora Estefania prepared glazed ham, roasted chicken, dinner rolls, *quezo de bola,* and hot chocolate. It was also a tradition in the household that the family presented gifts to the household staff.

"Yaya Helen, for your years of service and love, this is for you." Daria handed her nanny a manila envelope.

Yaya Helen burst into tears after she opened the envelope and saw the note from Señor Enrique promising her a home. "Señor, Señora, Daria, how can I accept this gift?"

"You have been part of this family, Helen, and your love for Daria is something for which I will always be thankful. This land is just a small way to thank you," said Señor Enrique.

"Helen, it's time for you to find a husband," teased Christina Valderrama.

"Señorita, I don't think I'll ever get married. I am happy to take care of Daria for the rest of my life," Yaya Helen said, giving Daria a hug.

The rest of the household received their presents of clothes, food, and extra pay and as part of the tradition joined the Hernandezes at the table for Noche Buena.

Señor Hernandez then made an announcement. "My dear family, it is indeed a gift to have all of you here. To my staff, I am thankful for your loyalty and service. Daria, I have a surprise for you, my dear."

Her papa gestured for her to stand next to him. Daria went next to her father and looked at him with curiosity.

"I know we usually exchange presents on Christmas Day, but I want to give you my present tonight," said Señor Enrique to his daughter. "Daria, I am unsure if what I have prepared for you will be a present that delights you or scares you," Señor Enrique began. "Last month, a young man came up to me and asked me for my greatest treasure. I do not want to give up the most precious person in my life, but I agreed because I know you will be happy and be loved."

Daria looked a bit confused by what her father said but at the same time felt nervous. Her heart fluttered.

Her aunt seemed to catch on what her brother was saying, but her son and husband pulled her back to her seat and shook their heads at her.

"Daria, a young man arrived tonight to see you. He has something to ask you." Señor Enrique reached for Daria's hand and squeezed it. He then turned Daria around. Half surprised, half nervous, she saw Marco smiling at them.

"Marco! I thought you couldn't make it?" Daria could not hide the excitement in her voice.

"Your dad and I planned it," replied Marco, taking a step toward Daria.

Marco turned to Señor Enrique. "Tito Enrique, thank you for accepting me and for giving me your blessing."

Marco turned to Daria and took her hands. Daria gasped, and the household members started to get excited.

Marco dropped to one knee. "Daria Hernandez, I love you. The first time I saw you I knew there would be no one in this world I would want to spend the rest of my life with and be the mother of my children. Daria, will you do me the honor of being my wife?" Marco opened a box with a round diamond ring in it.

Daria was quiet, trying to absorb everything that had happened.

"Daria, will you marry me?" Marco asked again, nervous about Daria's silence.

Daria started tearing up. She looked at her father, who gave her a smile and a soft nudge. She turned to Marco, smiling, and reached to help him stand up.

"Marco, I love you too, and yes, I will be honored to be your wife."

Karlos Vasquez decided to spend Christmas Eve alone. He reflected on his life, still in disbelief about what he'd accomplished. He walked around his study and reached for the pile of newspapers. A knock on his front door interrupted him.

"*Maligayang bati at kapayapaan para sa mundo,*" a man accompanied by his wife said.

"*Mag-kaisa tayo ngayon para sa kagandahang ng bukas,*" replied Karlos.

The trio made their way to Karlos's study. Karlos sat in his chair, and the couple made themselves comfortable on the couch. Karlos offered them sweets, and the man's wife went to the kitchen to make coffee.

"Karlos, we are nearing our triumph," said Ka Abel. "After the holidays, campaign season will be in full swing. I see you are catching up with some reading," Ka Abel said, pointing to the magazines and newspapers in front of Karlos.

"Sort of. The house I have built is ready to move into, so I'm packing too. Señor Enrique is giving this house to Yaya Helen, which I think is just right. She has been working with them since she was twelve."

"Why build a house here in Castellana when you will be in Malacañang Palace soon?" Ka Abel asked in a confident voice.

"Castellana will always be my home. This is where it all started," Karlos mused.

"It's not every day a haciendero gives land to a helper," Ka Abel commented.

"It was not solely the señor's decision. Daria convinced her father about this," said Karlos.

"Maybe you should dump Jocelyn and make Daria your first lady," suggested Ka Abel.

Karlos shook his head and changed the topic. "Since you are here you can fill me in on your plans. It would save me the headache of trying to decipher the messages in the paper," Karlos said, pointing to the tower of newspapers.

Ka Abel laughed. Ka Eden returned with the coffee and pulled the drapes.

"We have been successful so far with our group in Luzon. We got support from the union and labor. The higher-ups suggested that we can plant protesters against VP Aragon's factory and have them ask for you to negotiate," Ka Abel advised.

"I don't want to use fake protesters. What about the farmers in Luzon?" asked Karlos.

"Since the main organization is there, they will surely come up with something. I suggest keep up with your reading."

Ka Eden said, "I can see fate is with you, Karlos. Even though the typhoon caused so much loss it helped you become a hero to the people. The hacienderos for sure will have no problem telling their people to vote for you."

"Ka Abel, thanks for your help in Mindanao. I spoke with the Muslim militant group. In exchange for financial support, they are asking for the emancipation of Mindanao," Karlos shared. "I am not entirely sure if I could deliver that. The Congress and Senate would need to approve."

"We will get there after you win the presidency. It is crucial that we get Muslim support," pushed Ka Abel.

Karlos remained silent.

"Karlos, we have come this far. Remember your father's sacrifice and your promise to make this country a country where everyone will be treated with equality," Ka Abel reminded him.

Karlos looked at Ka Abel. "I have never forgotten. We are getting close to fulfilling our promises. I will show them who the real puppet is," Karlos said. "We will make our goal for a stronger and happier Philippines into reality."

Christmas Day at the Hernandez home was indeed merry. The Gutierrezes called from overseas and were overjoyed with the news, especially Marie Gutierrez. They congratulated Marco and Daria.

The family exchanged gifts before the ladies headed to the kitchen. On Christmas Day, the household staff had the day off to celebrate with their families, so the Hernandez ladies prepared lunch themselves.

"I hope my mom and Tita Estefania will remember 'Goodwill toward men'—or should I say women—while working together in the kitchen," Vicente remarked.

"That's why, gentlemen, our goal is to stay as far as possible away from the kitchen," instructed Ambassador Valderrama.

Attention then turned to Marco.

"Marco, I always wanted an older brother," Vicente teased his friend. "I knew from the start that you and I would someday be family."

"Marco, just a piece of advice—say yes to everything to avoid problems," Jaime Lacson said.

"I'll leave it up to Daria. I want her to be the happiest with our wedding. Whatever she decides, I'll go along with that," answered Marco.

"I suggested you get married on January second," said Señor Hernandez.

The gentlemen turned to him, surprised.

"The sooner the better! That way, Marco, I can have a grandchild before I die," explained Señor Hernandez.

The room was quiet. All the men except Vicente knew why Señor Hernandez was trying to rush the date.

"Tito, Marco's parents are still in the States. Don't you think it's too soon?" asked Vicente, surprised that his uncle wanted the wedding to happen right away.

"We can have the wedding here first at Castellana. When Marco's parents arrive they can host a reception in Manila," said Señor Hernandez in a serious voice.

"If that is what you want, Tito, I have no problem with it," answered Marco. "We need to ask Daria first."

Just then, Daria came in. "Did I just hear my name? Lunch is almost ready. Tita Christina is done setting the table, and Yaya Helen and Mama are finishing with the food," said Daria. "It has been peaceful so far."

The family entered the dining room and were delighted to see Christina and Estefania working together. The table was decorated with a red and green crocheted tablecloth. The gold advent candles nestled in the silver candelabra were all lit.

The guests arrived. Jocelyn and Dr. Gonzaga brought a Christmas basket filled with apples and oranges. Karlos Vasquez and Father Armando came next.

"Daria, where are you going to sit, next to Marco or Tito Enrique?" teased her cousin.

"How about next to you, Vicente?" Daria answered.

Daria took a seat next to Vicente, and her cousin playfully pinched her cheeks.

Father Armando led the prayer. He blessed the Hernandez family and thanked them for their support and contributions to helping him become a priest.

"Armando, it is good that you will be part of the parish now along with Father Jose," said Señor Hernandez. "As your benefactor, I would like to request that you marry Daria and Marco on January second."

"Papa, Marco and I have not agreed on a date yet. How can we prepare for a wedding just a week from now?" asked a surprised Daria.

"Well, what's the point in delaying? I will talk to your in-laws. You can have another wedding in Manila," Señor Hernandez said. "The wedding you envisioned was pretty simple. I am sure your mama and aunt can make it happen."

"But Papa, Marco and I still need to discuss this," said Daria.

"Marco agreed when I spoke with him earlier."

Daria looked at Marco. Her fiancé squeezed her hand under the table.

"Your papa is right, Daria," agreed Señora Estefania. "We can make this wedding happen in a week. Your papa is just sentimental. You know he is a man of action and wants to get things done right away."

Daria could not understand the rush. She wondered to herself, *Is there something going on that I am not aware of?*

"Well, this is all too sudden, my brother. I don't see why we need to rush," said Cristina Valderrama.

"Daria, Marco, can you do this for me?" asked Señor Hernandez, almost pleading.

From her father's expression, Daria knew in her heart that her father was hiding something from her. She gave him a hug. "Papa, if this would make you happy, then okay. I'll do as you say."

As the New Year approached, Daria's wedding preparations were running more smoothly than she had ever expected. Due to the Hernandez's influence, the catering, cake, and party favors were easily arranged. The invitations were sent out to a few guests four days before the wedding.

The people of Castellana and Hacienda Corazon were surprised by the sudden occasion. They gossiped that Daria might be with child, but the rumor was squashed right away by Father Armando.

Daria went with the flow, although she was overwhelmed. She noticed her father avoided her every time she tried to talk to him alone. Marco, noticing Daria was in a daze, took her to the garden where they could be alone.

"Daria, for someone getting married you surely don't look happy," observed Marco.

"Sorry, Marco. Of course I am happy that I will be marrying you, but something about Papa is bothering me," Daria sighed.

Marco had been contemplating whether to tell Daria the truth about her father's condition. He finally came to terms with himself. "Daria, there is something you need to know."

Daria looked at Marco with a worried and curious look.

"I love you, and whether we get married on the second, next month, or next year, I am just happy that we will become man and wife," Marco said, trying to find the right things to say. "As for your papa's request that we get married as soon as possible, he does have his reasons," Marco said, catching Daria's full attention. Marco took Daria's hand and sat her on the garden bench. He sat next to her.

"Daria, your papa is very ill and has little time left. When I was here last month he told me that and asked if I would like to walk you down the aisle before—"

"Why did you not tell me? Who else knows? Does Mama know? What kind of sickness does he have?" Daria stood, in a panic, and Marco held her.

"I promised your papa not to tell you. I am not sure exactly what is wrong with him, but he wants to see you happy and secure," Marco said, letting Daria sob on his chest. "You know your papa better than anyone else, Daria. I am sorry that I kept it from you."

The New Year's celebration was a blur to Daria. While Castellana was enjoying festivities and fireworks as it entered a new decade, the Hernandez household and Hacienda Corazon were rushing to prepare for Daria's wedding.

1970

The Hernandez garden was ready for Daria's wedding. A gazebo stood at the end of the garden walkway for the bride, adorned with yellow and pink flower petals. Chairs covered in white with bows were arranged in front of the gazebo. The luncheon tables were set with cream linen. Bells with two doves were placed on each guest's name plate. The cake was a simple three-tiered chocolate cake with white icing decorated with fresh yellow daisies.

Due to the short notice, the Hernandez invited only close family and friends and expected about fifty guests. As the guests starting appearing, Father Armando arrived with Father Jose, looking respectable in his robe and vestments. The children's choir began to sing hymns, and Señora Estefania, dressed in a yellow *Filipiñana*, greeted the guests. Christina Valderrama made her way toward the guests wearing an off-the-shoulder, knee-length beige dress, a yellow fascinator on her head.

Marco appeared alongside Vicente, both wearing Barong Tagalog and looking dashing. Karlos Vasquez congratulated them. They walked up to the gazebo to greet Father Armando and Father Jose.

"Don't mess this up, Mando," Vicente teased the new priest.

"*Father* Armando now, Vicente. I would not let Marco and Daria down," Mando answered back.

The pianist played Johann Pachelbel's *Canon in D,* and the guests headed toward their designated seats. Señora Estefania sat in the front row, Jocelyn next to her. Christina and Jaime sat behind them.

Marco stood at the bottom steps of the gazebo next to Vicente. Father Armando stood on the landing.

During the second half of the music, Señor Hernandez stepped out from the side in his Barong Tagalog, looking composed. He made his way down the steps to the middle of the walkway. Then, as the choir began humming, the grand front door of the Hernandez home opened, and Daria appeared. She wore a simple long-sleeved white lace gown, a bouquet of white roses in her hands, her hair up and held in place by a tiara that was once her grandmother's. A simple veil covered her face. Glowing, she walked toward her father.

Señor Hernandez, a man who did not show his emotions, became teary-eyed when he saw his daughter. He reached out and embraced her. He gazed into her eyes and wondered how time had passed so quickly. Daria was once just a little girl in his arms, and now she was a beautiful young lady, ready to start a new chapter in her life.

Daria took her father's arm and whispered, "Papa, don't let me fall."

Señor Hernandez began to shed tears, grateful and happy tears, because he had the opportunity to walk his daughter down the aisle. Whatever life brought him, he was confident that Marco would take good care of Daria. The next thing the señor knew, Marco was facing them, smiling. Daria's father embraced his daughter and then embraced his son-in-law. He slowly removed his daughter's hand from his arm and handed Daria to Marco.

CHAPTER 12

Daria and Marco flew to the island of Oahu for their honeymoon, a gift from Daria's papa. Daria was hesitant to leave her father, but she had promised herself to make her father happy and keep to herself the knowledge about his health. Señor Hernandez was relieved that his daughter was off on her honeymoon and would be away for a month. The election campaign was now at full speed.

Señor Hernandez went to his property that was once home to Mayor Karlos Vasquez. The three-bedroom, one-story house was within the city proper, close to city hall. Felix and Nelson accompanied their señor, along with the family lawyer, Attorney Delgado. Señor Hernandez was surprised to see that the house was empty, devoid of any of Karlos's belongings.

"Mayor Vasquez surely moves fast," commented Atty. Delgado.

"Which means he can get things done!" answered Señor Enrique.

The señor ordered Felix and Nelson to double check the rooms in case Karlos had forgotten any items.

"Señor, it looks like everything has been packed except Mayor Vasquez's study," Felix informed him. "His desk and some office chairs are still in there, but other than that everything seems ready."

"Check the back of the house and the lines, and stay outside until I call you," ordered Señor Hernandez. "Attorney, let's head to the study."

Señor Hernandez sat in the chair behind the desk. The room seemed bare without the bookshelves that once occupied Karlos's office.

Atty. Delgado sat in front of Señor Hernandez. "Señor, I understand you want your will revised," said the attorney. "Are you really sure that this is what you want? I think you should discuss this with Señora Estefania first."

"I am the sole proprietor of Hacienda Corazon and the azucarera. She cannot question my decision," Señor Hernandez said firmly.

"Señor, to give a piece of farm land to sixty families in Hacienda Corazon means about a quarter of the hacienda," noted Atty. Delgado. "I told the surveyor and my people in the land title office to keep this private, as you requested."

"I don't want the other hacienderos to know, especially this close to the election. If I am already dead, there is really nothing they can do about my decision," said Señor Hernandez.

He stood and noticed newspapers in the corner of the room.

"Well, Señor, I will go ahead and finish the paperwork. I will deliver it to you as soon as everything is ready," Atty. Delgado said as he stood to leave.

After the lawyer closed the door, Señor Hernandez picked up a newspaper from the pile and looked at it. It was outdated. He was about to call Felix to clear it away, but something caught his eye. He noticed the paper was opened to the classified ads section. He looked at the ads, wondering what Karlos would be looking for. He thought maybe Karlos needed an assistant or secretary. Some ads were check-marked.

Why would Karlos need a hairdresser? He then noticed another ad with a mark that read, "Looking for land to buy to build chicken coop." Señor Hernandez shook his head and threw the paper on the floor. He noticed that there were markings in another paper, this time an ad seeking pig farmers. The dates were circled, and that intrigued Señor Hernandez.

He picked up the first paper from the floor and went back to the desk. There was something inconsistent about the ads. The advertisement date for the hairdresser was Sept. 3, 1969; the position needed to be filled by Sept. 5, 1969. He thought about the dates and recalled the rebels attacked the Daza and Jison haciendas around that date. Señor Hernandez shook his head. *This must just be a coincidence,* he thought. He then looked at the piggery ad in the second paper: "looking to be filled by Sept 20." Señor Hernandez shuddered. He thought about the pigs stolen from the hacienda. The pig's head offering at his birthday party at the hacienda had been on the same date.

Why would Karlos have this underlined in the paper? wondered Señor Hernandez. He recalled the conversation he'd had with Karlos at the city hall. He remembered clearly that Mayor Vasquez had no leads about the rebel attacks.

His thoughts were interrupted when Felix knocked on the door to report about the areas of the house that needed repair. Señor Hernandez ordered Felix to get the car ready. The señor folded the newspapers and thought to himself that maybe he really did not know the real Karlos Vasquez.

LUZON

The first stop on the Nationalist Party campaign was in Ilocos Province. The farmland was not dominated by landowners but by small farmers who owned their own land and farmed rice, grain, and corn crops. Ilocos farmers were able to obtain their land after the administration, pressured by working farmers helped by the rebel group, had declared land reform. The success of the rebels in winning land for the farmers built confidence in the other rebel groups to continue with their causes but also allowed rebels in Ilocos to live peacefully with the farmers.

The party supporters had set up a platform on a makeshift basketball court, and the crowds were steadily entering. Karlos Vasquez and Aristotle Lacson were accepted by the farmers, who thought of Karlos as one of them. Karlos's popularity with the union groups gave him the edge.

"Mayor Vasquez, farming offers equal opportunity for many," said Aristotle Lacson. "Imagine what possibilities it can offer if the haciendéros share their land with their workers."

"It's not like the landowners here in Ilocos wanted to give up their land. They were forced to give it up," Señor Jamora observed. "There is a big difference between donating or selling land and the government forcing owners to give it up. In my opinion that's stealing."

"We can use this as an advantage. Vice President Aragon was one of those who opposed land reform," replied Aristotle.

Karlos was not interested in the conversation, so he looked over his talking points. He also thought land reform could be good for the farmers. Probably forcing the haciendaros to give up their land wasn't best, but the government could compensate land owners who could no longer manage their land and then give it to the people.

The crowd started cheering for Karlos as he and his running mate took the stage. Karlos smiled and waved and took his seat when Aristotle took the center stage to talk to the crowd.

"Ilocos is indeed a model for what modern farming should be," Aristotle began. "The farmers here truly love their land, and it shows in the quality of crops they produce. I was once a senator, and now I'm a farmer in Mindanao. In my years of experience I have seen progress in our land. Industry and factories started to take over, forgetting that farming has been the stronghold of this nation," Aristotle said. "Which is why our farmers need to be protected by government. With that, my friends, I present to you the future president of our republic, Karlos Vasquez."

The crowd cheered, which energized Karlos. These were the people he wanted to help. Farming was part of Karlos's heritage.

"My friends and fellow farmers, what an honor," Karlos said, raising his hand to quiet the crowd. "The drive to Ilocos was an eye opener. As we passed through different provinces I saw that farming is indeed still our country's asset. I have seen happy farmers here in Ilocos. Happy because working in your fields, able to sell your own crops to gain profit, is very rewarding." Karlos smiled and heard the crowd clap. Farmers agreed with what he was saying.

"When I win the presidency, on the first day in office I will create a law that will give incentives to landowners who can no longer manage their land to surrender their farms to the government," Karlos continued. "My government will distribute these lands to the farmers."

This caused the farmers to cheer even louder.

But Señor Jamora was not amused. He confronted Karlos about his statement after his speech. "Karlos, I do not agree with your earlier statements. You better clear this up, my boy, or the haciendaros might misconstrue you," Señor Jamora advised.

"Señor, there is nothing wrong with what I said. What I am offering is that the poorer haciendas have an option to sell their land to the government, and the government will then give the land to the farmers. This is a win-win situation.".

The van ride to their next destination was quiet. The group got some rest while Karlos and Aristotle reviewed which points were relevant and which issues to attack in the next province they were campaigning in.

Señor Jamora observed Karlos and his actions and persona and realized how much Karlos had changed. He thought that Mayor Vasquez had grown too confident and did not seem to accept his suggestions as openly as before. The señor also wondered if Karlos had gained support elsewhere without sharing it with him. He made a note to himself to observe Karlos more closely.

The campaign crew continued to Central Luzon and made its way to Pampanga, Tarlac, and Bulacan. The reception was lukewarm in these provinces, which reflected their support for Vice President Aragon. They also campaigned in Laguna and Cavite. To Karlos's credit, the union and labor groups made their presence and support felt in both towns.

After a long three weeks of campaigning, Karlos and his party were glad to be back in Manila for a break. As they reached the Nationalist headquarters, Karlos saw a group of media people waiting for him. When Karlos got out of the vehicle he was bombarded by a question.

"Mayor Vasquez, what can you say about the claims of Vice President Aragon that the Communist Party is behind you?"

Karlos was caught off guard by the question.

"Did you know that the rebels are being funded by the communist and Muslim militants? Vice President Aragon said he has proof."

Aristotle and Señor Jamora came to Karlos's side, urging him to enter the building, but Karlos did not budge. Karlos faced the media and made a challenging statement. "If Vice President Aragon has proof, then I ask him to show the public that proof."

The following day the media was all over the issue of Karlos Vasquez being a communist. Karlos was having breakfast with Jocelyn and other party members. The issue did not seem to bother him.

"We need damage control. We need to spin this issue around," said Congressman Saison. "I wonder what proof Aragon has."

"We will challenge him to openly show what he has. After all, you have nothing to hide, right, Karlos?" Señor Jamora said.

To Karlos's surprise, Jocelyn defended him. "Gentlemen, we all know who Karlos is, his background and accomplishments. It is obvious that Aragon could not think of anything else to use to put Karlos down."

Karlos smiled at Jocelyn and held her hand. Jocelyn accepted his hand.

"We have gathered information about Aragon, but it might be too early to release our propaganda against him," Congressman Saison said, thinking of ways to counterattack.

"I have a suggestion," Aristotle offered. "Gentlemen, we still have one card that we can use, and that is the personal life of Karlos Vasquez." The table was quiet, all ears on Aristotle. "I think it is time for us to use the love story angle. Who better to defend Karlos than Jocelyn? Jocelyn, do you think you can accept the challenge and help Karlos?"

Jocelyn beamed, thinking she could finally get the spotlight to shine on her.

Señor Jamora and Governor Escalante asked Christina Valderrama to help introduce Jocelyn to the press and the lady's circle. She refused to help because she said she could not tolerate Jocelyn and did not want anything to do with her. Christina, however, gave them a contact at *W*, a weekly magazine show, to arrange an interview with Jocelyn.

Jocelyn was ecstatic to be interviewed. She was led to the dressing room, and a stylist helped her with her wardrobe: a pink pencil skirt and a white cardigan, her hair swept in a low ponytail. Jocelyn was pleased with the results. She reminded herself of the talking points that Señor Jamora had practiced with her. She told herself that she needed to impress the host and the audience to help clear Karlos's name.

Jocelyn entered the studio and was introduced as the fiancée of presidential candidate Karlos Vasquez. She waved and smiled to the audience, trying to project a demure and feminine image. The host of the show, Vivian Romero, ushered Jocelyn to her seat. She sat with her back straight and legs crossed at the ankles.

"Jocelyn Gonzaga, welcome to *W*."

"Thank you for having me," answered Jocelyn, trying her best to maintain her posture.

"A lot of young women out there would probably want to be in your shoes right now, for Karlos Vasquez is indeed one of the most eligible bachelors of the country."

"Yes, I am indeed lucky. I have known Karlos since we were children, and I am glad to be able to stand next to him as he is running for president."

"Can you tell us about your love story with Karlos Vasquez? asked Vivan. "You are probably one of the people closest to him and know him best,"

Jocelyn let out a demure laugh. "When I was young, Karlos was a hardworking boy in the hacienda. At a young age, he was already helping his parents work the farm, and he went to school at the same time. I remember he would gather fruit for me and leave them at our house. He would always pick the perfect ones. I could tell it was him even if he denied it," made up Jocelyn.

"So you were young and in love with each other?" Vivian pried.

"Well, it was not until he graduated from law school that he actually started courting me. He wanted to prove to my family that he was capable, and he has done only so—not only to my family but to the people of Castellana," Jocelyn said, looking up trying to fight back tears.

"Are you all right, Jocelyn? It seems you have gotten emotional," Vivian commented.

"I'm sorry, Vivian. I came here today hoping that I could share my advice with young women, but talking about Karlos is making me …" Jocelyn paused, trying to find the right words to move the audience. "Well, talking about Karlos and how he's loving and giving makes it hurt me to hear about people calling him—"

"A communist? Part of the rebel group?" ended Vivian.

The audience gasped. In Jocelyn's mind, Vivian would someday be sorry for saying that.

"That accusation has no merit," Jocelyn told Vivian. "I came here not to talk about that issue but rather share with your audience that my fiancé is an honest and hardworking man. No matter what black propaganda the other party uses, my fiancé will not retaliate but instead prove that if you vote for him, he will the best president this country will ever have."

The host was not expecting Karlos's fiancée to introduce a political campaign to the interview.

"You are a girl in love, Jocelyn," quipped Vivian.

"Yes, Vivian. I am a girl in love, and like anyone who is in love or has been in love, we can see the good in that person, and we will stand by them in failure or success," Jocelyn answered proudly.

The audience stood up and gave Jocelyn a big round of applause. It was clear that Jocelyn, at least for today, had played her part well and helped boost Karlos Vasquez's popularity.

Jocelyn became an overnight sensation, much to her delight. The issue of Karlos being a communist seemed to be overshadowed by Jocelyn's interview. A beautiful crying fiancée standing behind her man and their love story sparked the masses' interest. They called them the Susan Roces and Fernando Poe Jr. of politics. The Nationalist Party made good use of the rising popularity of the couple and had Jocelyn join Karlos's campaign around the city.

March quickly followed, and the election was only a week away. The party decided to hold their *miting de avance* for Karlos in Castellana.

"Karlos, the election is around the corner. Soon you will be president and me the first lady," an overjoyed Jocelyn said. "We can have our wedding right after they pronounce you president!"

Karlos hugged her from behind, kissing her neck and saying, "Patience, my dear. After we win the election, then we can talk about our wedding. It will happen. You will become queen of this country."

After what she had experienced, Jocelyn would do everything she could to stay in the spotlight. Karlos turned Jocelyn to him and kissed her passionately, and Jocelyn returned his affection. Slowly they made their way to Karlos's bedroom. Much to Karlos's delight, the lovers spent their first night together.

CASTELLANA

Señor Hernandez and Señora Estefania watched the telecast of Jocelyn's interview. Estefania was quite proud of Jocelyn and asked Enrique if he could ask the station to replay it again.

Señor Enrique commented, "Estefania, I did not expect she had it in her. She sure is a good actress."

"She sure is. What I mean is she is radiant and poised. She is indeed fit to be first lady," Señora Estefania said to her husband.

Señor Hernandez got up and went to his studio as Estefania kept on praising her niece.

Attorney Delgado was waiting for the señor, his suitcase filled with documents.

"I see you've got things ready for me?" asked Señor Hernandez.

"Yes, Señor. I have sixty titles ready, and that is for about 300 hectares of land. I also have the deed for Helen." Delgado handed him the paperwork. "All it needs is your signature, and I'll have it notarized."

"I heard about Mayor's Vasquez plan. When he becomes president, he will be willing to buy farmland and give it to the farmers. Shouldn't you wait and see first?" Delgado asked.

Señor Hernandez looked at the paperwork and for a moment felt hesitant. He then remembered what Marco said about making the workers happy to avoid them revolting. If this could help Daria retain the loyalty of his people, he would do what was needed.

Señor Hernandez reached for his fountain pen and started signing the land title for Yaya Helen.

"It sounds like a good plan, but to whom will he give the land? Well, that we cannot guarantee," said Señor Hernandez.

He continued to sign the land titles. As he signed he felt uplifted, almost freed, from the burden of being a haciendero. The names on the title were workers who had been working for his family for generations. He had come to believe that they deserved a piece of Hacienda Corazon too.

Señor Hernandez handed the titles back to his lawyer. "Attorney Delgado, I have trusted you for many years. Keep this between us until my last breath."

Ka Abel was reading the classified ads in the *National Free Press*, checking if Karlos had left any messages for them. He saw an ad seeking information about a missing relative. Ka Abel set the paper down and reread the ad.

Missing relative, date of birth 1-1-1915, hard of hearing and partially blind, last seen in Pampanga. Contact K. Salva with any information.

The message was from Karlos Vasquez, using his pseudonym K. Salva. Ka Abel deciphered the message, which sent him to the first page of the newspaper, line twenty of the headline news. Karlos sought information about where the news of him being a communist came from.

Ka Abel called Ka Eden and showed her the message from Karlos. She nodded to her husband, accepting the mission to discover the root of the issue.

Daria and Marco arrived in Manila and headed toward the Gutierrez home. Marie Gutierrez was excited to see her son and daughter-in-law and welcomed them with an embrace with tears in her eyes.

"Finally, Daria, welcome to the family!" Marie Gutierrez told Daria warmly.

"Well, if it isn't Mr. and Mrs. Marco Gutierrez!" Miguel Gutierrez gave each of them a hug.

"Daria, thank you for making my wife's dreams of having a daughter come true," Mr. Gutierrez said, teasing his wife.

"Thank you for openly accepting me to your family, Tita—" Daria said before she was interrupted by Mrs. Gutierrez.

"Mom and Dad, my dear Daria," Marie said. "Thank you for coming into Marco's life."

"Okay, we are tired and hungry! What's for dinner?" Marco asked.

Marco did not receive an answer but was happy to see his parents walking with Daria with their arms around his wife as he headed toward the living room.

After dinner, Marco and Daria retreated to Marco's room, which had been redecorated with new wallpaper and furniture to accommodate the couple.

"My mom did a good job throwing all my stuff away. I guess she would not want you to find traces of my past." Marco looked at Daria, who stood by the door.

"If you have secrets, Mr. Gutierrez, better spill them. You know your parents are my allies," said Daria.

"Why are you standing there? Don't you want to come in our room?" Marco said, lying on the bed. He gestured for Daria to sit next to him. As she did, she looked at her husband.

"So this is it. Reality," mused Daria.

"Sure is. You'll get used to it here. I promise once I get back to work I will find us a place of our own," Marco told his wife.

Daria was quiet. She thought about Castellana and Hacienda Corazon. She had never envisioned herself living elsewhere, but she understood that she needed to be by Marco's side.

Marco sensed his wife's reverie and kissed her on the cheek. "I know you miss Castellana, especially your papa. We will be back there in a few days. Rest up now," Marco said, trying to comfort his wife.

Daria turned to Marco and laid her head on his chest. "Marco, do you think Papa is all right? I haven't seen him for three weeks. Considering his health…"

"You can not bring yourself to be apart from him?" Marco finished his wife's sentence.

Daria nodded, and her tears started to flow.

"Daria, in February our Hacienda Corazon project will begin. I think it would be best for you to stay with your family until the project is finished," Marco offered.

"But, Marco we are married! I have to be where you are," Daria replied.

"Right now, our father needs you, and I know that you will only be burdened if you are not by his side," Marco said, kissing Daria's forehead. "Don't worry, and don't feel guilty. I will fly to see you every weekend. As the project progresses, I will stay in Castellana longer."

Daria embraced her husband and kissed him. "Thank you, Marco, thank you," Daria said, feeling relieved.

CHAPTER 13

CASTELLANA

In a few days, the people would cast their votes and determine the fate of the country. Señor Enrique had spearheaded the idea of making Mayor Vasquez the next president. Recently Señor Hernandez had lost interest in Karlos's campaign. He slowly took the backseat and allowed Señor Jamora to take lead. For the past month Señor Hernandez's headaches had worsened, and his eyesight began to get blurry. The medicines that Dr. Jimena gave him had little effect, but the señor did his best not to let anyone notice. He continued with his routines around Hacienda Corazon but reserved his strength for only important things.

Señor Hernandez reached into his desk drawer and took out the new pills that Dr. Jimena had prescribed for him. He told himself he need to focus on Daria and Marco's arrival and decided to take three instead of the two the doctor had directed. When he returned the bottle, he noticed the classified ads he'd found in Karlos Vasquez's study. He told himself that now was not the best time to think about that. He gathered himself and headed to the main house when he heard the voice of an excited Yaya Helen greeting Daria and Marco.

Daria beamed when she saw her father and ran toward him to give him a big embrace.

"Whoa, hold your horses, Daria! Remember that you are a married woman now. You don't want to your husband seeing you hugging another man so eagerly," Señor Hernandez said, giving Marco a smile.

"How are you, my son?" He offered his hand to Marco, but his son-in-law hugged Señor Hernandez too.

"We are well, Papa. We had a great time in Oahu. Thank you for sending us," replied Marco.

"Papa, it looks like you have lost weight. You look tired," Daria remarked with a concerned look on her face.

"I'm all right, Daria. Let me look at you, my darling. Will I be expecting a grandchild soon?" asked Señor Hernandez, diverting her attention.

Daria Hernandez-Gutierrez turned red, a bit embarrassed about her father's question.

Her husband wittily replied, "We are working on it, Papa."

"Papa, I don't see Mama. She knows we were arriving today, right?" asked Daria, not surprised that her mother was not there to greet them.

"She is at church helping Father Jose and Mando. She is organizing a prayer rally for Karlos before his *miting de avance*," answered her father, who unconsciously rubbed his neck. "Which is great because I get to focus my whole attention on you and my son-in-law."

Daria notice her papa's action but did not say anything. She was trying her best to be strong for her father, to continue to pretend that she did not know about his condition.

"Papa, so what have we missed?" Daria asked, leading her father to sit on the couch.

"Nothing much. Hacienda Corazon has been replanted and is back on track. We also cleared the land where Marco and Vicente will be building their project. The surveyor and Atty. Delgado have processed the permit for construction and put a new land title under your name and Vicente and Marco's."

"Papa, I appreciate the gesture, but there's no need to add my name to the title. The land belongs to Daria and Vicente," Marco said.

"You are my son now, Marco, and I don't think it will be a problem for Daria and Vicente. Besides, Daria told me over the phone that you are allowing her to stay here with me for a while until your project is finished."

"I want Daria to be happy, Papa. If she needs time here in Castellana, then I will give that to her. As for the title, thank you," Marco said, grateful for Señor Hernandez's gesture.

"What about Karlos's campaign, Papa?" Daria asked. "Tonight is his *miting de avance*. Are we attending?"

"Señor Jamora and Governor Escalante are doing a fantastic job of handling him," said Señor Hernandez. "As a matter of fact, he has gained a lot of followers and supporters. He has a good probability of winning the election."

"You must be proud of him, Papa," said Daria. "You always had faith in Karlos, and you nurtured him. It would be your success too."

Señor Hernandez was silent for a few seconds. His thoughts went back to his theory about Karlos being involved with the rebels.

"Papa, are you all right?" Daria asked her father. "You are quiet all of a sudden."

"Sorry, I just had a passing thought," said Señor Hernandez. He straightened up. "I don't think I can attend Karlos's big event tonight. Would it be okay if both of you stay with me?"

"Of course, Papa. I'd rather stay here with you anyway," Daria said, putting her head on her papa's shoulders.

"Oh! And did I mention Jocelyn? Her dream of being in the limelight has finally come true. I wish you'd seen her interview. She could win an award for best actress. Even I was convinced by her acting," said Señor Hernandez.

Daria and Marco knew that Señor Hernandez was putting on an act too. Daria could tell that in her three weeks' absence her papa had suddenly became fragile and weak. His once robust personality was replaced by a weary persona, that of a man who was concealing his pain.

Señora Estefania's prayer rally for Karlos was well attended by the people of Castellana. The elites of Castellana were seated comfortably in front of the makeshift stadium in the plaza, the canopy shielding them from the sun. The people stood behind them, some snickering and some disapproving, but they showed their solidarity with prayer. Their intentions are all the same: to pray for a peaceful election and for Karlos Vasquez to be the next president.

Father Armando led the rosary. Señora Estefania, Jocelyn, and Dr. Gonzaga were on stage with their rosaries, their heads covered in lace chapel veils. Jocelyn gave a short speech after the prayer rally. She noticed that the crowd from Castellana was not giving her the same warmth and support as the crowd had in Manila.

Señora Estefania excused herself, headed toward the parish office, and knocked on Father Jose's office door.

"Father, may I have a moment of your time?" she asked.

"Of course, Señora. Come in. Please make yourself comfortable," answered Father Jose.

Señora Estefania closed the door firmly and took the seat across from Father Jose's desk.

"Is everything all right, Estefania? You look bothered. How is Señor Hernandez? He seems to be quiet lately," asked the concerned Father Jose.

"Father, I don't know what to with Enrique," Señora Estefania began. "I accepted long ago that he has no love for me. I quietly stood by him and did not say a word when he said he wanted to adopt Daria."

Father Jose sat back in his chair, giving Señora Estefania his undivided attention.

"I am used to him ignoring me and brushing aside my suggestions. Sometimes in my heart I would curse him and wish him ill, but here I am, still waiting, longing that one day he will need me and love me," Señora Estefania said, in tears.

"You have been a generous and good wife to him, Estefania. I am certain that even if he does not use words to express his affections, he loves you and he needs you," Father Jose said to console Estefania.

"Father, I want him to need me, but despite his poor health now, he still refuses to," Estefania said. "I have noticed in the last months that he has been having headaches, and I caught him taking medication. I took it upon myself to talk to Dr. Jimena. At first he refused, but finally he confessed and told me that Enrique has a tumor in his brain."

"Estefania!" Father Jose stood up and sat next to her.

"Dr. Jimena told me that he has about six months and that the cancer might have spread. There is no treatment for him," Estefania sobbed.

"Estefania, I am sorry to hear this. I too feel burdened hearing this," said Father Jose. "That he did not tell you is his way of coping with all of this. He did not tell you to avoid to worrying you."

"Father, I pray that in his last days he will at last acknowledge me and tell me that he loves me so I can let go of this anger I have been holding on to for so long," cried Estefania.

Father Jose allowed Estefania to cry and said a silent prayer for her. Neither knew that Karlos Vasquez had silently passed by and overheard everything they'd talked about.

Marco escorted his father-in-law to his studio while Daria helped Yaya Helen make dinner. Señor Enrique was relieved that his headaches did not bother him as much when he was talking to Daria.

"Thank you, Marco," Señor Hernandez said as Marco helped him ease into his chair. "Please sit."

Marco complied and sat in the chair in front of Señor Hernandez's desk.

"How are you feeling, Papa?" asked Marco.

"Seeing you and Daria makes me feel happy and well," answered Señor Hernandez. "Marco, there is something I want to show you." Señor Hernandez opened his drawer, took out the classified ads, and handed them to Marco, "I was checking Karlos's house with Atty. Delgado, and I found this in his study. Maybe the tumor in my brain is making me hallucinate. Take a good look."

Marco read the ads, trying to make sense of the underlined words. The other ads did not make sense to him, but the piggery ad did. "Papa, if I recall correctly, the date of your party at the azucarera was September 20, and it ended with the …"

"Yes, Marco, that's what I thought too. The other ad tells the date around the time the Jison and Daza farms were attacked," added Señor Hernandez.

"Have you seen anything else lately?" asked Marco.

"The other day I saw that a K. Salva was looking for a relative and gave his birthdate. My head started to hurt, trying to figure out what the date meant before I realized." Señor Hernandez showed him the front page of the paper. "The code means to read the story on the front page, which was about Vice President Aragon's accusation that Karlos is a communist."

Marco read looked at the ads again. He wondered if his father-in-law might have overanalyzed the words, but Marco then thought it might not be a coincidence. "How about the ad regarding the chicken coop? It has markings on it. Have you decoded it?

"Why don't you give it a try? Maybe I'm just going insane," said Señor Hernandez.

Marco looked at the wording. He saw that the ad was posted by K. Salva, and a thought came to him. *K. Salva? Could it be Karlos's pseudonym?* he thought to himself before he shook his head in disbelief.

"K. Salva is Karlos Vasquez—is that what you are thinking, Marco?"

"Yes. But this is impossible. How could Karlos be part of the rebellion?"

"I sent an anonymous telegram to Aragon, hoping he would investigate, but instead the idiot just threw it out there without even verifying it."

"Papa, you have known Karlos for a long time. Surely he would not deceive you like this," said Marco in disbelief.

Señor Hernandez took a set of keys from his drawer and handed them to Marco. He stood up and walked toward the picture of Daria in pigtails and asked Marco to remove the picture. "Marco, those keys are for this safe. In there are my last will and testament and the land titles for the people. I hope that my will can someday protect Daria. I entrust this to you."

"Papa, you should really share this with Daria," Marco said.

"Marco, after your project in Hacienda Corazon is done, promise me you'll take Daria away, far away from Castellana. This is my last request to you"

Ka Eden reported to Ka Abel about who had given information about Karlos's ties to the rebels. Ka Abel was astonished to hear the news.

"We need to send word to Karlos," said Ka Abel.

"It can wait for tomorrow. Tonight is his night," suggested Ka Eden.

"No, he has to know now. I have a plan." Ka Abel called his son Egoy and some of his men. "Tonight we will attend Mayor Vasquez's *miting de avance.*"

The plaza of the city of Castellana was flooded with Karlos Vasquez and Aristotle Lacson supporters wearing blue shirts waving blue and white flags. The mass of people came from all over the province of Azusa. Hacienderos from the Visayas made appearances, and Aristotle's family and loyalists from Davao came to support them. The incumbent senators and congressmen of the Nationalist Party also went out of their way, for they had noticed the people's support for Karlos. The seasoned politicians saw how the people embraced Karlos Vasquez, and they took the opportunity to make their presence felt; Karlos did have a good chance of becoming president. The media started their coverage; film cameras and photographers positioned themselves to catch the Nationalist Party candidates.

Señora Estefania was accompanied by Jocelyn and Congressman Saison. She told people that Señor Hernandez was feeling ill. She told the hacienderos that Daria and Marco had just arrived and it was just her husband's excuse to spend time with his daughter.

The church choir and the Castellana marching band started entertaining the crowd. The crowd was also delighted by the appearance of the night's event host, Vivian Romero, the show host who'd interviewed Jocelyn. Vivian shared a couple of songs to entertain the crowd.

"This is it, Karlos. Your destiny awaits." Señor Jamora praised the former mayor as he fixed Karlos's collar. "It is such a shame that Señor Hernandez could not make it. He would have been proud to see you and what you have accomplished these past months."

"Señor Hernandez may not be present, but he is always with me in here," Karlos said, pointing to his heart.

The band finished another number, and Vivian took over, addressing the crowd, "City of Castellana, you are blessed. You are blessed to have a son who is humble, giving, and indeed a born leader. Are we ready to see him as our next president?"

The crowd cheered and chanted, "Karlos, Karlos!"

"My countrymen, may I present to you the next president and vice president of the Republic of the Philippines, Karlos Vasquez and Aristotle Lacson!"

Karlos and Artistole entered and waved to the people, and the crowd's cheer became louder.

"My brothers and sisters, in two days we will be casting our votes. I hope you have decided who would be the best choice to lead this country," Aristotle called.

"Vasquez, Lacson!" cheered the crowd.

"Tonight, I will not bore you with promises and long speeches. From the beginning of the campaign we have been very consistent in our mission, and that is to serve the Filipino people," Aristotle said.

"Karlos Vasquez's administration will provide opportunities for many and help the poor earn a living through honest work. We will not be like the traditional politicians who want to gain their selfish desires. We stand in front of you to offer equal opportunity to all, to listen to the unheard voices and make them heard," promised Aristotle Lacson.

"So, my brothers and sister, out with the old politics and in with the new! For what we need is change. A change in government, and a fresher outlook, and I know only one man who can make this happen."

The crowd's cheers exploded because they knew the son of Castellana would soon be making his speech.

"My friends, let us welcome our next president, President Karlos Vasquez!"

The crowd welcomed him, chanting, "Vasquez! Vasquez!"

Karlos Vasquez walked to the stage, raising his fist and bowing to the crowd. He allowed the crowd's cheers to continue before he raised his right hand to quiet them.

"Thank you, everyone—thank you, my beloved people of Castellana and of our province, Azusa. Some politicians might think of the Visayas as just a landmark on their campaign trail, but I am proud to be in front of all of you as a son of the Visayas, a native of Azusa and a servant to the people of Castellana. I came here today ready with a speech to encourage your decision and to win over your votes, but the welcome I have received deserves no premade speeches or empty promises. I stand here in front of all of you to say what is in my thoughts and in my heart," promised Mayor Vasquez.

"Every election year, a politician stands in front of the voters promising progress, promising change, but have we really felt the changes that they have promised?" Karlos asked the crowd.

"During my campaign, I see that people are weary of the election. I have been asked by many, what point is there in voting, for there is no sanctity in our ballots? Elections are won not by the voice of the people but by powerful people who force their workers to choose the candidate that would benefit them. I urge each and every one of you to let your voices be heard by practicing your right to vote." Karlos Vasquez said the lines directly to the video camera that was broadcasting his campaign.

"I am a man who came from humble beginnings. Though I've been supported by many hacienderos and business people, I assure you that no one will be favored and be above the law when I become the president of this country," Karlos assured the people.

"This is also one of the reason I wanted my *miting de avance* held in my hometown. To show the entire country the support and love of my constituents, that I can be president. This is also to show the traditional politicians that even a man from the provinces who was born poor can run and will win the highest position of our land," strongly making his point to the people.

The crowd applauded Karlos.

"In my administration, I will hear the voice of the people and will take action. I will give the people opportunities to improve their lives, and no one will be above the law," promised Karlos. "I am thankful for the trust and support of the union, students, and professionals have bestowed on me. I also thank the hacienderos and the business sector who have showed their support. I will give you my word that I will serve as a bridge so that all may come to understanding and unite to make our country one of the most prosperous countries in Asia and the world."

The crowd's cheers got stronger, and the hacienderos joined the crowd in cheering.

"As for Aragon's accusation against me, I will not resort to black propaganda against him," Karlos said, shaking his head. "He has been in politics for years, but what contributions has he made? I will let his resumé speak for him," Karlos challenged his rival. "As a legislator, he did not pass any laws. He did not show strong support for any issues. When he was elected as vice president, all he did was enjoy his travels to different nations, saying they were for goodwill, but he brought nothing back to his motherland."

The crowd yelled, "No more traitor Aragon."

"Aragon called me a communist."

Karlos heard the crowd's cries. "No! we don't believe him! We know the truth."

"I would not stand for hostile and treacherous acts. I ask my brothers and sisters who are blinded by the foreign communist's empty promises to please put down your arms," declared Karlos. "In my administration, I will provide pardon and programs that will help the rebels transition back to society and rejoin the nation. If you dream of peace and equality, know that I believe in the same cause. But in order for us to reach these dreams, both parties need to work for peaceful talks," Karlos continued, getting the crowd more involved and passionate.

"This is why I ask you to use your hard-earned right to vote to choose the most fitting candidate. I believe and claim that I will win this election, and I trust that the Filipino people will join me in making change happen to our country, with peace and prosperity to all. Thank you, and may God bless us all!"

The applause exploded, and Karlos made his way to the crowd. He shook hands with the hacienderos and the Nationalist Party group and made his way to the people. The people rushed for the opportunity to shake his hand, and some of his constituents cried, for they were all hopeful for his win.

Karlos was then surrounded by children. "This is the future of our nation," said Karlos, placing his arm around a young boy. "Let us remove the problems and corruption that face us today so that they will enjoy opportunities and reap the benefits of our future." Karlos waved his last wave and felt the young boy tap on his leg. He counted the taps; it was a code from Ka Abel.

Karlos then entered the campaign van and opened the window to wave to the crowd. When the van sped up, Karlos recalled the order of the boy's taps. Karlos now knew who was behind the controversy that was thrown against him.

CHAPTER 14

ELECTION DAY

Monday, March 12, 1970

E lection Day was a national holiday in the Philippines. The law was passed to ensure people could practice their right to vote. The doors of the voting precincts opened at six in the morning and closed at two in the afternoon. The Hernandezes and half their household staff were first to enter the precincts to cast their votes, placing their ballots inside the ballot box. Their fingers were inked to show that they had finished voting. Representatives from the Commission on Elections and poll watchers from the Nationalist and Democratic parties were present to ensure proper reading and vote counting.

The citizens of Castellana showed their support for Vasquez and Lacson; the voting places were crowded with people wearing blue. The haciendero did their part as truckloads of people arrived at different precincts. The Hernandezes were confident that their people from Hacienda Corazon would vote for Karlos, but some haciendero handed carbon-copy papers as proof that their workers had voted for the chosen candidates.

Karlos Vasquez made his appearance in his designated voting precinct around seven, and the crowd cheered and told him they are praying for his victory.

The Nationalist Party members cheered as Karlos entered Governor Escalante's estate. Señor Jamora and Congressman Saison welcomed their candidate and patted him on the shoulders.

"The polls have officially closed, and we guarantee you a landslide in the Visayas," said Señor Jamora. "The hacienderos have sent word. Based on the carbon copies, you, my boy, have the lead here in the Visayas."

"The official counting has not started yet, and we cannot win this election with the Visayas alone," answered Karlos.

"Think positive, Karlos," said Governor Escalante. "I just got off the phone with Aristotle. Zamboanga, Davao, and General Santos were flooded in blue today too."

"Anything from Luzon and Manila?" asked Karlos.

"The Nationalist office said that there are mixed votes in the exit polls, and they are keeping a close eye on the provinces. Knowing Aragon and his dirty antics, we have to be vigilant," said the governor.

The official counting of ballots started on time an hour after the polls closed. The Nationalist Party in the Visayas and their volunteers had their eyes and ears glued on different media outlets.

"I wonder what happened to Enrique Hernandez," said Señor Jamora. "He started this whole thing, but he is nowhere to be seen."

"His daughter just got back. Knowing Enrique, his daughter is always his number one priority," Congressman Saison pointed out.

"He started it, but we placed the plan into action. Our friend Enrique sure is smart. He made us work hard, and he will be reaping the benefits," said Señor Jamora with a laugh.

"We will all benefit, am I right, Karlos?" commented Congressman Saison, looking at Karlos.

Karlos pretended he did not hear the conversation and set his eyes on the newscast when the news outlet announced partial results from several provinces and towns.

"Relax, Karlos, the report is mostly from municipalities in Manila and neighboring provinces. We already projected that Aragon would get the votes from these areas," Señor Jamora said.

Around eight, one of the volunteers turned in a note for Governor Escalante.

"Gentleman, as projected, a landslide in Castellana for Karlos. The COMELEC representatives have approved and tallied a total of 33,657 votes for Vasquez and 30,409 for Lacson," announced the governor.

"How many votes for Aragon? Zero?" asked Señor Jamora.

"He got thirty-nine votes," laughed Governor Escalante.

"We were expecting a landslide from Castellana," said Karlos. "It's going to be a long night."

The results for the province of Azusa were released the following day. By noon the COMELEC had stamped and verified Karlos and Aristotle's win in the in the province of Azusa, with 765,987 votes, which was 95 percent of the registered votes counted.

Around midnight the total vote tally from Western and Central Visayas came in. Vasquez won the Visayas with 635,867 votes. The official tally for Vasquez came in at 1,401,854 votes, only 139,185 for Aragon.

"We got Visayas's final count. If there are about ten million registered voters—" calculated Señor Jamora.

"That is only 10 percent of the tally," finished Karlos.

"Let's not lose hope. We still have Mindanao and parts of Luzon coming," encouraged Governor Escalante.

The tally from the city of Manila concluded, with Aragon leading with 182,000 votes and 153,540 votes for Vasquez. The provincial votes from Luzon also started to come in; Aragon got the majority of the votes, putting the two candidates in a close and tight race.

"This leaves us Mindanao," said Karlos. "Any word from Lacson?"

"We spoke this morning. It's a mess in Mindanao. Militant groups started attacking precincts, and some ballot boxes are missing," Congressman Saison reported.

"As for the entire Zamboanga province, Karlos has been leading, but there's no official tally yet," said Governor Escalante. "This is the time for us to be vigilant. Aragon has ties to the military, and who knows what dirty tactics he'll use."

At the Hernandez household, Señora Estefania, Jocelyn, and Dr. Gonzaga were eagerly watching the newscast. Jocelyn was excited to see Karlos's numbers and was already fantasizing about her wedding and what kind of first lady she would be.

"Tita, I believe Karlos will win this election!" cheered Jocelyn. "You think I can have my wedding at the Manila Cathedral? I want the top designers in Manila to design my gown. The wedding will be filled with flowers and dancing and—" Jocelyn's daydream was interrupted by Señor Hernandez.

"Who will be paying for this extravagance, Jocelyn?" asked Señor Hernandez as he entered the library with Daria and Marco.

Jocelyn sat down next to her aunt and laid her head on Tita Estefania's shoulders.

"Let the girl dream, Enrique," Estefania said to her husband.

"Looks like Karlos does have the chance to win. The numbers are so close," observed Marco.

"Marco, if Karlos loses by one vote, then it will be all your fault," Daria said to her husband, who was not able to vote because he was not a registered voter in Castellana.

"Mindanao is the key for this election. Knowing Aragon, he probably had the army change the ballots by now," Señor Hernandez commented.

Señora Estefania turned to her husband. "Are you saying Karlos has a chance to lose the election because of Mindanao?"

"This is just my opinion. The COMELEC has issued a statement about militant attacks in Mindanao delaying the vote count," said Señor Hernandez. "The only way for those votes to be counted fairly is if Karlos and the party have allies in Mindanao."

On the third day of the vote counting, Aragon was in the lead by only ten thousand votes. Only 25 percent of the votes had been counted and approved by the COMELEC in Mindanao; they needed 75 percent to announce the winner of the presidential election.

The national media had little coverage on what was happening, but the local media outlets were vocal about the ballot swapping that had been done in the precinct. Aristotle Lacson called Governor Escalante and told him that the military were the ones changing the ballot boxes, not the militant groups.

"We have to get the media to report about Aragon's action," said Governor Escalante.

"But how? Aragon has control of the national media," a fuming Señor Jamora replied.

"Governor, could you have one of your men adjust the radio antenna? Is there a way we can get a signal from the local radio station in Zamboanga?" asked Karlos.

"Karlos, I see what you are getting at," said Señor Jamora. "Let's go to town and visit the local radio station."

After hearing Karlos Vasquez's plan, Castellana's local radio station was in chaos. Reporters, engineers, and technicians dropped everything they had scheduled to get in contact with Rudy Magbanua in Zamboanga. Karlos was on the phone with Aristotle, who was in the local radio station with Rudy. The Nationalist Party members were on high alert and sent word to different local provincial radio stations to set their signals to capture the reporter's news.

"This is the plan—we need to let the people know on what is going on in Mindanao. If they find out about Aragon's plan it will anger them," said Señor Jamora.

"I agree. The elections were quiet and fair until Mindanao was cut off," said Romeo Barredo, one of the station hosts.

One of the engineers set the signal to capture Rudy Magbanua's show. Karlos asked the technicians to place speakers outside the radio station so that the crowd could hear what he was about to reveal.

"Karlos, it's working. Come in the booth," said Señor Jamora.

Inside the booth, Karlos and the local news commentator took their positions. Karlos then heard Rudy's voice in his earphones.

"Rudy, are we clear? Can you hear us?" asked Karlos.

"Yes. Aristotle had his men place speakers outside the station," answered Rudy.

"Okay, we will go live. Are you ready? In five-four-three-two-one ... The lights inside the studio turned green.

"This is Rudy Magbanua, reporting from our station in Zamboanga. Visayas, welcome to our show," the host announced.

"Rudy, this is Romeo Barredo in Castellana. There has been no news about what is happening in Mindanao, but we have received reports that ballot boxes were stolen by the militant groups. What is happening around there?"

"Yes, the military presence is strong here in Zamboanga and most parts of Mindanao. I have seen a report on television that the militant groups are causing the attack, but to be honest, Romeo, the group has been cooperative with this election. What we see are men in camouflage entering the precincts and removing the ballots."

"We know that Aragon has a narrow lead against Vasquez. In your opinion, who is directing the military?" Romeo asked leadingly.

"I have no actual proof to answer your question, Romeo, but we all know that Vasquez has no ties with the military."

A crowd started to build outside the radio stations in Castellana and in Zamboanga. The people muttered that this was the works of Aragon and that he needed to be stopped.

"I can see people are leaving their houses to come to the station to listen to this broadcast. I hear angry cries out there about Aragon," reported Romeo. "I hope this broadcast can reach the proper channels, Aragon owns a couple of media outlets. As responsible broadcast journalists, it is our responsibility to let the people know the truth."

The show was interrupted by noisy feedback, and gunshots rang out.

"Romeo, I can see outside that the military is heading toward our studio," Rudy Magbanua informed listeners.

"Romeo, this is Aristotle Lacson. The military is reaching the station right now, and gunshots were fired outside," said the vice-presidential candidate. "News of our broadcast might have reached the higher-ups."

Señor Jamora tapped the window and pointed toward the television. Two networks had turned their programing off, and one small local network started to talk about the radio coverage and Mindanao. The picture was blurry and the voices unclear.

"Looks like news has spread to Manila," said Señor Jamora.

The snowy picture on the television showed crowds marching toward the Democratic Party headquarters, calling to Aragon for an explanation. The newscaster explained that Malacañang Palace was surrounded by protesters asking for the military to withdraw from Mindanao.

"The truth is reaching the people," commented Romeo Barredo. "We just got word that people are gathering and protesting, calling for fair elections."

"Rudy? Rudy, can you hear us?"

There was no reply from the Zamboanga station, only silence.

"Ladies and gentlemen, we have lost contact with host Rudy Magbanua and Aristotle Lacson in Zamboanga. We heard gunshots on air. Let us pray for their safety."

The news had reached Manila, and the people were fueled by anger about Aragon's actions. The protesters and the masses started to gather in different areas, becoming so large and strong that even Aragon and President Mendoza feared them.

Romeo Barredo attempted to update the people about the events in Manila as telegrams and phone calls started to bombard the radio station. To his relief, one of the technicians signaled that they were getting a signal from Zamboanga's station.

"Ladies and gentlemen, it looks like that our friend Rudy Magbanua is back on air! Rudy? Rudy, can you tell us what happened?" asked Romeo.

"Romeo, can you hear me? Yes, the military were barricaded by the people from entering the station," said Rudy. "This is an amazing act by the people! This election has truly shown that the people are rising up and want their voices to be heard. I think the country is ready for a fresh, new government."

"It's good to hear that you are safe. I agree. The masses in Manila have spoken also. We got news that protesters are heading to Malacañang."

"Romeo, sorry, I have to interrupt you. Romeo, it has come to our attention that the people have reached the president. The military is pulling their presence from the station," Rudy reported. The crowds cheered outside the Zamboanga station and were heard over the radio. "Can you hear the crowd, Romeo?"

"We sure can! Same here in Castellana!"

"Hopefully the confiscated ballot boxes will be returned and not exchanged for tampered ones," said Romeo.

"The people know who they voted for. From the support of the crowd, it looks like they voted for Karlos Vasquez," replied Rudy.

"It's too early to say, my friend, but for sure soon we will know who the next president of our country will be," ended Romeo Barredo.

CHAPTER 15

T he COMELEC regained control in Mindanao and retrieved the ballot boxes. President Mendoza made an announcement that the military would not interfere with the elections but would remain in post in the event the militant groups might attack.

The people did not accept the president's explanation. The majority believed that Aragon planned everything, and the militant group was their scapegoat. The masses continued their vigilance, making their presence felt while the ballot boxes were opened and tallied.

Karlos and his party assembled at Governor Escalante's home the next day. Señor Jamora paced back and forth, and the governor and Congressman Saison played a game of checkers.

"How can the two of you play a game right now?" said the worried Señor Jamora.

"Calm down, Señor Jamora. The people have spoken. Don't you have confidence that this is a win for us?" asked the congressman.

"I am with Señor Jamora on this one," said Karlos. "We cannot rest easy until the COMELEC announces the final count."

"Governor, you need to come and see the newscast," said one of the volunteers.

"The Commission on Elections has counted 65 percent of the ballots, representing five provinces in Mindanao. The numbers are: Aragon 60,362 votes and Vasquez 101,762 votes, giving Mayor Karlos Vasquez the lead. Looks like we are on our way to declaring our next president."

The Nationalist Party members and volunteers cheered after hearing the news. They approached Karlos and congratulated him.

Karlos was stunned, not by the votes but the fact that he'd made it this far.

"Karlos, this is what we have been working for! All we need is for Aragon to concede. You did it, my boy! You did it!" cried Señor Jamora, kissing Karlos on both cheeks.

Vice President Aragon did not concede right away. He waited till the COMELEC reached 90 percent of precincts and ballots. Aragon then knew that it was time for him to accept the fact that a young mayor with no background or riches had won the presidency. He also realized and accepted the fact that it was indeed Karlos Vasquez's destiny to win. The people had indeed spoken.

On Monday, March 18, 1970, the Commission on Elections stamped and approved that the elections had concluded and named Karlos Vasquez as the president-elect of the Republic of the Philippines.

The entire country rejoiced over Karlos Vasquez's victory. The masses believed that indeed there would be a welcome change to the country. The citizens started to be optimistic about government again and believed that President-Elect Vasquez would be the leader who would help them better their lives.

No city could be happier than the city of Castellana. The people filled the church in thanksgiving, for in their hearts they believed that Karlos was indeed the one chosen to lead the country to prosperity and that the cries of the poor would be heard. A celebratory mass was held in St. Thomas Aquinas, officiated by Father Armando. In his homily, Father Armando shared his joy that his brother was elected but clearly stated that church would stand behind its principles. He was not afraid to criticize his brother if he became dishonest or corrupt.

The mass was attended by Daria and Marco without Señor Hernandez. His health had been deteriorating, and the señor was getting weaker. Señora Estefania and Jocelyn were front and center. Karlos's fiancée never missed an opportunity to revel in the spotlight.

After the mass, Congressman Saison and Governor Escalante invited the people to join them in the plaza. Daria and Marco followed the crowd and were ushered to sit near the stage.

"Marco, Daria, how are the newlyweds?" asked Governor Escalante. "Señor Hernandez has been quiet lately. I hope he is not ill or anything like that?"

"Papa is fine, Governor. He has been experiencing a lot of headaches lately, and for once he actually followed Dr. Jimena's advice to rest and take it easy," replied Daria.

The couple then turned to a familiar voice. "Why, if it isn't my favorite couple!" Father Armando said as he approached Daria for a hug. "I miss you both. My schedule is insane, but if you need me to officiate at your first-born's baptism I will drop everything to accommodate you."

Marco shook Father Armando's hand. "Thanks, Father. We will surely do that, but for now, we just ask you to bless us and pray for our marriage."

As they saw Karlos Vasquez enter the plaza, the crowds started cheering and clapping. He made his way through the crowd, chatting with people, receiving garlands, and shaking hands. When he arrived in front, Jocelyn stood, assisted him with the flowers, and then embraced her fiancé in front of the crowd. The crowd cheered, almost forgetting the real Jocelyn.

"Daria, Marco! Finally I have the chance to see you both," said Karlos.

"Our congratulations, President-Elect Vasquez," Marco said, shaking Karlos's hand.

Señora Estefania made her presence known, and Karlos gave her a kiss on both cheeks.

"Señora Hernandez, I would not be where I am today if not for Señor Hernandez," said Karlos. "Let me just finish with the celebration and I will personally come over to thank him."

Karlos then went up to the stage and waved to the crowd. He threw both of his fists in the air in honor of his victory. The crowds chanted, "Vasquez, Vasquez, Vasquez!"

"My beloved Castellana. This victory is for all of us!" Karlos began. "Your support and love are what gave me courage as I toured across our country during the campaign. My Castellana family have showed the entire country that anything is possible, and now sons and daughters of the poor can dream that one day they can become president." The crowd roared in approval.

"There are so many people to thank, starting with all of you. I thank the Nationalist Party for their confidence in me and for embracing my vision for the country. I would like the thank my vice president, Aristotle Lacson, who is in Zamboanga celebrating his triumph, for trusting me and for mentoring me on what kind of a leader I should be.

"I also thank all of the hacienderos and business leaders. I look forward to working with you to help my administration create jobs and opportunities to enrich the lives of our countrymen.

"And to the man who started it all. Without him, all of this would have not been possible. Señor Enrique Hernandez, though you are not with us today, I am eternally grateful. Your generosity and kindness enabled me to be the man I am today. To you and your family, thank you. Rest assured, people of Castellana, that I will never forget my roots. Even during my absence from our city, I will always have Castellana and the province of Azusa's best interests at heart."

The present administration was given fourteen days to transition the responsibilities of the government to the Vasquez administration.

Señor Hernandez was in his study reading the news about Karlos meeting President Mendoza, pleased to see that the cabinet members Karlos chose were the people who had helped him with his campaign. Señor Hernandez sent his regrets to the celebratory affairs for Karlos, sparking talk that Señor Hernandez might be seriously ill.

Señor Enrique felt a sudden chill, and his head started hurting. He reached toward his drawer but stopped when he heard a knock on the door. A familiar voice greeted him.

"We did it, Tito! All we planned and dreamed of is finally here." Karlos went up to Señor Hernandez and embraced him. "In one week, I will be inaugurated as the president of the republic," proudly said Karlos.

Señor Hernandez patted Karlos's back and gestured for him to take a seat.

"Karlos, I have always believed in you. I knew from the start that you would go places," said Señor Hernandez.

"Tito, you have been my mentor, my inspiration. As I promised you before, I will protect Hacienda Corazon," Karlos said, looking at Señor Hernandez. "Tito, may I ask why you chose me?"

Señor Hernandez looked at Karlos, not sure what he just asked him or what answer he was looking for.

"You father has been like a brother and a friend to me," cautiously answered Enrique Hernandez. "I watched your father die in front of me, and with his last words he asked me to take care of you," Señor Hernandez shared. "I am certain your father is smiling in heaven right now."

"What happened to Tatay was senseless, Señor. He was killed trying to save you from the rebels," recalled Karlos.

"I know that, Karlos. That is why I kept my promise to your father."

"Which is why… Which is why you believe that I am a communist?" Karlos asked, showing him a copy of the telegram he'd sent to Vice President Aragon.

Señor Hernandez did not reply and retained his composure.

"What made you believe that I am a rebel, Señor Hernandez?" asked Karlos. "You were the one who made me. What made you believe this accusation?"

"You tell me, Karlos," answered Señor Hernandez. He then pulled out the classified ads and showed them to the newly elected president.

"You have played this charade all too well, Karlos. This is a betrayal of your father," accused Señor Hernandez.

"Betrayal? How can this be betrayal? Wasn't it you who betrayed him?" Karlos yelled at Señor Hernandez.

Señor Hernandez looked up, surprised by Karlos's reaction. "Betrayal? What betrayal are you talking about, Karlos?"

"Here you are, the great señor of Hacienda Corazon, pretending he does not know what he did wrong. You do know, Señor. My grandfather and my father worked for your family for generations. They asked you for a piece of land to call their own, but what did you do?" accused Karlos. "My father got tired of your empty promises. He had enough of you and your greed, and he decided to go against you."

"Karlos, I know what I promised your father, and he knew that it could not be done at that time due to open trade," Señor Hernandez said calmly, feeling his head become heavy and his vision blurry.

"Do you know why the rebels are residing on the north side of the Hacienda, close to Mt. Mansilay—?"

"Karlos, please listen to me …" interrupted Señor Hernandez, but he could not get Karlos to hear him.

"The rebels are the people you betrayed with your greed, Señor Hernandez. They are former Hacienda Corazon workers, and my father he was the leader of the rebellion," blurted an angry Karlos.

This revelation shocked Señor Enrique Hernandez. "Karlos, you are not in your right mind. I don't know how these ideas came into your head, but you have it all wrong. Your father had it all wrong."

"Señor Hernandez, all of your life you thought my father saved you from the rebels. How ironic. My father was running toward you not to shield but to kill you!" Karlos yelled. "One of the rebels missed and shot my father instead," cried Karlos.

"Karlos, listen to yourself. What has become of you …" Señor Hernandez felt a sharp pain his head.

"I have become your puppet to protect your interests, but now you know that it is *you* who are *my* puppet," Karlos said, mocking Señor Hernandez as he saw him weakening from the pain.

Señor Enrique Hernandez's body gave in to the pain and collapsed on the floor. Karlos looked at the once-powerful Señor and remembered how people use to revere him. "Look at you now, Señor Hernandez. What a pitiful sight. I finally got to defeat you with your own game."

Señor Hernandez heard Karlos's words. His last thought was, *What have I done? I created a monster.* The once-mighty señor of Castellana took his last breath.

Karlos Vasquez looked at the lifeless body of Señor Enrique Hernandez. For a short moment, he felt regret and even grief, but his hatred was stronger, and it swallowed the humanity inside him.

Daria and Marco arrived home after a day of riding horses at Hacienda Corazon. On their way to her father's study she heard Karlos's voice asking for help. The couple rushed toward Señor Hernandez's study, where Daria froze at what she saw.

Marco ran to Señor Hernandez's side and tried to find a pulse. Karlos rushed to Daria, offering her support.

"Karlos, get help. Tell Felix to get Dr. Jimena," said Marco.

Daria slowly walked to her father's lifeless body. Marco checked his father-in-law but could not feel his pulse. Daria started sobbing and called her father, with no response. Daria touched her father's cold hand and looked at Marco. Marco shook his head and stood close to his wife. Daria held her father and starting weeping.

CHAPTER 16

Señor Enrique Hernandez's death came as a shock to those of Hacienda Corazon and Castellana. The people and the workers could not help but mourn their dear Señor Hernandez's unexpected death. The operations at the azucarera were shut down to honor their fallen señor. Castellana mourned for the great Señor Hernandez, who had given so many opportunities to the people of the city.

Father Jose and Father Armando rushed to the Hernandez home after hearing the news and tried to console the grieving widow and his daughter. Marco broke the news to Christina Valderrama and Vicente, as well his parents. They were overcome by grief and concern for Daria and booked the first flights available to Castellana.

Señora Estefania and Daria were overtaken by intense sadness and disbelief that Señor Hernandez had left them. Both women were grief-stricken, and neither made any effort to decide what to do next. Marco asked Daria; he even asked Jocelyn to help talk to Señora Estefania, but to no avail.

Marco felt relief with the arrival of Christina and Vicente. Christina became emotional after seeing her brother, but she gathered herself and took charge of the wake and funeral arrangements. Vicente it took upon himself to assist with managing the azucarera and Hacienda Corazon.

Marco went in to his father-in-law's studio to fulfill his request that upon his death Marco secure the land deeds and Señor Hernandez's sealed copy of his last will and testament. Before he went to the safe, Marco noticed that one of the desk drawers was open. He recalled that it was the same drawer where Señor Hernandez had stored the classified ads he showed to Marco, revealing his suspicion toward Karlos Vasquez.

Marco checked the drawer and found it empty. He checked the other drawers but did not find the ads anywhere. Marco shook his head and went to the safe for the deeds and the will. Marco placed the items in a briefcase. He was about to leave the studio when a thought stopped him. He remembered that Karlos had been with his father-in-law the night he died. Marco shuddered as he tried to connect the events. *Could it be that Karlos is the reason that Enrique Hernandez died?*

Marco kept his thoughts to himself and entered their bedroom. He found Daria asleep on the bed. He placed the briefcase in one of his suitcases and sat next to his wife. He looked at Daria and stroked her hair. His thoughts returned to one of the conversations he'd had with Señor Hernandez. *Papa, I will stand by my promise to protect and take care of Daria and convince her to leave Castellana. I also promise you that I will keep an eye on Karlos. If I find out he had something to do with your death, I will seek justice.*

Christina Valderrama arranged her brother's three-day wake and decided that Hacienda Corazon's azucarera would be the best location. The family decided on a closed coffin, for they couldn't bear the sight of Señor Hernandez, who looked as though he was just sleeping. The coffin was placed in the covered courtyard, and people started lining up to pay their last respects. The hacienda and azucarera workers stayed with Daria and Señora Estefania, showing their loyalty and gratitude to their late señor.

The hacienderos and politicos also paid their respects and showed their grief openly, for they all had looked up to Señor Hernandez.

Karlos paid his respects, along with Jocelyn, and they stayed with Señora Estefania the whole time, giving her their full attention.

Marco and Yaya Helen took turns watching over Daria, who looked sick and pale but refused to leave her papa. Marco got a chance to talk to Vicente, only to hear bad news.

"Marco, the azucarera is not doing too well. I checked the finances, and I found out there is a loan against the azucarera."

"I don't think this is the right place and time for us to discuss this. Let us focus on the funeral first," said Marco.

Karlos Vasquez approached Vicente and Marco and extended his condolences to them. "Señor Hernandez was like a father to me. I can't believe he is gone," said Karlos.

Marco tried reading Karlos's expressions and actions, but nothing stood out.

"In a few days you will be proclaimed president, Karlos. The best remembrance you can offer Tito is to become the president he wanted you to be," said Vicente.

Señor Jamora made his entrance and approached Señor Hernandez's coffin. He captured the crowd's attention when he started howling and crying. His wife, embarrassed, led him to sit next to Señora Estefania.

Governor Escalante arrived, followed by Congressman Saison. Neither gentleman reserved their tears as they paid their final respects to their friend.

Señor Enrique Hernandez's funeral occurred on a Friday and was well attended. The mass was held in the Catholic cemetery's chapel. People of all walks of life were present, as many people had been touched by the late señor's generosity. Father Jose tried to hold back tears as he gave his friend and benefactor the final rites.

Señora Estefania and Daria wore black mourning clothes, their faces covered by veils. Mother and daughter sat next to each other quietly. Christina Valderrama sat next to them, also dressed in black. Vicente and Marco sat next to her. Marco's parents arrived on the day of the funeral, and Marco was grateful to see them.

When it was time for Señor Hernandez to be placed in his final resting place, Marco, Vicente, Karlos, and Armando assumed their places to carry the coffin to the Hernandez Mausoleum.

Father Jose ended the funeral with a final prayer and prayed that Señor Hernandez would have everlasting peace. Señora Estefania broke down in tears. If not for Jocelyn and her late husband's sister she would have fallen to the ground.

Daria cried silently as Marie Gutierrez held her daughter-in-law in her arms.

The crowd slowly faded, leaving Enrique's family behind. Daria sat next to her mother.

"Mama, it's just us now," said Daria.

Señora Estefania did not bother to look at her daughter. "Daria, now that your papa is gone, I have something to ask of you." She turned to Enrique Hernandez's daughter, "When your father was alive I held on and tried my best to accept you. However, Daria, now I can't. I only tolerated you because of your father, and now that he is no longer here I ask you to stop addressing me as your mama."

Daria, already stunned by grief, nodded and walked away from Señora Estefania. Daria's heart was crushed. On the same day she bid good-bye to her father, the woman she had looked up to as her mother also left her.

On the fortieth day after the late Señor Enrique Hernandez passed, Señora Estefania was in no mood for celebration. She hosted a lunch only for the family. Along with them was Atty. Delgado and Father Jose. Christina Valderrama and Vicente remained in Castellana for the entire mourning period, and they couldn't help but notice the tension between Estefania and Daria.

After the luncheon, they convened in the library. Atty. Delgado would read Señor Hernandez's last will and testament. Atty. Delgado began by making sure that everyone mentioned in the will was present. He requested Yaya Helen and Marco join them too. Señora Estefania was surprised that Jocelyn was not called in to the reading.

He opened the sealed brown envelope and started reading Señor Hernandez's will.

"I, Enrique Hernandez, a Filipino citizen of legal age, born on the September 21, 1910, a resident of the city of Castellana, being of sound mind and memory and not acting under undue influence and intimidation, do hereby declare my last will and testament.

"For my daughter, Daria Hernandez-Gutierrez, my son-in-law Marco Gutierrez, and my nephew Vicente Valderrama, I give and bequeath the following property:

"Three hundred hectares of Hacienda Corazon, which will be used for your project to further develop the land in accordance to your plans.

"To my daughter Daria and sister Christina Hernandez-Valderrama, I give and bequeath the land and the azucarera. I designate both my daughter and sister the privilege and freedom to maintain control of or sell the azucarera.

"To my sister, Christina, I bequeath to you the Hernandez family heirlooms, including the jewelry, photographs, and paintings that have been in our family for generations. These have been catalogued and appraised and are in the safe at the Banco Filipinas office in the city of Castellana." Atty. Delgado then handed Christina Valderrama the keys to the safe.

He continued. "To our loyal helper, Helen Casipe, I give and bequeath the property located 5010 Ilang Street in the city of Castellana, province of Azusa."

Attorney Delgado then handed the title to the tearful nanny. Yaya Helen went up to Daria and embraced her. Daria sat quietly and said a prayer to thank her papa for granting her request for her nanny.

Señora Estefania was not pleased with what she was hearing. *The land close to the city hall was promised to Jocelyn. And why is my name not mentioned yet?*

"To my wife, Estefania de Paz-Hernandez, I give to you and bequeath to you the amount of P$3,000,000 and the title of our house in Castellana and all the valuables the house contains.

"To my dear friend Father Jose Servando, I bequeath P$1,000,000, which will go toward your retirement and projects for the Church of St. Thomas de Aquinas.

"I also, bequeath P$500,000 to the Order of St. Dymphna for the building of their asylum and for whatever needs and projects they wish to allocate the funds."

"Why are the nuns included in his will? Are you sure he was in his right mind when he wrote this?" a furious Señora Estefania asked.

"My apologies, Señora. I will answer your questions after I finish reading the will," answered Atty. Delgado.

"For my people in Hacienda Corazon. For generations, your families have helped familia Hernandez and Hacienda Corazon become one of the most productive haciendas in the country. I appreciate your dedication, loyalty, and service, and with that I bequeath three hundred hectares of land in Hacienda Corazon to be given to the following families." Sixty families were named on the list.

"The land has been divided and titled for the families listed and are given freedom to do as they will with the land."

"This is insane! Had Enrique gone mad!" an angry Señora Estefania yelled.

Daria gasped with surprised. She started to tear up and smiled at Marco.

"Lastly, I hereby direct that Marco Gutierrez will be executor and administrator of this last will and testament."

Marco now understood why his father-in-law had left him the keys to his safe. Marco nodded to Atty. Delgado as a sign that he accepted the responsibility.

"I hereby revoke and annul any will that I have written preceding this last will and testament.

"Señor Enrique Hernandez signed this document on January 5, 1970, with Father Jose Servando, Father Armando Vasquez, and Dr. Jacobo Jimena as witnesses before me, Attorney Edgar Delgado. This ends the reading of the last will and testament of Señor Enrique Hernandez," closed Atty. Delgado.

There was silence before a raging Señora Estefania came up and pulled Daria's arm. "You, you *bastarda*! You put your father up to this, didn't you?"

Christina Valderrama rose and tried to hold Estefania back.

"*Puñeta*, Daria! You took advantage of your father's illness and asked him to give away to the farmers the land that was owned by this family. This is your doing!"

"Ma ... Señora, I did not ask my father for this. I was not aware that Papa was sick," answered Daria.

"Edgar, the land that was given to the people, that land belongs to me! After all that I have suffered from Enrique, I deserve that land!" said Señora Estefania, who was out of control.

"Señora, please! The title for the entire Hacienda Corazon was in Señor Enrique's name. The title is clean," explained the lawyer.

"Then I do not accept this will—this will is false!" All eyes turned to Estefania Hernandez. "I will contest this will!"

"Señora, the will of Señor Hernandez is clearly set. The land titles are all signed and notarized. There is nothing I can do," Atty. Delgado replied.

"Then if that is so, all of you get out of my house!" yelled Estefania.

"Estefania, please be reasonable. It is not like you were left with nothing. My brother made sure that you are taken care of," said Christina.

"You heard what I said, Christina." Estefania looked at her sister-in-law and then at Daria. "Get out of my house!"

MALACAÑANG PALACE

The palace accommodated the media in the press room when President Karlos Vasquez's thirty days in office had passed. He'd appointed Señor Jorge Montevista as his press secretary as a token of thanks for the haciendero's support during his campaign. Secretary Montevista welcomed the press and thanked them for their presence. He handed them instructions and explained the protocol for the press conference.

President Vasquez entered the room, followed by Jocelyn, who took her seat in the front row.

"This makes me recall the tension when I was in college and had to defend my thesis in front of my professors," President Vasquez joked.

The members of the press laughed.

"One of the gifts of democracy is freedom of the press. The press and other media have an obligation to tell the citizens of our nation the truth, and that is why I welcome all of you today. I hope that you can also give me insight into your views of my administration's first thirty days in office."

"We will now take questions. Please approach the mic with your questions," Secretary Montevista explained.

"I am from the *National Free Press*. Mr. President, one of the first agendas when you took office was to minimize the military presence in Mindanao. There are still reports of Muslim militant insurgence. What influenced your decision?"

"Thank you for the question. We focused on the hot issues right away," Karlos responded. "During the elections, we saw how a military presence can be abused. Some news broadcasts were too quick to judge our Muslim brothers. As I said during my campaign, and I stand by my words, instead of arms I offer an olive branch to the militants. I believe that if we approach them with sincerity we can achieve more than by attacking them."

"I am from *Philippines Today*. Mr. President, in your first thirty days you have been criticized for your lack of foreign diplomacy and have been very vocal about your Philippines First program. Are you not afraid that you might be cutting ties with our allies?"

"In order to better the lives of our countrymen, we need jobs. If we accept imports and cater to the foreign investors, we are not giving people the chance to be innovative. We need to give local businesses a boost by supporting locally made products," Karlos said.

"Following up, Mr. President, was this also the reason you did not agree to joint military exercises with the American forces?"

Karlos was not pleased with the question. "We are Filipinos, and we must learn how to best protect our country the way we are supposed to, without other countries dictating how to protect our country. If we need to build foreign relations, we need to start with our neighboring countries," President Vasquez answered, trying to show the press he was not avoiding topics. "Thank you for the question."

Secretary Montevista interrupted. "Thank you, *Philippines Today*. Can we have the next question?"

"President Vasquez, I am from *Abante Visayas*."

"Oh, a fellow Visayan! It's nice to see that we are represented," said Karlos, smiling.

"What are your plans for the Visayas? We have seen that in your first thirty days your administration has focused on the business sector and Mindanao. What can we expect from our fellow Visayan?"

"I am glad you asked that question. I am encouraging Congress to come up with legislation that can be beneficial to both landowners and workers. The legislation is in the works and hopefully will be passed soon," President Vasquez shared.

Secretary Montevista faced the press and told them the president would answer two more questions.

"Mr. President, I'm from *Entertainment Press*. When will you be getting married to Jocelyn Gonzaga?"

Karlos's mood lightened. "When I took my oath, I promised the people that I would serve my country first. I am grateful for Jocelyn's love and patience but definitely not during my term."

Jocelyn was shocked by Karlos's answer. *How dare you, Karlos Vasquez!* thought his fiancée.

Secretary Montevista raised his hand, signaling the last question.

"Mr. President, I am Juan Silverio from *Republika*. I understand that you want to build relations with our neighboring countries. During your campaign, you never addressed the accusation made about your ties to the rebels. Do you, sir, have a personal agenda or relationship with the Communist Party?"

President Vasquez's expression changed. He looked ready to charge the reporter before Secretary Montevista interrupted. "Esteemed members of the press, this is all the time we have for today. We thank you for your presence."

"Mr. President, you did not answer my question …"

The *Republika* reporter was ushered out by the presidential guards as President Vasquez waved to the press and made his exit.

Karlos Vasquez retreated to his office, trying to keep his composure. He lost his temper when Secretary Montevista entered.

"*'Tang Ina*, I thought you filtered the press invited today. Why did you invite *Republika*?"

"I did screen the invited press, Karlos, but *Republika* came anyway. If I don't let them in, they would surely think you were hiding from them and all of this was just for show," Montevista answered.

"It is for show! Our goal was to make my first thirty days a success to reassure the people and show them that their votes were not wasted," complained Karlos. "Montevista, your hacienda, is losing money, and this is the only way I can think to help you. If you want to keep your position, then make sure you do your job right! Do what you need to do make sure that reporter will keep his mouth shut," President Vasquez ordered.

"Understood, sir," Montevista said before he left the president's office.

Karlos shook his head and sat in his chair, trying to calm himself down. He pressed the intercom to ask his secretary for something to drink. Instead, Jocelyn entered his office, looking furious.

"How dare you, Karlos?" fumed Jocelyn.

"Not now, Jocelyn," Karlos warned.

Jocelyn ignored the warning. "You made me look like an idiot! You said we would get married during your term to make me first lady."

"I said shut up!" Karlos yelled.

Jocelyn was shocked by Karlos's reaction and took a step back.

"If you think you are in control of this relationship, you are all wrong. If you don't want to wait, then go back to Castellana," said Karlos. "Don't think you are irreplaceable, my dear."

Jocelyn had never seen Karlos Vasquez angry. Even when she whined and ignored him he had always been persistent and patient with her.

"I am sorry, Karlos, I was out of line," Jocelyn said. She walked up to him to massage his shoulders.

Karlos stood up, dragged Jocelyn to the couch, and pushed her down. Señora Estefania's niece struggled, but the president held her down.

"Karlos, what are you doing? Get off me!"

"I know what you are after, Jocelyn. You chose to follow me. If you think you can control me, you are wrong. I own you." Karlos then made that clear to Jocelyn.

Jocelyn stopped struggling, knowing that she could not win. She allowed Karlos Vasquez to take over her body.

CASTELLANA

Daria and Marco settled in Yaya Helen's house in the city after Señora Estefania asked them to leave. Marco asked Vicente to go back to Manila to handle GGC in his absence. Vicente complied and agreed that they would alternate taking care of business in Manila and Castellana.

Christina Valderrama returned to Manila and planned to fly to New York to join her husband, Ambassador Jaime Valderrama. Christina was at ease when she left, knowing that her niece would be safe in the care of Marco and Yaya Helen.

"Yaya, thank you for letting us stay with you," Daria said to her nanny, hugging Yaya Helen tightly.

"My baby, if not for you I would not have this blessing. My home is your home," her nanny answered, hugging her back.

"What is all this? Can I join in?" Marco asked.

Daria went up to her husband and gave him a kiss on the cheek. "Did everything go well with your meeting?"

Marco looked at his wife and shook his head. "The intestate proceedings did not go well, Daria. Señora Estefania is disputing the will, insisting that your papa was not of sound mind when he wrote it. Even with Dr. Jimena and Father Jose's testimony, she still refuses to settle."

Daria let out a sigh. "I am willing to give her the azucarera, Marco. I want the workers to have the land. I am willing to give up my shares."

Marco took Daria's hand and led her to the living room. He opened his briefcase and showed Daria a statement. "Daria, Vicente found this statement. It shows that the bank is about to foreclose on the azucarera," Marco reported slowly.

"Daria, I know this might be a shock. I went to meet with the bank manager earlier, and he verified the loan. He told me your papa used the hacienda as collateral to borrow money for Karlos's campaign."

"How could this happen? Does Mama know?" Daria asked, confused.

"It was brought up earlier. Señora Estefania said she would save the azucarera in exchange for the land titles," said Marco. "There are some hacienderos who are willing to buy the azucarera. However, they agree with Señora Hernandez that the land should not be given to the people."

"Marco, we can't let this happen. We have the land deeds. Why can't we just have Atty. Delgado hand them over to the people?" asked Daria.

"I wish it was that simple, Daria. The hacienderos are siding with Señora Estefania. They are afraid that if the farm workers from Hacienda Corazon receive land, their workers might expect them to follow."

"What about if we ask for help from Governor Escalante or Congressman Saison?"

"I went to see them, but they have been giving me the runaround. They are hacienderos too, Daria,"

"What about if we ask Karlos for help? If he finds out what Papa did for him, I'm sure he will help us," Daria told her husband, a hopeful look on her face.

Marco kept quiet. He was trying to think of a way to discourage Daria from contacting Karlos Vasquez. "Jocelyn is Karlos fiancée. Don't you think he will side with them?"

"Marco, I have known Karlos all my life. I know if it is for the people of Hacienda Corazon, he will help us," Daria stated.

Marco saw how hopeful his wife was and told himself this is not the time to tell Daria about what Señor Enrique had discovered about Karlos Vasquez. He held his wife and prayed for protection, for he knew that if Karlos became involved it would be harder for him to protect his wife and keep his promise to Señor Hernandez to have Daria leave Castellana.

MALACAÑANG

"Tell me one good reason why you will not write this bill for me, Congressman Saison," President Vasquez demanded.

"Karlos, this is not a good idea. This will anger the haciendaros for sure!" answered Congressman Saison.

"This is a fair deal, especially for the smaller haciendas and the struggling haciendas! We are offering to buy part of their land for agrarian reform. It's not like we are taking it," replied the president.

"Karlos, you owe them a lot for winning this election, and this is an insult. Do you really think they would willingly sell their land for such a small fee?" countered Congressman Saison.

"Do you think it would be better if I ask you to create a land reform bill? That way they will be forced to give up their land," Karlos Vasquez threatened.

"Karlos, tell me the truth. Why are you doing this? You told the haciendaros that if you became president you would protect their interests," the congressman reminded him.

"That was when I was mayor. I am now the president, in case you forgot, Congressman."

"Well then," Congressman Saison said. He stood and walked toward the door. "If you will excuse me, Mr. President."

Karlos pounded a fist on his desk. He knew what Congressman Saison's next step would be: to gather the congressmen from the Visayas and ask them not to support him. He could already see that Saison would report to Governor Escalante; soon the haciendaros would know what Karlos was planning.

"Mr. President, Vice President Lacson is here to meet with you," announced his secretary.

"Send him in."

Aristotle took a seat in front of Karlos and placed his cane at the side of his chair.

"I saw Saison leave. It looks like he was not happy with your plan," said the vice president. "His reaction is what we were expecting. We can find other representatives that can help you," assured Aristotle. "I still have friends in Congress who share our sentiments."

Congressman Saison did not waste time before he contacted Governor Escalante about Karlos's plan. The governor advised the congressman that it would be best for now to follow the president's order.

"Governor, I don't see any reason why we should agree to this. People might revolt and pressure us to give up our haciendas," said Saison.

"I know Karlos. He will not fail us. There are haciendas that can actually benefit from his plan. As for us, we can command how much the government pays us," answered the governor.

"I am not sure about this. I have a bad feeling for where this could lead to, but all right. I'll see what I can do," said Congressman Saison.

As soon as Congressman Saison hung up the phone, the governor's phone rang again.

"Karlos, I have convinced Saison. As long as you keep your end of the bargain, I can see that your Agrarian Reform bill passes."

MANILA

Marie and Miguel Gutierrez were overjoyed to see Marco and Daria. Vicente was also present at his friend's house to welcome the couple. Marco's mother noticed that her daughter-in-law was pale, and Daria admitted that she felt lightheaded. Marie led Daria to the couple's bedroom so she could rest.

Marco took the opportunity to talk to his father and his friend.

"Is there any other way we can help Daria without asking Karlos for help?" asked Miguel Gutierrez.

"I have been thinking, Marco. I think we should give Tita Estefania the land Tito left us. Maybe she will be satisfied with that and give the other land to the people," Vicente suggested.

"I suggested that to Atty. Delgado. But Señora Hernandez insists that she does not want to give the land to the workers and that Papa was not in his right mind when he wrote it in his will," Marco answered.

"Maybe asking for Karlos help is not such a bad idea," Vicente said. "Marco, I understand your suspicions toward the president, but maybe we can ask for his help just this once."

"I don't trust him," Marco said, looked at his father and his friend. "I really believe that he had something to do with Papa's death and that he is working with the rebels."

"I asked Juan if he can investigate Karlos," said Miguel Gutierrez. "He brought it up at the press conference. Karlos did not answer the question he asked, and he could not find any proof either."

The men changed the topic when they heard Marie Gutierrez's footsteps approaching.

"Marco, have you been taking care of Daria?" scolded his mother. "My poor daughter is so sick that she can't take anything!"

"She must be tired from the flight, Mom, and all the things that have been happening," replied Marco.

"Well, at least she is here with me. Have you contacted President Vasquez?" asked Marie.

"Señor Jamora and the governor are not helping us out. We hope that Father Armando can reach him," said Marco.

CHAPTER 17

A week passed, and even with Father Armando's help Daria still could not reach President Vasquez. The Gutierrezes asked for help from their friends in the business, but they couldn't get through to the president either.

"Why do I have a feeling that someone is blocking our way to reach Karlos?" said Mr. Gutierrez.

"I think you are right, Papa. To think that even Father Armando can't get a hold of his brother ... It *is* odd," Marco observed.

Mrs. Gutierrez entered. "Good morning, my boys. Marco, where is Daria?"

"She was complaining of a headache last night, so I thought letting her sleep in would be good for her," Marco answered his mother.

Daria appeared in the doorway. "Good morning. Sorry I overslept," she apologized.

"It's all right, my dear. Come have breakfast. You skipped dinner last night—you must be hungry," her mother-in-law said.

Daria reached for the seat next to Marco but felt her head spin.

"Daria, are you all right?" asked her husband.

"My head, Marco. I feel like it's spinning." Daria then collapsed in her husband's arms.

Marco's heart sunk as he held his wife. He heard his mother call to the driver to get the car.

Marco carried his pale wife into the car and told the driver to take them to the hospital. Daria regained consciousness and insisted she was fine, but Marco would not accept her argument. Marie Gutierrez went in with Daria to the emergency room.

Marie informed his son that his wife needed to be examined and told them she would let them know as soon as the doctor had Daria's results.

Marco paced in the waiting area and did not notice a man with a cane approaching him.

"Marco Gutierrez?"

Marco looked up. Miguel Gutierrez stood next to his son.

"Vice President Lacson!" Marco said, surprised. "I'm sorry, sir. My wife is in the emergency room, and I did not notice you."

"Daria is here? What a coincidence. I am here for a check-up," said Aristotle. "I hope she is all right."

Marco introduced his father to the vice president.

"How long have you been in Manila? Have you had the chance to meet with Karlos?" asked the vice president.

"We have been trying to get in contact with him, but we understand that he is a busy man," said Marco.

"Nonsense! He would be happy to see you and Daria," Aristotle replied. "Give me your contact information, and I will give it to him personally."

Marco gave the vice president his calling card.

"Well, I hope Daria is all right, and I hope to see you both soon," Aristotle Lacson said, handing Marco his personal card.

As Vice President Lacson made his exit, Marie Gutierrez appeared and told Marco that Daria would be transferred to a private room.

"Is Daria all right, Mom?"

"I think it's best you hear it from her," Marie answered with a big smile on her face.

After Daria was transferred to a VIP private room, Marco rushed to his wife's side, looking concerned when he saw his Daria hooked up to an IV and other things.

"Daria, you had me worried! What did the doctor say?" Marco asked his wife, holding her hand.

"We are all right, Marco. We just need to rest," Daria answered.

"A lot of rest, Daria," added her mother-in-law.

"I'll stay with you. What exactly is wrong?" asked Marco, not getting his wife and mother's hint.

Miguel Gutierrez understood what Daria said perfectly and clapped his hands, to Marco's confusion.

"Marco, *we* are fine," Daria said, placing Marco's hand on her belly.

Marco was silent for moment. "You mean you and me, we are having a baby?"

"Finally, my son, you got it!" Miguel Gutierrez shook Marco's shoulder and reached out to Daria.

"I'm going to be a grandmother!" said Marie. "I am so happy right now!"

Marco turned to Daria. "Are you all right? How are you feeling? Is there anything you need?"

The doctor quietly entered the room, interrupting the Gutierrezes' celebration. "She needs rest. She needs to stay in the hospital for the next day or so or until she gets her appetite back. I suggest she needs to be on complete bed rest till the end of her first trimester."

"Yes, doctor," Daria answered.

Marco was overwhelmed and happy with the news. All he could think of was making sure that Daria and his child would be all right, so he decided to delay telling Daria that he'd run into Vice President Lacson.

The following day Vicente came to the hospital to visit Daria and Marco. He was so excited about becoming an uncle that he brought a huge teddy bear with him.

"Vicente, thanks for the gift, but I think you can wait till the baby is born for the next present," said Daria.

"Make sure you write in my nephew's baby book that Uncle Vicente was the first one to give him a present," said Vicente.

"Or niece," Daria corrected Vicente.

"My friend." Vicente turned to Marco. "I knew it! I knew that you and Daria were meant to be. You have to name your first-born son after me."

"Maybe we can return the favor by finding you a wife, Vicente," Marco teased.

"How can I find a wife if I can't even get out of work and shower?" answered Vicente.

Marco looked at his friend, feeling guilty. "Vicente, I'm sorry. I know I have not been doing my share of the work lately."

"It's okay. As long as I know you are busy taking care of our Daria, I will survive the work and will be your humble servant," Vicente said, bowing to Marco.

"Oh, I almost forgot, Daria. I brought someone here who I know you will be happy to see and share this moment with." Vicente walked to the door but before he opened it—

"Daria my baby is now having a baby!" cried Yaya Helen, running to Daria's side.

"Yaya, how did you …? I am so happy you are here," Daria told her nanny. "Vicente, thank you!"

"Well, it's actually more a surprise for Marco. My friend here needs to rest too, and he needs to earn a living to provide for his family," Vicente jokingly told his cousin.

"Whatever reason you might have had, Vicente, thank you," said Marco.

Daria ordered Vicente to take her husband out for air and to get him something good to eat. Marco complied, knowing that Daria was in good hands now that Yaya Helen was around.

Vicente took Marco to their favorite Japanese restaurant before they headed to the GGC office.

"I must say, Vicente, you did an awesome job! I think you deserve to be the vice president now, not me," said Marco.

"Flattery won't get you anywhere, my friend," Vicente said before his tone turned serious. "I know we had plans for Hacienda Corazon. I have to apologize for the mess we got you into."

Marco looked at his friend. "No need to apologize. We will be fine without that project, my friend. My only concern is Daria and our child. I would rather give up everything at Castellana and keep Daria here in Manila," Marco added.

"Knowing Daria, though, she won't rest until she fulfills her father's will," Vicente observed.

The intercom in Marco's office interrupted their conversation. "Mr. Gutierrez, welcome back, sir. You have a call in line one."

Marco picked up the phone. "This is Marco Gutierrez."

"Marco! It's nice to hear your voice. I heard from Aristotle that you and Daria are in Manila," said President Vasquez.

Marco felt uneasy. Now that he made contact, he had no choice but to schedule a meeting with the president.

Daria was released from the hospital, happy to be back at her in-laws' home. Marie and Yaya Helen took turns doting on Daria, making sure that all the doctor's orders were being followed. Daria understood the excitement of the family and did her best to be a good patient.

"It seems that I am outnumbered," Marco said to his wife. "Let me know if my mom and Yaya are driving you insane so I can kidnap you from them."

"Do you feel left out?" asked his wife.

Marco gave his wife a kiss on the forehead and rubbed her belly.

"No, it's just that I don't get to spend time with you."

"Wait till seven months from now," Daria said, putting her hand over her husband's. "We can probably schedule something for just the two of us after the baby is about three months old."

Marco laughed and shook his head, happy to see his wife relaxed and smiling. He did not want to ruin the mood by talking about her papa's will or the hacienda, but Marco knew that he could no longer delay President Vasquez's request to meet with them.

"Daria, I saw Vice President Lacson when you were in the hospital. We were able to reach Karlos."

Darla sat up and looked at her husband. "Marco, this is great! Why did you not tell me right away?"

"I wanted to make sure you were all right first. In your condition, I don't want you to get all worked up," said Marco. "I told Karlos that we've been trying to reach him but to no avail. I also told him that you are expecting and it might be difficult for us to get to Malcañang," Marco explained.

"Marco, this is our chance! I feel so much better, and it's not like I can't move or anything," Daria said with excitement. "Marco, why are you hesitating?" Daria asked, noticing that her husband did not seem eager to see Karlos.

"It's not that I am hesitating. I don't want you to be overwhelmed or emotional. It might make you or the baby sick," Marco said, knowing that he would not win this argument.

"Marco, I understand you are concerned about me. Let me promise you this. Once my papa's will is settled, I will not hesitate to leave Castellana and stay with you here," Daria told her husband.

Marco, surprised by her wife's reply, said, "Daria, I would never ask you to leave Castellana or the hacienda if you don't want to."

"Thank you, Marco. My home is where you are. It does not matter to me if we stay here or in Castellana, but for me to be at ease, I need to make sure that Papa's wishes will be followed. I need to give the land to the workers," Daria pleaded.

"All right, Daria, let's get this settled. Once everything is done, you, me, and our baby will start anew," Marco said, embracing his wife.

Due to Daria's delicate pregnancy, Karlos Vasquez and Aristotle Lacson accepted the Guitierrezes' invitation to have luncheon in their home on Sunday. The palace office contacted the family so the presidential security group could check their home and outline security protocol. When President Vasquez learned about the security check, he commanded them not to resume, because for him it was a family rather than political matter.

Karlos and Aristotle arrived casually at the Gutierrez residence with two palace guards. Marco and Vicente greeted the president and vice president and escorted them to the living room, where Daria and the senior Gutierrez were waiting.

Karlos was glad to see Daria. He felt like the old Mayor Vasquez and approached Daria, giving her a big hug.

"Daria Hernandez, look at you!" said Karlos. "I remembered when you were just a little girl, running around the azucarera and sitting on your papa's lap, and now you are expecting your first child."

"You did very well too, Karlos, changing from that nerdy boy in the hacienda to the president of the country," replied Daria. "Please have a seat."

Karlos and Aristotle made themselves comfortable.

"Aristotle told me that you have been trying to reach me. I do apologize, but I never received any of your or Armando's messages," said Karlos.

"We do understand how busy you are," said Vicente.

Karlos turned to Daria. "So how are Castellana and Hacienda Corazon?"

Daria looked at Marco, and her husband nodded to her encouragingly.

"Karlos, Papa's will has been read. We are having hard time executing what he wanted," Daria said.

The president looked at his former señor's daughter with concern and curiosity. Daria handed Karlos a copy of Señor Hernandez's will.

"As you can see, Papa left part of Hacienda Corazon to his people," Daria said.

Karlos looked stunned.

"Sixty families, Karlos, including Felix and Nelson and the people you grew up with in Castellana—Papa left them what he promised them, their own land to farm."

Karlos's last conversation with his future father-in-law flashed back to him. Marco noticed that the president looked uncomfortable and turned pale. Karlos regained his composure and read the last part of the will. He looked at Daria.

"I am in awe that Señor Hernandez would actually do this for the people of Hacienda Corazon," Karlos said. "Never did it cross my mind that he had this planned."

"Karlos, my papa took a loan against the azucarera to help fund your campaign," Daria added.

"We all agree that we are ready to give up the azucarera and the land that was left to us so the people can get the land they deserve," Vicente said.

"Is Señora Estefania the problem?" asked Karlos.

"She is contesting the will. Plus, the haciende ros are not too keen on the fact that Señor Enrique left land to the people," Marco added.

"The haciende ros must feel threatened," said Vice President Lacson. "This could be the perfect opportunity to put your bill into action, Karlos."

"Daria, I owe your father so much," said the president. "I will help you and make sure that his last wish is granted."

Karlos Vasquez stood on the balcony overlooking the palace gardens and thought about what had been revealed to him earlier. A wave of guilt rushed through him.

"Was I wrong about Señor Hernandez?" Karlos asked himself. "Maybe I was too young to understand the entire truth."

Karlos shook his head. *It's too late for regrets now. Everything has been set up*, he thought. *I can no longer ask for Señor Hernandez's forgiveness. The only way I know right now to atone for what I did is to help Daria.*

The following day the president summoned Congressman Saison and the Nationalist Party House of Representative members.

"I requested your presence today, gentlemen, to ask you to help me fulfill one of my campaign promises," stated President Vasquez.

Congressman Saison looked at Karlos and nodded. He then handed out the bill that he'd written, as requested by President Vasquez.

"Gentlemen, I present to you my draft for the Agrarian Reform bill," said Congressman Saison.

The Nationalist Party congressmen read the bill. It was direct, to the point, and quite controversial.

"Karlos, we need time to think about this. If we support this bill we need to answer to a lot of people who placed us in office," mentioned Congressman Baylon from Cebu.

"For how long should you allow your puppeteers to control you, Congressman?" asked Karlos. "I know some of you are hacienderos. The bill is written so no one is forced to sell their land. It is also a business opportunity, gentlemen."

"How soon would you like this bill approved?"

"I want the bill on the House floor as soon as possible," the president demanded.

The day of President Karlos Vasquez's first State of the Nation address was well covered by various sectors of the media.

The president was briefed by Secretary Jorge Montevista, who instructed Karlos on the points he needed to focus on and the lines he needed to emphasize. The president showed his disinterest, for he had other plans in mind.

President Vasquez's first stop was to meet with the Chief of Staff of the Armed Forces of the Republic. He was escorted to Batasang Pambansa and welcomed by the committee. The speaker of the House, Congressman Araneta from the Diplomatic Party, announced the arrival of the president of the republic and called for a joint session of Congress.

Karlos Vasquez stood dignified and composed as "Lupang Hinirang," the Philippine National Anthem, was sang by St. John's Boys Chorus. President Vasquez then made his way to the rostrum to deliver his first State of the Nation address.

President Karlos Vasquez's State of Nation Address was not without its controversies and highlights. The following day he got mixed reviews in several editorials, but the masses embraced his promises.

The union and labor organization were satisfied with the president's proclamation he'd increase pay for teachers, public servants, and police to help boost the public servants' morale. He also ordered the Department of Labor to strictly enforce the law to protect the common worker by fining business who did not follow the government's laws regarding social security and overtime pay. The president also created a committee to check factories and manufacturing plants to ensure safe working conditions for the workers and that the environments they worked in were not detrimental to their health.

President Vasquez also appealed to the business sector to support his "Philippines First" program by encouraging them to create quality affordable products. He also offered government assistance to businesses facing financial difficulties, as long as their services and products were made from 80 percent domestic materials.

He began receiving calls from his ambassadors for his statements about minimizing the American presence and the removal of their bases from the country and the imposition of increased taxes on foreign goods. He was criticized for his plan to strengthen ties and friendship with China and to grant amnesty and opportunity for citizenship to the Chinese who'd entered the country illegally. He emphasized tightening the country's relations with China and other Asian countries by supporting the Asia and Southeast Asian associations rather than putting extra effort toward the United Nations.

The sentiments of the foreign allies and the ambassadors' questions were overshadowed by two of President Vasquez's proposals. Newspapers and other media outlets highlighted his decision to pull out 50 percent of the military presence in Mindanao and his Agrarian Reform Program.

President Vasquez efforts at putting the average and working Filipinos' needs first was reflected in his first

State of Nation address. This signifies the truth of the promises he made during the campaign.
—*Philippines Today*

The plan of the president is ambitious. President Vasquez, our countrymen and the world will be watching your every move. May you do your work with humility and grace. Remember: you cannot please everyone, but we commend your efforts for putting our country first.
—*National Press*

Mr. President, removing the presence of our military in Mindanao because of your belief that the militant group is not a grave threat to your people in the south has no basis. We question your interest in China and your Agrarian Reform Program. How can be we assured that your so-called agrarian reform is not to camouflage communistic interest in gaining control of our farmlands?"
—*Republika* editor Jose Silverio.

"You need to do something about the *Republika*, Secretary Montevista," Karlos warned his press secretary.

"Mr. President, your speech is well accepted, especially by the union organizations and the masses," said Secretary Montevista, trying to divert Karlos's attention.

"How about the press from Visayas and Mindanao?" asked Karlos.

"Mindanao press accepted it very well. The majority of the people in the area are in favor of your Agrarian Reform proposal. Also, the Muslim groups are grateful for your action in minimizing the military presence in Mindanao," reported the press secretary.

"Good. Aristotle has agreed to go to Zamboanga to oversee the plan," stated Karlos Vasquez.

"The Visayas though—well, response is mixed," said Montevista. "There are hacienderos who want it, and there are some who are afraid that it is a precedent to land reform," informed the press secretary.

"I am giving the hacienderos a chance here," said Karlos. "I think it's time I go visit our beloved Castellana."

Daria was in her second trimester and couldn't be more excited. She had regained her strength and was allowed to move around under the watchful of eyes of her mother-in-law and nanny. Daria had settled into her life in Manila with Marco, but her mind was still at Hacienda Corazon.

The intestate proceedings had not progressed. Talk about the late Señor Hernandez's will had reached the workers. Daria promised Marco that she would leave matters to him, Vicente and Atty. Delgado for now.

She heard Yaya Helen announce, "Daria, there is call for you. It's from the president's office."

"This is Daria Gutierrez," Daria answered the phone.

"Daria, Karlos here. How are you?" Karlos Vasquez said.

"I'm doing well, Mr. President. Congratulations on your State of the Nation address," answered Daria.

"Thank you. Daria, this might be too much to ask from you in your delicate condition, but I must ask if you would you join me in Castellana," President Vasquez asked.

"I have to ask Marco if I can go," said Daria.

"In my speech, I mentioned the Agrarian Reform bill. To be honest, this bill was created with your papa in mind," answered Karlos. "Daria, when we get back to Castellana, I will make sure that the Hacienda Corazon workers receive the land that Señor Hernandez promised them."

"When do you plan to leave?" asked Daria.

"First thing tomorrow morning," answered President Vasquez.

CHAPTER 18

aria put all her efforts into convincing her husband to accept President Vasquez's proposal. Marco agreed only after Vicente offered to travel with Daria and Yaya Helen.

The group arrived with Jocelyn in tow. Vicente forced Daria to rest at Yaya Helen's house. He'd noticed that his cousin had a difficult time during the flight. Jocelyn went directly to Tita Estefania's house. Karlos dropped in on his brother and Father Jose.

"Well, if it isn't the pride of Castellana!" Father Jose greeted Karlos.

"To what do we owe the honor of your visit, Mr. President?" Father Armando said, teasing his brother.

"You are my only brother, Mando. I don't think I need any reason to visit you," said Karlos, embracing his brother. "I just miss you, that's all."

"Karlos, we heard about your Agrarian Reform bill. Is that why you came to Castellana?" Father Jose asked.

"Separation of church and state, Father," Karlos reminded him in a joking voice. "Partly, yes. I am sure the hacienderos are probably angry at me right now. But mostly I'm here about Señor Enrique Hernandez's last will and testament," Karlos informed him.

"Karlos, Señora Estefania is fighting the will. Daria is having a hard time because the hacienderos are blocking her attempts. As for the presiding judge, well, he is of course a haciendero too," said Father Jose.

"Father, would you come with me to meet with Señora Estefania?" asked Karlos.

"Karlos, like you said, the church will not commit itself to serve politics," Father Jose said. "But if this is just about asking Señora Hernandez about the will, then yes."

Jocelyn was happy to see Señora Estefania. The reunion of niece and aunt also gave Señora Hernandez comfort.

"Tita, the house is so quiet, but I guess it's better than having Daria here. I know how much it must pain you to see her every day over the years," Jocelyn observed.

Señora Hernandez smiled. "Jocelyn, I am sorry that your tito decided to give the house to Helen, but I promise you, dear, this house and this land will be all yours."

Jocelyn smiled, rejoicing over that the fact she would inherit a mansion.

"I am your daughter, Tita Estefania. No matter what, I will be by your side," said Jocelyn.

"So what brings Karlos back to Castellana? It must the bill that was signed, or perhaps wedding plans?" inquired the señora.

Jocelyn tried to hide the truth from her aunt. "No talks or wedding date yet, but Karlos and I are practically married. It will happen soon enough," said Jocelyn.

Their conversation was interrupted when the maid came in to announce the arrival of President Vasquez and Father Jose.

Jocelyn was worried that her aunt would not face Karlos, but to her relief Señora Estefania welcomed them.

"Karlos, it has been awhile. Welcome back home," Señora Estefania said.

Jocelyn approached Father Jose to show her respect and took Karlos's hands.

"Karlos, Tita Estefania promised me the mansion," she told her fiancé.

Karlos Hernandez, paying no attention to Jocelyn, took a seat across from Señora Estefania. "Señora Hernandez, it has been made known to me that Señor Hernandez left land for his workers," started Karlos. "I came here to ask you to please give the land to the rightful owners and respect Señor Hernandez's last request."

"Do you think all of this is fair to me, Karlos?" asked Señora Hernandez, trying to keep her temper in check. "My family owned that land. Enrique betrayed me by giving it to those people."

"Don't you think it's a small price to pay? Daria and Vicente are giving up their rights to the land left to them, as well as the azucarera. Isn't this enough for you?"

"Karlos, please. Tita has the right, after all the suffering she went through with Tito, not to mention the pain of seeing Tito's *bastarda* every day," Jocelyn said.

Karlos looked at her sternly. "This has nothing to do with you, Jocelyn," Karlos said. "You and I need to talk later too."

"Karlos, I don't think you will win this. The hacienderos and Governor Escalante are helping me. They don't want the land to be given to the people. Do you know what chaos this might bring?" Señora Estefania challenged.

"What you are doing, Señora Hernandez, is an obstruction of justice," Karlos answered. "I am not afraid with what the hacienderos might say or do. Whether you like it or not, the people will get their land."

Señora Hernandez was surprised by Karlos's speech. She realized that she had no power over him. "Karlos, I will fight this, no matter who stands in my way," countered Señora Estefania.

"Fine. You will lose this battle for sure. Don't say I did not warn you," said President Vasquez.

The following day Daria, Vicente, and President Vasquez headed to Hacienda Corazon with two palace guards. They were also joined by Karlos's former vice mayor, Antonio Lizan, and the police chief.

Daria was displeased when she saw the condition of the hacienda. In her short absence, Hacienda Corazon had lost its charm. The workers were idle due to the lack of leadership from Señora Estefania. The green sugarcane that once grew healthily on the land were now unattended.

The fruit trees with abundant fruits were uprooted and the ones standing seems to have lost its desire to share its bounty. The stables that housed her horses were lifeless. Señora Estefania had ordered all the horses be sold, including her beloved Silvestre.

Daria also learned that the workers' wages were not being paid on time, creating conflict between the workers and Señora Hernandez. Daria was horrified when they reached the azucarera. The once-magnificent iron fortress that milled the hacienda's sugarcane was lifeless and rusty. Rebels had looted steel and machinery, leaving the azucarera empty. The workers were threatened by the rebels. Without Señor Enrique Hernandez to protect them, all they could do was flee to find another livelihood.

Daria went inside her father's office and was devastated. She started crying when she saw that her father's picture and awards were destroyed. She tried looking for her father's nameplate, but Vicente stopped her.

"Enough, Daria. There is nothing left here," said Vicente.

"I shouldn't have left, Vicente," Daria, crying and shaking, answered.

Vicente escorted Daria to the courtyard, where they saw Karlos Vasquez talking to the workers. The workers rushed to Daria. Yaya Helen and Vicente tried to stop the mob from coming near her. Daria saw the fear in the people's eyes, but what President Vasquez saw was hope.

"Miss Daria, we are glad you are here," said Felix. Señor Hernandez's loyal bodyguard looked displaced and weak. "My men and I tried to stop the rebels, but we were outnumbered. Señora Hernandez refuses to pay the stipend. I am sorry, Miss Daria."

"Felix, I know you did what you could," said Daria.

President Karlos Vasquez was saddened and angry about the plight of the workers in Hacienda Corazon. It was once his home too.

"Hacienda Corazon is where I was born, where I grew up. This is where my family worked for generations," said Karlos. "My father protected this land and was killed here."

Everyone turned their attention to Karlos.

"Daria, Vicente, and I understand your frustration and anger," Karlos continued. "If the late Señor Enrique Hernandez saw this he would be angry for sure. My family in Hacienda Corazon, we are here to make it known that Señor Hernandez never forgot you," Karlos said, pulling out the señor's last will and testament.

"It says here in his last will and testament that sixty families will each receive five hectares of land!"

The people gasped and started whispering.

"So the rumor is true," said one of the workers.

"Daria and Vicente have the signed and ready land deeds. Our señor never once forgot you and your fathers' efforts to make Hacienda Corazon great. He wanted to give all of you the chance to farm your *own* land," said Karlos Vasquez.

I hope this atones for my sins against you, Señor Hernandez, thought the president.

The people found renewed hope and purpose. They stood in front of the house of Señora Estefania and made their voices heard, asking her to free their late señor's last will and testament.

"That *bastarda* Daria," said Señora Estefania. "Jocelyn, can you talk to Karlos about this?"

Jocelyn was quiet. She was afraid of what Karlos might do to her if she interfered.

Señora Jamora and the other hacienderos had their men protecting Señora Estefania, but it was harder for them once the president and the mayor of Castellana were involved.

The crowd spent the night in vigil in front of the Hernandez house, preventing Estefania and her niece from leaving the premises. The following day Vicente and Atty. Delgado came to see Señora Estefania to persuade her to stop her attempts to block Señor Hernandez's last will and testament, but she continued to be stubborn.

"I will never give in to Daria or you, Vicente," answered Señora Hernandez.

"Tita, we will give you the land Tito has left us and the azucarera too. Just please release the will and let the people have their land," Vicente advised. "The people already know, and they are angry—you don't want this to get worse than it is."

"You should hear their pleas, señora. Not to mention they have President Vasquez on their side," added Atty. Delgado.

"Jocelyn, talk to Karlos. Persuade him," pleaded her aunt.

"I think we should give the people their land," Jocelyn said quietly.

"You too, Jocelyn?" asked Señora Estefania.

Jocelyn avoided her aunt's gaze. "Tita, it's not like you will be left with nothing. I will stay here with you and help you rebuild."

The cries of the crowd got louder as Governor Escalante tried to make his way onto the Hernandez property.

"Estefania, it's a riot out there!" said the governor at the door, shaking his head.

"Governor, please tell everyone here what could happen to the other haciendas and Castellana if I give in," Señora Hernandez requested.

The governor was quiet, trying to find words to tell her that she had lost this battle.

"Señora Hernandez, with all due respect—"

"Oh, please, Escalante, do not tell me you are betraying me too?" an angry Estefania said.

"Listen to me, Estefania," said Governor Escalante. "You need to let the people have their land. I also suggest that you accept Daria and Vicente's offer and accept the land they are willingly giving you. Set an example for Karlos's Agrarian Reform Program."

"Have you gone mad, Governor? You want me to sacrifice my land to save you and the other haciorceros?" Señora Estefania angrily asked.

"It is a sacrifice that could give you peace, Estefania. I understand why you want the land so much, but do you even know how to run a hacienda? And with all this you have lost your workers. Admit it, Estefania, you have lost," said Governor Escalante.

Vicente and Atty. Delgado looked at Señora Estefania, hoping she would concede.

"Never—even if this kills me!" said the angry señora. She stormed out of the house to face the crowd.

Jocelyn ran after her aunt to try to stop her, but it was too late.

"You imbeciles! Get off my property!" yelled Señora Estefania.

"Señora Hernandez, we mean you no harm. We just want what is rightfully ours," cried a man in the crowd.

"What is rightfully yours? Ha! Señor Hernandez was sick when he wrote his will. He was not in his right mind. Do you think he would be pleased with your behavior toward me if he was still alive?

Señora Estefania moved closer to the crowd, and someone threw a rock at her.

Jocelyn moved next to her aunt and saw blood on Señora Hernandez's forehead.

"Stop this, all of you! Karlos won't have this! Do you know who I am?" Jocelyn said, trying to intimidate the crowd.

"You are nobody, Jocelyn Gonzaga, only the president's whore!" yelled a voice in the crowd.

Governor Escalante, Vicente, and Atty. Delgado tried to pacify the crowd. Vicente noticed that not all the people were from Hacienda Corazon.

"My friends, please, let's not resort to violence," said Governor Escalante. "Señora Estefania has agreed to concede and give the land that Señor Hernandez promised to the people."

"Governor, I never agreed to that!"

"Estefania, look at the crowd. This is your only chance to redeem yourself," advised the governor.

Señora Estefania was enraged. She pushed Governor Escalante and grabbed the gun from the governor's holster. She starting shooting at the crowd.

The crowd panicked, and so did Jocelyn.

"My son! You killed my son!" cried a woman from the crowd.

The situation maddened the crowd, and they started to thrown stones at Señora Hernandez and Jocelyn. The hacienderos bodyguards tried to barricade the crowd, but they were outnumbered.

Señora Hernandez aimed the gun again at the crowd, but this time a gun shot rang out before a bullet pierced Estefania's chest.

Jocelyn screamed at the sight as her aunt dropped to the ground.

The news of Señora Estefania's death reached Daria and Karlos Vasquez in city hall. Daria, shocked by the news, started to have contractions.

Karlos took Daria back to Yaya Helen's house and had Dr. Jimena check on her.

"I did not want this to happen, Karlos! Mama—I can't believe she's dead," cried Daria. "Perhaps if she was not stubborn and had given the people their land ..."

"Daria, this is not your fault. Señora Hernandez's greed consumed her," said Karlos.

"What do I do now?" asked Daria.

"Right now, you need to rest, Daria," Vicente suggested as he entered Daria's room.

"Vicente, I am glad you are all right. I don't know what to do. I can't just stay here, Mama her remains and Jocelyn?" a distressed Daria asked.

"Daria, we will take this one step at a time. This is a shock, not only for us but for all of Castellana," said Vicente. "You need to think about you and your baby first."

Daria nodded and asked if she could have time alone.

Karlos and Vicente went to the living room. Vicente had many questions but decided to be wary of Karlos Vasquez.

"This is a tragedy, Karlos," said Vicente. "I cannot even fathom with what just happened."

"I spoke with Mayor Lizan. We will enforce a media blackout," said Karlos. "I'll also speak with the governor and the hacienderos."

Vicente was debating whether to tell Karlos about what he'd seen: that the people who'd attacked Señora Estefania were not from Hacienda Corazon. He remembered Marco's words and decided not to say anything.

Señora Estefania's wake was arranged by her brother-in-law. Dr. Gonzaga decided to lay Estefania to rest after the third day of her wake to avoid additional controversy. Aside from Father Jose and Father Armando, only Vicente and Jocelyn attended the funeral. No haciendero or politicos went.

Dr. Gonzaga was worried for his daughter. He noticed that Jocelyn had become paranoid and fearful. Her personality changed, and she became manic. When Karlos Vasquez visited his fiancée, Jocelyn screamed at him, calling him a rapist and a liar. Dr. Gonzaga was surprised by his daughter's outburst and gave her some sedatives to calm her down.

"I'm sorry for this, Dr. Gonzaga," apologized Karlos.

"Jocelyn has been under a lot of stress. To see her aunt shot in front of her was indeed traumatic," answered Dr. Gonazaga.

"I came to apologize for my absence from Señora Estefania's funeral. I don't think she would have wanted me there after all the events that have happened," said Karlos.

"The dead don't know or mind, Karlos," answered the doctor.

"Dr. Gonzaga, Daria was advised about Señora Estefania's last will and testament," Karlos said. "Daria said she won't contest the will and will give Jocelyn everything her aunt promised her. Daria also said she will give Jocelyn the rights to the azucarera and the land that was left to her."

"Daria has a kind soul. I am not a businessman but a doctor," said Dr. Gonzaga. "I am afraid that my daughter is not in the best condition at the moment."

"That is why I urge you to please consider my plan," said Karlos

Dr. Gonzaga looked at Karlos. "What are you asking for, Karlos?"

"I ask that the remaining Hacienda Corazon land be part of the Agrarian Reform Program," said Karlos.

Marco arrived in Castellana as soon as the flight hold order was suspended. Marco was afraid for his wife after Vicente told him with what happened to Señora Estefania. Atty. Delgado had called to say that he needed to come to Castellana to complete his role as the executor of Señor Hernandez's last will and testament.

The Gutierrezes arrived at Yaya Helen's house, relieved to see Daria resting comfortably on her bed.

Marco sat by his wife and held her. "I'm sorry I couldn't make it sooner."

"Marco, I'm glad you are here." Daria looked at her husband. "Hacienda Corazon and Castellana have always been where I felt safe and loved, but not now. Marco, let's finish everything we need to finish. Take me and Yaya Helen back with you."

Marco held his wife tighter. He was relieved to hear that his wife was willingly to leave Castellana. He just hoped and prayed that after this ordeal Hacienda Corazon would also let Daria go.

The hacienderos gathered at Governor Escalante's home, furious over recent events.

"We have been deceived by a traitor!" said one haciendero.

"Jamora, you said you had him under control," said Señor Porras.

"I did. I was deceived too! I am angrier than any of you because I was the one who made the most effort to help him win the presidency," Señor Jamora answered back.

"Gentlemen, please. If we fight among ourselves then we will not come up with a plan to get rid of Karlos Vasquez," said the governor.

"What's the status in the neighboring province?"

"There are hacienderos who agree that this so-called land reform is actually good for them," said Señor Jamora.

"It's probably the poorer haciendas or those land owners who have debts to pay," said one señor.

"One thing we should be grateful for is the media blackout Karlos ordered. If word came out about what actually happened, it could cause the people to revolt over the haciendas," said Governor Escalante.

"Señor Enrique Hernandez is the one to blame for all this!" cried another haciendero.

"There is no point in blaming the dead. I knew Enrique for a long time. To be honest, I expected this from him," Señor Jamora offered.

"Jocelyn Gonzaga was named the benefactor of all of Señora Estefania properties, and Karlos Vasquez was seen talking with Dr. Gonzaga," said Señor Porras.

"I think we should not focus on Hacienda Corazon. Let us allow Karlos to enjoy this victory. Perhaps there is something we can do to make him realize who placed him in power," Governor Escalante said.

The people of Hacienda Corazon gathered at the city hall as they were instructed. Daria, Marco, and Vicente were completing the final paperwork to release the land titles to the people. Marco and Vicente questioned Karlos Vasquez's motives after noticing media people outside.

"How can this be news? All we need to do is give the people their titles and get out of here," Vicente said to Marco.

"Be careful, my friend. We don't want anyone to sense that we are suspicious of the president's actions. Our goal is to get this over and done with," Marco answered.

When everything was signed and sealed, Daria asked Atty. Delgado to send the families receiving the titles in one at a time, but President Vasquez interrupted.

"Daria, this is historic. Your father's good will needs to be shown to the entire country to give people inspiration," Karlos said persuasively.

"I don't see the need, Karlos," Daria answered, but Karlos Vasquez insisted.

"Daria is right, Karlos. We prefer this be done in private," Marco said.

President Vasquez ignored Marco's words.

"Daria, lives have been sacrificed to win this for the people. Please, I ask you allow me to share this," said Karlos Vasquez.

Before Vicente or Marco could react, Karlos Vasquez led Daria out to the city hall steps.

Karlos addressed the crowd. "Hacienda Corazon has been my home and will always be my home. That is why today marks a historic win for my people. Through the kindness of our late Señor Enrique Hernandez, sixty families will be given the right and privilege to farm their own land."

The crowd cheered.

"Our late Señor Hernandez's daughter bravely fought against her father's so-called friends and other politicians to ensure that Señor Hernandez's last request is executed to benefit his people."

The crowd started chanting Daria's name. Marco and Vicente stood protectively beside Daria.

"Daria, if I may?" asked the president. Daria handed the land deeds to Karlos.

"In my hand, I hold the titles that represent not only ownership but also the hope that people who have slaved and toiled over land that is not theirs be given an opportunity. For these families, may your dreams be fulfilled and may prosperity find you."

President Vasquez started to read the family names on the land titles. The families shook hands with Karlos but turned their attention to Daria as they cried, holding her hand and thanking her and her father.

"This act of Señor Hernandez is indeed heroic and righteous. I also want to announce that Jocelyn Gonzaga, the benefactor of the remaining lands of Hacienda Corazon, has agreed to sign an agreement and take part in my Agrarian Reform Program."

Marco looked at Vicente. They both understood that they were only pawns in Karlos's charades.

"In return, my administration will build a modern public hospital and improve, as well as add classrooms, to our school."

The crowd applauded and cheered, calling President Vasquez's name.

"To the haciendros, please consider my administration offer to share your land. Señor Hernandez wrote his will out of generosity, not expecting anything in return. Daria, sweet Daria, fought for the people of Hacienda Corazon using her own resources.

"If someone could give this much to their people, receiving nothing in return, then I ask why is it difficult for others to share part of their land when I am offering them just compensation. Let us not be greedy, gentlemen. The world is changing, and the country is opening its door for change. I ask all of you to take part in making our republic a country that offers its people fair opportunities."

Ka Abel was in the crowd along with his people. He was proud of Karlos. He believed this was the chance that the rebels too could claim lands; equality would be spread all over the country. Ka Abel instructed Ka Eden to gather the rebels and other rebel leaders at Mt. Mansilay.

Ka Abel knew that now was the time they needed to make their presence known.

President Vasquez headed back to Malacañang the following day after his act had been covered by the primetime newscasts. Karlos Vasquez once again became the center of attention for different media outlets. His mass support was becoming evident. The once-quiet workers were starting to question their landowners, pressuring for reform.

Karlos accepted the phone call from Ambassador Valderrama, who was in dire need for Karlos to pacify the United States.

"Karlos, I understand you want the country to prosper of its own accord, but you need to make a statement to our allies," said the ambassador.

"Which allies?" asked Karlos.

"Mr. President, the American government is concerned about the propositions and activities of your administration. It was bold of you to minimize ties with them, but they are responding to your pride by putting a quota on our sugar exports here in the United States," Ambassador Valderrama informed him. "They are also concerned about the military pullout in Mindanao and that your Agrarian Reform Program is, well, a ..."

"Communist plot?" finished Karlos. "Let me remind you, ambassador, you are a delegate of our country. Do not forget which country you are serving," President Vasquez said before ending the call.

Karlos Vasquez called Secretary Montevista into his office. "I need you to call a press conference. I want to address our so-called allies," ordered the president.

Before Daria, Marco, and Vicente returned to Manila, Daria visited Jocelyn at the asylum in the Order of St. Dymphna.

Jocelyn never returned to her usual self after the events she experienced. Her father decided that it would be best, and safer for his daughter, if she were brought to the asylum.

Daria was disheartened to see Jocelyn strapped to the bed in her room. Jocelyn was anxious and nervous, as well as confused. She claimed to have been raped by Karlos Vasquez and that she was the daughter of Señor and Señora Hernandez.

"Daria, Daria, you *bastarda*, you caused all of this! You killed Tita Estefania. I will kill you too," Jocelyn yelled. The restrains made it difficult for Jocelyn to move.

"My dear, as you can see she is not in her right mind. We will continue to provide medical help for her, as well as pray for her," the nun in charge of the asylum said.

"Jocelyn, I came here to bid you farewell. I will be leaving Castellana. I pray that one day you will find peace," said Daria.

"Peace? You only have peace when you are dead," Jocelyn said. She laughed. Her mood suddenly changed.

"Daria, Daria, please let me out of here. This is all Karlos's doing. That man is the one who is insane, not me," pleaded Jocelyn. "He tricked me, Daria. He took advantage of me. He planned all of this! Do not be stupid. See the evil he is."

"Jocelyn, thank you for your concern. As I said, I will continue to pray for you," Daria said, turning toward the door.

"Ha ha ha ha ha ha! Daria, naïve Daria. One day you will find out the truth. Don't say I didn't warn you"

Daria left the asylum with a heavy heart. Jocelyn and Daria had never had a bond or even tried to like each other or become friends. Neither had made the effort. They had been pitted against each other for as long Daria could remember. However, Jocelyn's last words haunted Daria. For some reason, Daria felt that Jocelyn was telling her the truth.

CHAPTER 19

D aria and Yaya Helen settled in the Gutierrez home. Marie was overjoyed that Daria decided to stay and told Marco that they couldn't leave the house until after the baby was born. Daria and Marco agreed on the condition the soon-to-be-grandparents did not spoil their child.

The family was about to eat dinner but was delayed by the telecast of President Karlos Vasquez addressing the issue of Philippine-American relations.

Karlos's words were bold. He stated that the country was capable and would no longer accept being called "my little brown brother" by the Americans. He was firm about increasing tariffs and shocked everyone when he asked the Americans to leave the country.

"This is a disgrace!" Marie Gutierrez, who was half American, said. "I do not understand his hatred or agenda."

"This is not the Karlos Vasquez I used to know," said Daria quietly.

Marco was tempted to tell his wife everything he had discovered about Karlos Vasquez but was afraid that it might affect her pregnancy.

The headlines in the paper the next day hailed Karlos as a true Filipino. Some papers viewed him as a hero who would bring the country into a new era. The attention was not without criticism. The *Republika* once again questioned the president's action, saying he was like a spoiled child throwing a tantrum and his views on international diplomacy were elementary.

The US ambassador to the Philippines urged the president to sit down and talk, but Karlos told him he had no interest in doing so.

The masses embraced President Karlos Vasquez's views about the president's standoff with United States. In response to President Vasquez, the United States did not renew the open trade agreement with the Philippines. The United States also posted travel warnings to citizens traveling to the Philippines and urged citizens who resided in the country to return to the United States for their safety. The once-strong ties between both countries slowly crumbled as President Vasquez continued his verbal tirades against the western country.

The misinformed masses were moved by President Vasquez's endeavors. They embraced the changes the administration was delivering, believing they needed to show their patriotism with action. Crowds formed in front of the United States embassy, asking them to leave. Labor unions and the masses started attacking multinational companies, calling them opportunists, and harassing the American companies, asserting they would not support their businesses and products. Even the Gutierrez Group of Companies was not spared.

Marie Gutierrez received a letter from the United States embassy, asking them to leave the Philippines and return to the States for their safety.

"Marie, I think it's a good idea for you to join our sons in the States. We will process Daria and Helen's papers as soon as she gives birth," Miguel Gutierrez advised.

"I do not understand how all of this happened! Miguel, I want our family to be safe, but we have to leave together," said Marie.

"I still have a lot of things to attend to. Marco and I will be at ease if you and Daria leave the country first," said Miguel.

"I think it is a good idea for the women to leave, Papa. Vicente can go with them," said Marco.

Vicente added, "My dad told me he and Mama have filed for political asylum. They fear that if they head back here, they will be prosecuted as traitors."

"How can your father be a traitor, Vicente, when all he did was preserve whatever relationship we have with the United States?" said Miguel Gutierrez.

Marco and Vicente had been forced to leave their workplace due to the riots. "It was a horror at the site today, Dad. We had to shut everything down. I was surprised to see some of our workers joined the protesters," said Marco.

"When we expanded GGC, I made it the company's mission to provide quality jobs and protect our workers," said Marco's father. "We are proud that GGC is the leading company for giving workers benefits."

"Which is why I am saddened by how quickly they turned against us," said Marie.

"I don't have any interest in politics, but with everything that is going on, I feel that people were misled by false promises and information," Marco said.

"I understand that the people are angry and tired and they want to improve their lives in the quickest way, but I don't think Karlos's approach is correct," said Vicente. "President Vasquez should know very well that progress takes time. He is misleading the people."

"Rome wasn't built in a day," Marie answered.

Daria, now seven months' pregnant, entered the living room. She had heard the conversation all the way from her room and was concerned for the family's safety. "I am shocked how Karlos is acting right now. He is no longer the same person I knew," said Daria. "I called Father Armando, but he said he has not heard a word from his brother.

"I noticed there was a change in Karlos. I always thought it was his passion to help the people, but it's more like is he possessed and can't think straight," Daria added.

"Daria, we have to cut our ties with Karlos. I think his obsession with equality and change has led him to seek aid elsewhere," Marco said.

"What do you mean, Marco?" asked his mother.

Marco was silent for a moment. Vicente placed his hands on Marco's shoulders. "I think we should tell them what we discovered, Marco," said Vicente.

Marco looked at his parents and then his wife.

"Daria, I am sorry for hiding this from you. I do hope you won't hold it against me," started Marco. "Your papa suspected that Karlos Vasquez was being supported by the communist rebels," said Marco. "Señor Hernandez found proof that Karlos was communicating with the rebels. I think Karlos confronted your father the night of Señor Hernandez's death."

Daria turned pale and tried to make sense of what her husband had just said.

"Daria, I know this is difficult to accept. I have a friend who works for a newspaper, and I asked him to investigate Karlos," Marco said. "He learned that Karlos and his family have always been involved with the rebels. He is their patron."

"How could he? My papa adored him, and my poor mama's life was sacrificed for his cause. Jocelyn …" Daria came to a realization. "Jocelyn told me at the asylum to be careful of Karlos. She said that she was abused and …"

Marco held his wife. "Daria, as of now we are safe. We will act as fast as we can to leave the country."

"Marco, Daria, you know I love you both, but I don't think I can join you," Vicente said.

"Vicente, do you think Tita Chris and Tito Jaime will allow you?" asked his cousin.

Vicente looked at the worried faces looking at him. "I am a Filipino. I cannot desert my country in times like these," he said.

"This is not the time to be patriotic, Vicente," observed Marco.

"This is the time to be patriotic," Vicente answered his friend. "The people have been deceived by a leader they think is their savior. President Vasquez promised our countrymen a better life. Amidst poverty and hopelessness, the people have found hope in Karlos."

"Vicente … Please, think about our family," Daria pleaded.

"I feel the responsibility to challenge President Vasquez. I want the people to learn of his true intentions. As stubborn as the majority may be, they need to know the false hope that is being offered to them. This is my obligation as a Filipino," said Vicente.

"Vicente, I respect your views and admire your devotion to our country," said Miguel Gutierrez. "But I will continue to plead for you to change your mind and come with us."

The situation in Manila turned for the worse. The press was silenced; media blackouts were ordered by Malacañang. Word reached Marco that his friend Juan Silverio had gone missing, and the *Republika* office was set on fire. There was no coverage about the journalist's disappearance or the fire that killed and injured employees of the paper.

"I am glad that you finally did your job right, Secretary Montevista," praised President Vasquez.

"I just did what I was told," answered his nervous press secretary. "Mr. President, if I may, I would like to resign from my position as your press secretary." Secretary Montevista handed him his resignation letter.

"I remember you begged for a position in my administration during my campaign. What is the reason for your resignation?" asked the president.

"I don't think I am fit for the position, and …" answered Secretary Montevista.

"And … you are afraid that something might happen to you and your family?" finished President Vasquez. "Why won't you think it over?" said Karlos, tearing the resignation letter. "May I suggest the cell where your friend Juan Silverio is?"

Secretary Montevista turned pale and started sweating, not knowing what to say. "I am sorry if I upset you, Mr. President. If I may, I would like to return to my duties," said Secretary Montevista.

"Good! It's settled then. I know you won't leave me," smiled Karlos. "Now, be a good boy and continue your work."

"Mr. President, there are gentlemen here who say that they made an appointment to talk with you, but I don't see it in your schedule," Karlos secretary announced over the intercom.

"Let them in," President Vasquez ordered.

"*Maligayang bati at kapayapaan sa ating lahat,*" the group greeted him.

"*Mag-kaisa tayo ngayon para sa kagandahang ng bukas,*" replied Karlos.

Ka Abel walked up to Karlos and shook his hand. The rebel leaders saluted Karlos.

"Patron, this is it. We are near the victory," Ka Abel said. "It is now time to put our plan into full action."

"Karlos, you have gone this far in the game. We cannot back out now," encouraged the leaders.

"I understand what I need to do," President Vasquez said, a slight hesitation in his voice.

"Karlos, your tatay gave up his life for our cause," Ka Abel reminded him. "I understand you have grown fond of the people around you, but it is their destiny to give up their lives for the sake of the majority."

Karlos closed his eyes and nodded.

"Let our brothers know it's time to move our plan into action. *Sulong!*" ordered Karlos.

The evening newscasts filled every Filipino household with horror and fear. Mindanao was overtaken by militant groups that, to everyone's horror, killed Vice President Aristotle Lacson's entire family. President Karlos Vasquez sent troops to Mindanao that were ambushed and killed by the rebels.

The militant group told the president that they would murder every Christian in Mindanao if the government did not agree to their demands. They began the murders, including reporter Rudy Magbanua.

President Vasquez asked the leaders of the Muslim militant groups to meet him in Malacañang, only to be refused. To show he was sincere in offering open talks with the Muslim rebels meant to arrive at terms for peace, Karlos Vasquez met with them in Zamboanga.

For days there was no news about the president. Then President Vasquez made an appearance and called the media to Zamboanga to cover the announcement of the agreement between him and the Muslim leaders. The live telecast from Mindanao reached the living rooms of the Filipino people.

"My countrymen, I, Karlos Vasquez, elected president of the republic, have come to terms with Muslim leaders in Mindanao. In order to preserve the lives of millions in Mindanao, I signed Proclamation 1926, declaring the separation of Mindanao from the Republic of the Philippines," announced President Vasquez. "In exchange for the lives of millions of non-Muslim Filipinos in Mindanao, I proclaim that Mindanao will be returned to its original state as the Sultanate of Maguindanao."

President Vasquez's announcement shocked the entire nation. The Congress and Senate kept silent, for the politicians understood the repercussions if their responses angered the president. A handful of politicians and social groups protested, only to be lambasted by the military and arrested for treason.

The Sultanate of Maguindanao signed the peace treaty and gave the Vasquez administration thirty days to evacuate the non-Muslims.

Panic and fear swept the nation. President Vasquez accomplished his first victory toward paving the way for the Republic of the Philippines to enter a new form of government.

The Vasquez administration ordered each province to open an evacuation center for the people leaving Mindanao. The president also promised that the evacuees would be given five hectares of land per family from the land the government had purchased under the Agrarian Reform Program.

The haciendros in the Visayas and Luzon, as well as farmers in other regions, were dismayed with Karlos. The farmers who had received land under the Agrarian Reform Program were furious at having to share their land with the migrants. The haciendros, who were already in conflict with the administration, the rebels and the new farmers, decided to plot toward a way to throw the president out of office.

"What has become of Karlos? We created a monster!" exclaimed Señor Jamora.

"I am still his press secretary, though he dared to threaten me when I gave him my resignation," Señor Montevista said.

"We've already lost so much because of the sugar cap ordered by the United States, and now this?" Señor Porras added.

"We indeed made a mistake, gentlemen. I would have never thought Karlos Vasquez would betray us like this," said Governor Escalante.

"We were all fooled! Look at all the damage he has done to us and the country. He has only been in office for less than a year" said Señor Jamora. "We should have someone assassinate him."

"Mind your words, Señor Jamora," warned Governor Escalante.

"We put him in power—we can take away his power," Señor Jamora stated.

"The politicians who went against him are either in prison or dead. Congressman Saison is in Camp Crame. Who would think Karlos would put him there," said Secretary Montevista.

"What about Father Armando?" asked Señor Porras.

"I was told that he has no contact with his brother," answered the governor.

"Why won't we use him and the church to make our voices heard?" Señor Jamora suggested.

"We can give it a try. In the state everyone is in right now, all we can do is pray and have faith," answered Governor Escalante.

MANILA

Marco and Vicente were forced to stop operations at GGC as the riots and protest heightened. The business sector was in turmoil, unable to continue production and distribute their goods. The stock market hit record lows, and the panicking people started to withdraw their money from the banks, causing a temporary bank run.

Amidst the chaos, the Gutierrez household focused on Daria as she got ready to deliver her child. The hospitals were crowded and doctors scarce. Daria was left with no choice but to deliver the baby at home with the assistance of Yaya Helen and her mother-in-law.

Marco and Mr. Gutierrez waited helplessly as they heard Daria's cries of pain. When they heard the loud cry of an infant and the joyous voice of Marie Gutierrez, they were relieved.

Marco's mother emerged from Daria's room and smiled at her son. She beckoned for him to come and meet his newborn child.

"Marco, it's a boy!" Daria said tearfully.

Marco was overcome with joy. Daria handed Marco their son, and the new father accepted his newborn as carefully as he could.

"What do you want to name him?" Marco asked Daria.

"I have thought about it. I want to name him after the two men I love most," said Daria. "Everyone, may we introduce to you Enrico Hernandez-Gutierrez?" Daria beamed.

Baby Enrico was the light and hope of the Gutierrez household. The chaos in the streets and the riots seemed to be diminished by the joy the newest member of the family brought.

Vicente had not changed his mind about leaving. He'd joined a secret movement to overthrow President Vasquez. He was seen less often until he got word that Daria had given birth to a baby boy.

"I thought you were naming him Vicente," chided the new uncle. "How about you use my name as his middle name?"

"We have not registered his birth certificate yet so there is still a possibility," Marco answered.

"It's impossible to get anything through right now, but I do have some good news," said Vicente. "I was able to gain access to the American Embassy. I want to personally deliver this to you," Vicente said, handing Marco an envelope.

Marco was pleased with what he saw.

"Daria, we have your papers, as well as Enrico and Yaya Helen's. We can leave soon," Marco announced.

"Well, it says Baby Boy Gutierrez. Our little Enrico here does not have a birth certificate yet, but I was told that would not be a problem as long as a parent and a witness can sign the affidavit," relayed Vicente.

"Vicente, please, I beg you to come with us," Daria pleaded.

Vicente turned to his nephew to tickle and kiss Enrico. He ignored Daria's words.

"If everything works out, you will be out of here at the end of the month," said Vicente.

CASTELLANA

Father Jose and Father Armando organized a prayer rally seeking acceptance and tolerance for those who were displaced by the emancipation of Mindanao. Father Armando tried to reach his brother, but to no avail. Mando been openly challenged the president in his homilies. He prayed that the real Karlos Vasquez, a man with dignity and honor, a lover of peace, would overcome his greed and false morals.

The prayer rally was attended by the haciendores and their families. A small group of farmers, religious orders, and immigrants attended as well. Aside from Governor Escalante and Señor Jamora, no other politicians made an appearance.

"Father, it's a not as big as the prayer rally we had for Karlos when he was running for president. The church is only half full," Father Armando observed.

"We live by faith, not by sight," Father Jose reminded Mando.

The prayer began with the rosary. Father Jose went to the pulpit to talk to those present.

"To those who came here to pray with us, thank you," Father Jose began. "Let us pray that the migrants are welcomed to our city and that they may start their new lives in peace and with hope. Let us also call upon the Holy Spirit to enlighten the hearts and the minds of the people that we may seek the truth and not be intimidated about questioning the actions of our leaders."

The faithful heard the voices of protesters coming toward the plaza.

Father Armando took over. "My brothers and sisters, in times of disconnect and unease may we be reminded: *For our struggle is not against flesh and blood, but against the rulers, against the authorities, against the powers of this dark world and against the spiritual forces of evil in the heavenly realms.* Ephesians 6:12."

The protesters arrived at St Thomas de Aquinas church. Some were armed, ready to threaten the people and the priests. "Separation of church and state!" cried the crowd.

The people in the church started to panic.

Governor Escalante and Father Armando went outside to talk to the protesters.

"We are here today to pray for peace and for our president. I come here as a man of faith and not to represent the government," said Governor Escalante.

"Then what are you praying for? To have President Vasquez impeached? Or perhaps praying for his death?" answered one of the rebels.

"We are praying for peace and for my brother's heart to be to be moved to do what is right," answered Father Armando.

"Priests will always support the rich. The hacienderos built your churches and support you!" said the angry rebel.

"We answer to God, not to anyone else," said Father Armando.

The rebels turned to Governor Escalante. "If you hacienderos were not so selfish about sharing your land and treated your workers with dignity and respect, none of this would have happened. It is you, the rich, who should be blamed, not Karlos Vasquez," said the rebel.

"I say this to you and your cause: someday you will know the truth, and the truth will set you free," said Father Armando to the rebels.

"Go inside your church and pray. We don't need your prayers. It's the people who decide the fate of this nation, not the hacienderos or priests," said another rebel. He pushed Father Armando and Governor Escalante inside the church.

The people inside the church were frightened. They panicked as they heard the church doors being barricaded by the rebels. There were no other exits for a retreat.

"My brothers and sisters, let's surrender our fears to God and ask forgiveness for our sins. Let us forgive those who have sinned against us," Father Jose suggested, knowing that the end was nearing for those inside the church.

"*Our Father who art in Heaven, hallowed be thy name. Thy kingdom come, thy will be done on earth as it is in heaven. Give us this day our daily bread and forgive us our trespasses, as we forgive those who trespassed against us—*"

The glass windows shattered as gas bombs were thrown inside the church.

"Separation of state and church!"

"*Lead us not into temptation but deliver us from evil …*"

The people in the church started coughing and began to lose their breath.

"*For thine is the kingdom and the power and the glory …now and forever.* My brothers and sisters, let us put our trust in God and remember in this world there is no lasting peace, only in the kingdom of heaven," Father Jose said before he released his last breath.

As Father Armando fell to the floor, he saw the suffering of the people. He thought of his brother. *Brother, I forgive you, and I will take my death with ease. I will now be closer to God to pray for you.* Father

Armando then closed his eyes. The screams of the people in the church faded.

News of the death of the haciendaros and the martyrdom of Father Jose and Father Armando reached the neighboring towns. The rebels were in full force and started attacking haciendas, forcing the haciendaros to give up their land to avoid their wrath.

The country was in turmoil, but President Karlos Vasquez did not allow his conscience to distract his intentions. Karlos learned about his brother's death. He mourned and asked his brother for forgiveness. He convinced himself that his cause, to equally distribute opportunities for all, outweighed his brother's life.

"We are close to making this country the People's Republic of the Philippines," said Ka Abel. "This is not the time for regrets, Karlos."

Karlos looked at Ka Abel. "I don't have any regrets. I accepted this position and worked my damned hardest to get here."

"Karlos, we are so close to obtaining what we have fought for. Be prepared, for tomorrow we will rise as a nation of the people," said Ka Abel.

CHAPTER 20

M arie and Miguel arrived at the American Embassy before
Daria. The Gutierrezes abandoned their home and
properties to ensure the safety of their family. All they
brought were their necessities and property titles. They were scheduled
to leave the country on the 11:00 p.m. flight.

Daria held baby Enrico. They and Yaya Helen were on their way
to the embassy, escorted by Vicente. Daria could not reach Marco and
tried to reassure herself; he must be in the embassy with his parents.

Vicente stepped on the brakes suddenly when their car was blocked
by two military personnel trucks.

"Daria Gutierrez, Vicente Valderrama, you are requested to come
with us," said one of the soldiers.

"By who? She is not going anywhere!" said Vicente.

"We were ordered by the president," answered the soldier, "and we
will use any means necessary if you resist this order."

Daria, Vicente, and Yaya Helen were taken to Camp Crame. Daria
held her baby tight and prayed for their protection. She tried to make
sense of why they were brought to the prison. Her question was answered
when she saw Karlos Vasquez coming toward them.

"Daria, I see you had your baby," President Vasquez. He moved
close to Daria to look at Enrico.

Daria stepped back and held her child tightly. Vicente moved in
front of Daria and his baby cousin only to be pushed down on his knees
by the guards.

"No need to be afraid. I am this child's uncle, after all," said Karlos. "What is his name?"

"Enrico," Daria answered quickly.

"Enrico. Nice name. I get it—Enrique and Marco. He's named after the two men who adore you." Karlos laughed.

The baby started to cry, and Daria rocked her son, trying to pacify him.

"Oh, I think little Enrico must be hungry, or perhaps he misses someone," Karlos said, looking at Daria.

Daria shuddered at what Karlos said, afraid to ask what he meant.

"Daria, why won't you have Yaya Helen hold Enrico and come with me?" ordered Karlos.

Daria followed Karlos's instructions and handed her crying son to her nanny. Vicente struggled to get away from the guards, but Karlos signaled the guard to control Daria's cousin.

"I really don't want to hurt you, Vicente. Don't worry. I just need to talk with Daria," said President Vasquez. "I have no intentions of harming her."

Daria followed Karlos toward the prison facilities. She felt faint when she saw the beaten and weak prisoners in their cells. Then Daria heard a familiar voice calling her.

"Daria, Daria, leave this place!" Daria turned around and saw the bloody Congressman Saison inside a prison cell with other men. Daria thought they were the other members of the Senate who'd tried to overthrow Karlos. Daria gasped and approached her father's friend in his cell.

"Señor Saison, who did this to you?" asked Daria.

The weakened haciendero pointed to Karlos. "Daria, he used all of us. He is a traitor to this country."

A prison guard moved toward Congressman Saison's cell and hit the haciendero's hand with his crop.

"Karlos ..." Daria said the president's name as though he were the devil.

"Let's move on, Daria," said Karlos, not looking back at the cries of Congressman Saison.

When Secretary Montevista saw Karlos and Daria, he rushed to Daria's side.

"Daria, please forgive me," the guilty Señor Montevista said.

Before Daria could ask any questions, she heard the faint sound of Marco's voice calling her.

Secretary Montevista stepped aside, and Daria rushed toward her bruised and bloodied husband, who was tied to a chair.

"Daria, I never wanted to reach this point, but Marco left me with no choice," said Karlos. "I found out your husband was the one who started the rumor about me being a communist. Apparently he was right."

"Karlos, you insane coward," Marco said.

"Your friend from *Republika* endured much for you, but what can I say? When a man's family is at stake he simply gives in," Karlos responded.

"What do you want from us, Karlos?" Daria bravely asked.

"Daria, Daria. You see, every leader needs a courageous and yet gentle woman next to him," explained Karlos. "Someone who can be the mother of this new nation. I always thought Jocelyn would be perfect for that position, but her selfishness and ambition got in the way."

Karlos walked closer to Daria, to the dismay of Marco.

"Daria, you have been a role model for our people. You have been sincere and courageous in fighting for your people's rights," Karlos praised. "Which is why I sincerely believe no one is more fit to stand next to me and be the mother of our new country."

"Never!" Marco yelled.

One of the guards took Daria aside. Karlos ordered his people to put electrodes on Marco.

"Karlos, stop this!" cried Daria.

President Vasquez walked toward the control box and adjusted the voltage. Karlos then pulled the lever. Marco let out a scream. Marco weakened, and his head dropped forward. Daria, fearful for her husband's life, pleaded with President Vasquez.

"Karlos, please let Marco go. I will do what you ask of me. Just let my family go."

Marco looked up. "No, Daria!"

Daria went to her husband. "Marco, please. You need to survive for Enrico's sake."

"If it's any consolation, Marco, I promise not to lay a hand on your wife."

Marco shook his head. "I would rather die."

"I can let you die, Marco, along with your son and Vicente. I am really being nice to you right now," said President Hernandez.

Daria stood up and faced Karlos. "Can you assure me you will release my husband and child?"

"I give you my word that they can leave the country safely," Karlos promised.

Daria turned to Marco. "Marco, always remember that I love you. Take good care of Enrico," Daria said to her husband, in tears.

"Okay then." Karlos pulled Daria to his side and ordered his men to release Marco. Daria tried to go to Marco, but President Vasquez pulled her arm.

"You have already said your farewell," Karlos said.

Daria saw the guards walk away with her husband. Her heart broke. She told herself not to let her emotions get the best of her and turned to Karlos.

"Thank you for staying with me, Daria," said President Hernandez. "Even if it is against your will."

"Are you satisfied with all that happened, Karlos?" asked Daria. "Do you have any regrets? Your brother died for your cause. So did people who believed in you. How can you be this cruel?"

"All of us have a part to play in achieving peace and prosperity for our countrymen," said Karlos.

"Is this what you call peace, Karlos? Killing and torturing people?" Daria asked directly.

"We need to destroy the evil that prevents progress for everyone," answered Karlos. "The people wanted me to be their leader because I promised them equality and a better life."

"You are insane! If your view of equality is getting rid of democracy, Karlos, your plan will fail," Daria said.

"How can I fail, Daria? Have you seen the people revolting against the tyrants? They believe in my cause," answered Karlos.

"The people are desperate. One day they will suffer the repercussions of their actions and realize that all of this was a mistake."

Karlos laughed in her face.

Daria heard a familiar voice in the room.

"Daria, my baby! I told Vicente I cannot leave you here," Yaya Helen said, crying and clutching Daria.

"Daria, I have been very generous with you. Please don't abuse my generosity," Karlos warned.

"Yaya, we need to be strong now. We have to survive this," said Daria.

"I still need your assurance that my family is safe," Daria told Karlos.

"As you know, Daria, I am a man of my word," answered President Vasquez.

An hour later President Hernandez received a phone call. He handed the phone to Daria.

"Daria, we are safe in the embassy. Marco and Enrico too—we are all here," Vicente said over the phone.

"Take care, Vicente, and please watch over Enrico," Daria asked.

Daria heard the speaker in the background asking the citizens in the American Embassy to get ready for boarding.

"You go now, Vicente. I love you," said Daria to her cousin before the line went dead.

The rebellion had won victory. Karlos Vasquez's plans succeeded. Businessmen and landowners surrendered after numerous attacks from the communist insurgents. In his mind, Karlos had fulfilled his promise to create equality for all citizens.

In celebration of their victory, the crowd in front of the palace joined the soldiers and greeted President Vasquez, now the great leader of the republic, by cheering his name.

"Today we mark a new era in our beloved republic. We are no longer a nation of inequality, and no country will dare look down on us," said Karlos. He faced the people on a balcony at Malacañang. "Today we establish a new government. A government that is represented by the people, with equality for all its citizens. I present to the world the People's Republic of the Philippines."

Karlos turned to Daria and offered his hand. Daria took the hand of the great leader of the new republic. Emotionless, she stood next to Karlos. Daria then placed her hand on her heart as the people sang the new national anthem and saluted the new Philippine flag.

NOVEMBER 1971

With Karlos's permission, Daria returned to Castellana to pay respects to her father. The great leader asked his men to escort her and Yaya Helen to Castellana and instructed the guards to bring Daria back before curfew.

Daria arrived in her hometown but could no longer recognize Castellana. The plaza and the city hall still stood, but gone were the music and bustle of the people. The gossip and laughter that once filled the city proper had been silenced. Instead military officers occupied the streets. St. Thomas de Aquinas Church, once a refuge to its citizen, was in ruins. The magnificent Spanish-style houses that lined the streets of the city had lost their elegance in their new role as residences to the rebel leaders and high officials.

The car passed by the Hernandez's former residence. Daria's once-beloved home had been turned into a hospital. Sick, hungry people lined up at the entrance, patiently waiting their turn to be seen by Dr. Gonazaga and Dr. Jimena. Daria watched a father who stepped out of the line, begging to have his son seen first, be hit by the guards. Others pulled him back in line.

Daria and Yaya Helen arrived at the Catholic cemetery. The once-manicured lawns were covered by tall grass and weeds. The once-celebrated All Soul's Day had been abolished by the Communist government, as had other religious traditions.

Daria stood in front of her father's tomb.

Papa, I am glad you are not here to witness what has become of Catellana, Hacienda Corazon, and the entire country, Daria thought. She lit a candle and said a silent prayer, not only for her papa and Señora Estefania but also for Father Armando, Father Jose, and all those who died and suffered for Karlos Vasquez's ambitions.

Daria's attention was caught by one of the guards, who reminded her that it was time for them to head back to Manila. Daria asked to pass by Hacienda Corazon, now known as Mt. Mansilay Farms. Daria couldn't help but shed tears for the land that was once her playground. Gone were the lush green sugarcane fields, replaced by dying rice fields. The azucarera was rusty, stripped, and dilapidated. The people working the fields were new faces to Daria. She wondered what had happened to the workers given land by her father. The farmers looked tired and weary. Due to the new law of equality, they could not profit from the crops they sowed.

Karlos's hope for the people was perfectly planned but poorly executed.

Was your fight for perfect equality worth it? thought Daria. *The workers don't look satisfied. They look hungry and helpless.* Their hope seemed empty; they worked aimlessly.

Daria and her loyal nanny walked to the car awaiting them, which drove them to the airfield. They entered the private plane, and the pilot prepared for takeoff. As the plane soared over the clouds covering Castellana, Daria looked beyond the horizon, and her heart ached. She might not be imprisoned in the fields with the workers, but her heart was imprisoned. She and her heart longed for the family she once had.

EPILOGUE

1975

Boston

The leaves turned orange and the wind blew cold as autumn started its reign. The Gutierrez's colonial residence had become a playground. Blue and red balloons and multicolored streamers decorated the patio.

Vicente Valderrama was trying to balance himself and put up the piñata. Children started laughing and running around him. Vicente's father, the former Philippine ambassador, tried to help his son and scare the kids off, but to no avail.

"You really have no talent with children, Papa," said Vicente.

"Maybe if you give me a grandchild I could harness my talent," replied Jaime Valderrama.

"I already have a son," said Vicente, looking at a five-year-old Enrico playing happily with his friends.

Christina Valderrama and Marie Gutierrez brought out the two-tiered blue and red birthday cake they'd made for their grandson and called Enrico and his friends.

Enrico happily ran to his grandmothers, revealing the dimples on his round face.

For a moment, Christina thought she saw a glimpse of her brother Enrique Hernandez before she realized it was Enrico who ran toward her.

"*Mamita*!" Enrico cried happily to Christina Valderrama. His grandmother picked him up and gave him a hug.

"Are you having fun?" asked Christina.

The little boy nodded, his eyes shining brightly. "*Lola* Marie, did you make this for me?" asked Enrico. "I hope it is chocolate."

"Of course it is," Camela Gutierrez happily answered, taking her grandson from Christina.

"Where's dad and *lolo*?" the birthday boy asked.

"Here, son. We went in to get you this," Marco Gutierrez pointed to a new red bicycle, a large bow wrapped around it.

"A new bike! Thanks, Dad!" Enrico cheered as he ran over to check the bike. "I am a big boy now—no more training wheels!"

His father walked over to him and patted him on the head. "Time indeed flies, my son," said Marco. "Now go and blow your candles."

The Valderrama family, Marco's parents and brothers, as well as Enrico's friends gathered around to sing "Happy Birthday."

"Make a wish," Marco told his son.

Enrico blew his candle out, but instead of smiling and being delighted, he hid his face against his father's chest.

Marie noticed the boy's reaction and cut the cake to divert the guests' attention. *Every year on his birthday he cries after he blows out his candle,* Marie thought.

Marco took his son inside the house and cuddled him until he stopped crying.

"Dad, when will my wish come true?" asked his son.

Marco looked at his son and remembered his wife Daria. He remembered that his wife was sentimental about holidays and her birthday. She longed to have known the mother she never knew.

Marco looked up at the picture of him and Daria on the wall and gave his son a kiss on the head.

"Let's continue hoping and wishing, my son," Marco said. "Someday your mom will be here with us."

GLOSSARY

Adobo: Pork and/or chicken dish cooked in soy sauce and vinegar

Azucarera: Sugar mill

Camp Crame: Internment camp for political prisoners

Chop suey: Mixed vegetables dish

COMELEC: Commission on Elections

Encargado: Right-hand man of the haciendero, manages fieldworkers

Hacienda: Family-owned farmland

Haciendero: Person who owns and runs family farmland

Lanzones: Round sweet fruit covered in yellow skin, common in the southern part of the Philippines

Lechon: Whole roasted pig

Maligayang bati at kapayapaan sa lahat: Greetings to you, and peace to all mankind.

Mag: kaisa tayo ngayon para sa kagandahang ng bukas: Unity for a brighter future

Malacañang Palace: Where the president has his office and resides

Merienda: Afternoon snack

Noche Buena: Christmas Eve midnight feast

Pan sit: Filipino noodle dish

Puñeta: Cuss word commonly used by the haciendaros

Rambutan: Fruit with red hairy skin from the lychee family

Suman: Sticky rice cooked in brown sugar and wrapped in banana leaves

Tambis: Juicy rose apple fruit

Tatay: Father

Tito: Uncle

Tita: Aunt

Valenciana: Sticky rice cooked with turmeric and meat

Yaya: Nanny

CPSIA information can be obtained
at www.ICGtesting.com
Printed in the USA
LVHW111220130223
739349LV00001B/10

9 781524 669522